THE SEASON

By Sophia Holloway

Kingscastle
The Season
Isabelle

a&b

THE SEASON

SOPHIA HOLLOWAY

Allison & Busby Limited
11 Wardour Mews
London W1F 8AN
allisonandbusby.com

First published in Great Britain by Allison & Busby in 2022.

A CIP catalogue record for this book is available from
the British Library.

First Edition

ISBN 978-0-7490-2798-8

Typeset in 11.25/16.25 pt Sabon LT Pro by
Allison & Busby Ltd.

Printed and bound by
CPI Group (UK) Ltd, Croydon, CR0 4YY

For K. M. L. B.

CHAPTER ONE

'I HAVE RECEIVED A LETTER FROM YOUR AUNT Elstead, my dear.' Sir John Gaydon looked up from his perusal of the missive, held at arm's length both to facilitate his reading and to keep the peculiarly scented paper from his nose. He smiled at his daughter.

'How is my aunt, Papa?' Miss Henrietta Gaydon put down the sock she was darning in a housewifely manner.

'Well, very well, as it appears you will be able to see for yourself, quite soon.'

'She is coming to visit us?' Henrietta was astounded, since she could not actually recall having met her aunt since her mother's funeral, some eight years previously.

'No, Henrietta, you are going to see her. I . . . you are eighteen, ready to make your curtsey before the polite world, and your aunt has kindly agreed to present you this Season, with your cousin Caroline.'

'You mean go to London?' Henrietta made it sound as if it were St Petersburg.

'Yes, of course. It would be unfair, even cruel of me, to keep you cooped up here, and prevent you making your mark, taking advantage of meeting . . . people.' In truth, Sir John did not relish the idea of losing his daughter to a husband, but recognised it was selfishness on his part.

'London,' repeated Henrietta, in an awed voice. 'Almack's?'

'I cannot conceive why not. I am sure your aunt will be procuring vouchers for your cousin.'

'But what shall I wear?'

'Gowns.' Sir John blinked at the question, which, as a man, he took quite literally. 'No need to fear there are not sufficient funds put by to cover your junketing about. Your aunt was always quite the fashionable lady, and will rig you out in fine style.'

Henrietta sat down in the nearest chair in a manner that the lady would no doubt have considered lacking in deportment.

'I cannot believe it, Papa. I had thought perhaps the local assemblies . . .'

'Your dear mama would have wanted you to have your Season, be presented at court as she was, and you are a dashed pretty girl, very like her in her youth. You will be a great success, as long as you remember not to consider yourself "a great success".' Observing her stunned expression, he rang for tea. However, when the door was opened, it was not the butler who entered, but a well-set-up young man of above average height, with dark chestnut hair, a ready smile and such ease as might have made him appear the son of the family. He came forward, hand outstretched, as Sir John rose from his chair.

'Good afternoon, sir. No, no, please do not get up. I thought I might drop by to tell you that I met Mr Preston on the Ludlow road, and he said his pointer bitch has had a fine litter, and you can have your pick, or rather Henry can, as promised.' He looked to Henrietta, who clapped her hands together.

'Oh, Charles, how wo . . . but if I am going to London . . .'

'London?'

'Yes, my boy, Henrietta is off to dazzle in the firmament of society. Oh, there you are, Stone.' The butler had entered. 'Would you bring tea, please.' His gaze reverted to his godson. 'You will stay and take "tea and excitement", won't you, Charles?'

'Er, yes, yes of course.' Lord Henfield appeared almost as taken aback as Henrietta, but made a recovery. 'Foolish of me not to have considered you disappearing for the Season, Henry. I am sure you will have a wonderful time. Just do not let some buck in yellow pantaloons turn your head with his finery, eh?' His smile was broad, but his eyes did not echo the pleasure to quite the same degree. He took a seat to the right of the fire, and extended cold hands to its warmth, feigning preoccupation with the act of getting the blood flowing back in them. He had known Henrietta from her infancy, and she and his godfather were as 'close family' to him, with both his parents having deceased in the first five years after he attained his majority. He would miss her.

'So what shall I do about the puppy? It was very kind of Mr Preston to remember how much I admired his pointer, and to offer us one of her litter, but if I am in London . . .' Henrietta bit her lip.

'I think he would understand, Henry, honestly. If you like I will take you over to The Chestnuts just before you go, and you can have a look at the litter and make your choice, assuming they are not yet ready to leave their mother. The Season is not so long that you will not be back within a few months, and if it is here already, well, you will have missed it looking all big eyes and uncoordinated paws but that is all. It will grow to accept you easily enough.' Like her sire, Lord Henfield preferred not to think that London would be other than an interlude of pleasure. 'The puppy might even keep your papa company in your absence.'

'Really, Charles?' Henrietta giggled. 'So I am as much company as a dog? Charming. Papa, I refuse to sit at your feet and beg for treats, just so as you know.'

'No, Henry, you know I didn't mean . . . obnoxious girl. You will have to learn to be much more formal and polite for London. No treating poor decent fellows as you do me.' Lord Henfield gave her a look of mock reproach, at which she wrinkled up her pretty little nose.

'I shall be very polite, because I shall be treated with politeness, sir.' She stuck her chin in the air, but her lips twitched.

Sir John shook his head and laughed at the pair of them.

'So when are you leaving?' Lord Henfield enquired.

'Papa?' Henrietta looked at her father. 'You did not say when.'

'You are expected in South Audley Street in three weeks.'

'Oh my goodness! What shall I do?'

'Start packing?' suggested her friend, his lips twitching at her expression.

'But I have not got clothes suitable for London.' One hand went to her cheek.

'That is why your Aunt Elstead wants you settled so soon, so that she may, let me see . . .' Sir John picked up the letter once more. 'Ah yes, "ensure her wardrobe does her justice".'

'Do not worry, Henry. You will take London by storm, not a doubt of it, and do us proud.' Lord Henfield gave her a wry grin.

She assured them she would try very hard to make them proud, but doubted very much that London would find her anything out of the ordinary.

* * *

Henrietta alternated between wild excitement, nervousness, and gloom. She was counting the days, but both eager for adventure, and cast into misery at the thought of leaving her papa. Lord Henfield was somewhat surprised to find her in the latter mood when he drove her over to The Chestnuts, and Mr Preston, to select the pointer puppy.

'You know, it may not be ideal, Henry, but it will soon recognise you as mistress once you get back, and it really will give your papa something to make a fuss of while you are away.'

'I told you before that he does not fondle my ears or tell me off for hiding bones under the library rug, you know, but you are right, and I ought to be pleased. We have missed a dog since old Rufus died, and he had got to be too old to go out with Papa when he went shooting.'

'Then why such a long face? I would think you would be like a cat on hot coals, eager to experience the capital.'

'Oh yes, yes I am, but . . .'

'But . . .?' He cast her a sidelong glance. She did have a most enchanting profile, he admitted to himself.

'I have never been away, not for more than a week with my grandmama, after Mama . . . It feels like . . . desertion.'

'Ah.'

'And I do not know my Aunt Elstead, beyond recognising her if she walked into the room.' Henrietta sighed.

'Ah.'

'The "ahs" are not helping, Charles.'

'Sorry, Henry. I suppose the nearest I can think of was going off to school, which was pretty dashed scary at the time. One wondered, as you do, about fitting in, making friends and all that, but you know, it just "happens", and you have to remember that all the other young ladies will be nervous and feeling vulnerable too. And there is even the advantage of not getting thrashed at all-too-frequent intervals.'

'It is different for men.'

'She says, from great experience.' He smiled at her.

'But when they "go to Town" they generally do so after university, and have a wide acquaintance among their peers.'

'And have less guidance, not that it would be popular at the time. We all thought ourselves very grown-up and were no more so than . . . pups. We therefore tumbled into a few scrapes, but learned a lot.'

'I cannot imagine you in a scrape, Charles.' She looked at him, his face open and honest. She could not think of him engaged in the least devilry.

'I do not know whether that delights me or horrifies me. Do you think I am too virtuous, or too boring?'

'You are never boring. Charles, and as for virtuous . . . virtue may sound boring but actually it is to be applauded, since vice is to be deplored.'

'I once let a chicken into the master's lodgings when I

was up at Oxford,' admitted Lord Henfield confidingly.

'Well, sir, if that is the limit of your vice . . .'

'Er, and its three "friends". One laid an egg under the master's wing chair.'

'Most reprehensible.' Henrietta's lips twitched. 'Were you apprehended?'

'I confessed, and did "penance" by clearing up the mess, and you would be amazed how much mess four hens can create, and having to write an ode, in the style of Horace, "To a Chicken".'

'Goodness! I am sure that taught you a lesson, and not in Latin.' She bit her lip to prevent herself giggling the more.

'It put me off poultry, unless cooked.' He had coaxed her from her sad mood, which had been his intention, and they arrived at Mr Preston's both in good humour.

Mr Preston greeted them with a combination of warmth and deference, having known both since childhood and himself being in the lower echelons of the local squirearchy. He escorted them personally to the hay-scented loose-box where Tilly, his pointer bitch, was suckling her litter of seven. She looked up at her master's arrival, and the thump of her docked tail showed her greeting. Henrietta was content to watch the family for a few minutes, then squatted down and spoke softly. Tilly appeared unconcerned, and the pups, sufficiently fed to start snuffling about, began to play. One puppy came towards her, cautiously at first, taking her scent, tail wagging in a hopeful manner. Henrietta extended her hand and the puppy nosed it, then licked it experimentally, and sneezed.

'I told you wearing pepper was not a normal perfume,' observed Lord Henfield mendaciously.

Mr Preston reached and picked the puppy up. Tilly watched, but did not move.

'Nice little bitch, this one. Not shy, interested in what is about, and nice short back and good head. She should make a good working dog like her mother.'

'She is very pretty also.' Henrietta stroked one velvety, liver-brown ear. The puppy had a light flea-bitten colour coat with splashes of liver-brown on shoulder and haunch, and a 'cap' that extended over both ears and cheeks. 'Might we have this one, when she is old enough to leave her mother?'

'Of course you may, Miss Henrietta. I will bring her over to The Court when weaned.'

'I am afraid I will be absent then, Mr Preston, for I am going to London, to stay with my aunt, Lady Elstead, but I do look forward to seeing this little one when I return. Dido, that will be her name.'

'Dido it is then, Miss Henrietta.'

'Remember to tell your papa, Henrietta, or the poor thing may get most confused if he names it Thistle.' Lord Henfield was in funning mood.

On the journey back, however, Henrietta, having extolled the visible virtues of the puppy all she might, became quiet. Eventually she spoke.

'When I am away, Charles, will you look after Papa for me?'

'He is scarcely in his dotage and enfeebled, my dear girl.'

'No, but it has been just us, him and me, for some years, and . . . He treats you as he would a son.'

'He has always been most kind and generous of time and advice, but a "son" . . .'

'You count as part of the family, to him, to me too, Charles. I trust nobody more than I do you.' Henrietta put his lack of response and compressed lips down to the taking of a sharp bend without much reduction in pace.

Came the day, came the tears, and if the majority were from Henrietta, then her father's eyes could not be said to be dry either. Lord Henfield, who had walked over to bid her farewell, remained dry-eyed, however. He said little, believing it a time for father and daughter, with himself upon the fringes, but when it came time to hand her up into the waiting post-chaise, it was he who took her hand. She looked up at him, her lashes wet, bravely trying to smile at him. His expression became of a sudden quite serious.

'Spread your wings, Henry, and enjoy all that is new, but remember we are here for you still,' he murmured, in his soft baritone. He paused, and then pressed something into her gloved hand. 'You will have jewels suitable for a young lady, items from your mama, but

16

this belonged to mine, and I would like you to have it.'

Henrietta blinked at the brooch in her palm, a gold disc in which a frond of leaves was set in pearls.

'Oh Charles, you should not. I cannot . . .'

'You can, and I beg that you will.' He closed her fingers over it, and she, blushing, stood upon tiptoe and kissed his cold cheek.

'I will miss you too, you know,' she said softly.

'Only until that first dance, fickle Miss Gaydon,' he replied, hiding his own embarrassment. 'Now, off with you.' He handed her into the chaise, and watched her arrange her skirts, then closed the door.

The horses were set in motion. Henrietta leaned to wave and keep her father in sight as long as possible, but the curve of the drive eventually hid the two gentlemen from view. She dabbed at her eyes, sniffed, and looked again at the brooch. She was, she decided, a very fortunate young woman to have a doting papa and such a kind friend.

When Henrietta reached South Audley Street on the third day, having spent two nights upon the road, she was weary of body, and disinclined to eat, her constitution, she decided, not being best suited to prolonged travel. Indeed, upon a few patches of post road she had felt quite unwell, and it was a rather pale young woman who alighted before the Elstead residence, and trod, a little stiffly, up the steps.

Her aunt greeted her warmly, and fussed over her tiredness, concealing at the same time her disappointment.

When last she had seen Henrietta, a formless little girl of ten years, she had features which clearly showed her maternal lineage, but had her sire's brown hair and looked likely to follow him in being, although not stocky, 'solid' in build. The young woman before her, despite a pallor from travelling, and a tired droop to her shoulders, was possessed of a figure that would draw admiring glances, and a face that would make those glances stares, at least among the impertinent. She was not, perhaps, as tall as some men liked, and her hair was still 'brown', but of a shade that made the word seem inappropriate for one so beautiful. Lady Elstead had expected to bring out her daughter with her niece a little in the background, but faced the fact, squarely, that Caroline, brunette and pretty as she was, could not hold a candle to her cousin. It was most lowering.

She voiced this complaint to her lord, having sent Henrietta up to rest and take supper in her room, if she could not face coming down to dinner.

'It is most vexatious, and it is no secret that Sir John's estate passes to her upon his demise, and a healthy estate that is. I almost wish I had not made the offer to bring her out . . . But my poor sister trusted me to do so, come the time, and one has one's duty to the family.' She sighed, both indicating the sorrow at the loss of her sibling, and at the burden now placed upon her.

'Well, my dear, in some ways it is no harm done. A girl can only marry one man, and a man may only marry one girl, so if there are plenty hovering about Henrietta, then Caroline will also be in their milieu, and . . .'

'You would have our daughter take her cousin's "cast offs"?' snorted Lady Elstead.

'No. I am simply saying there are enough young men to go around. Caroline is a pretty girl, and will do well.'

'"Well" may not be good enough, sir.'

'What is it you want for Caroline? Surely a decent husband, of good family and with sufficient wherewithal to keep her in comfort, is enough. The Season ought not to be a competition to see which girl "wins" the highest rank or the wealthiest husband.'

Lady Elstead did not reply, since she wisely realised that the male perspective was not that of every Society mama. Rank was not everything, nor was wealth, but both counted for more than their obvious advantages. Every woman sought to be a success at her own come-out, and then prove her worth by launching any daughters in such a way that they in turn achieved a brilliant marriage.

'Get Henrietta off your hands and you will see Caroline follow suit,' declared Lord Elstead. His lady looked thoughtful. 'Trust me on this.'

'I hope you are right, my lord, but . . . yes, I will trust you.'

Lady Elstead went to her bed, putting from her mind any unchristian thoughts of showing Henrietta off in unbecoming gowns, or hinting at an inclination to the consumptive habit. In fact, the opposite was true.

CHAPTER TWO

WHEN HENRIETTA AWOKE NEXT MORNING, it was only upon full consciousness that she realised where she lay. The bed was comfortable, much more so than those at the posting houses upon her journey, be the sheets never so aired, and she stretched luxuriously. A fire was already alight in the grate, and Henrietta, normally a light sleeper, acknowledged just how tired she must have been. She rang for her maid, and hoped Sewell, who had found fault with almost everything beyond the borders of Shropshire on their journey, would be in a more positive frame of mind. In this she was to be disappointed.

'Never have I been in such a noisy, unwholesome place in all my born days, Miss Henrietta.'

'I slept very well,' offered Henrietta.

'Yes, miss, but you was done to a cow's thumb, as well I know, and would have slept sound if the house itself had taken fire. Now, will you be wishful to take your breakfast in your bed or . . .'

'Oh no, I think it only polite to present myself properly before my aunt at a good hour. I fear that yesterday I was monosyllabic, and besides, I wish to make the acquaintance of my cousins.'

Her aunt had informed her that whilst of course the younger Felbridges were still at their studies, in school or at the Elstead family seat, both Caroline and James, Caroline's elder brother, were in residence, and eager to meet their cousin. It had only been a pity that Caroline was at a dressmaker's fitting, and James not yet returned from an engagement with one of his friends. Refreshed by slumber, Henrietta was hoping she would match their expectations.

When she went downstairs and was shown to the breakfast parlour by the butler, who introduced himself as Barlow, she found only the Honourable James Felbridge at his repast. He almost jumped to his feet, and, had anyone asked, would have instantly declared that his cousin far outstripped any expectations he had of her, although those had been very vague. That her gown was not in this year's fashion, and her hair styled in a manner that had echoes of the schoolroom about it, struck him not at all. What he beheld, as he later confided to his crony Mr Carshalton, was 'a vision'. He swallowed hard, twice, and made her a bow.

'I believe you must be my cousin James,' said Henrietta, making her curtsey and then offering him her hand. She had expected him to shake it, but he, after a moment's hesitation, bent over it and kissed it rather formally. Henrietta looked surprised. 'Oh.'

'Indeed, and mighty honoured I am to make your acquaintance, Cousin Henrietta. I was told you had arrived, but that you were fatigued by the journey.'

'Alas, I must sound very feeble.'

'Not at all. Long way from Staffordshire, and . . .'

'Shropshire,' she corrected.

'Long way from there too. You must have been fagged to death. You are recovered now, though?'

'Oh yes, and my appetite has returned also.'

'Appetite . . . breakfast, yes, must eat.' He showed her the selection of covered dishes, and was most attentive, to the point where she reminded him that his own breakfast was being neglected.

'It is of no matter, cousin.'

'You say that, but wait until your eggs are cold and congealed and you will not think so.' Henrietta smiled, and a dimple peeped.

When Lady Elstead entered the parlour a few minutes later it was to find the son and heir already in a fair way to being besotted, which was a thing she had not for an instant considered. Her arrival curtailed his adoration, and she had no compunction in dismissing him upon the excuse that he had evidently finished eating and she wished to discuss the day's plan with Henrietta. Once he had withdrawn, her ladyship settled herself with tea and toast, and looked at her niece.

'So, my dear. You look to be recovered.'

'Indeed, ma'am, I feel very much more the thing this morning and can only apologise if I seemed . . .'

'No, no, my dear child.' Her aunt raised a hand. 'I perfectly understand how exhausted you must have felt.' There was a short pause. 'You have not been to London before, have you.'

'No, ma'am, no further than Grandmama Gaydon, in Cheshire.'

'Well, I have no doubt it will seem very strange at the first, but you will soon get used to it. You must, of course, remember that going about alone is unthinkable, not as at home, where I am sure you were at liberty to exercise unescorted. Wherever you go, if you are not accompanied by myself, or another chaperone, you must take a maid, or a footman. To appear "forward" is an unforgivable sin in the eyes of society, and would blight any chance you have of making a suitable connection.'

For one moment Henrietta's mind went blank, and then the full import of what had been said hit her. She had, in some strange way, thought of this visit as an adventure, a rite of passage even, but here was the nub of the matter. Her aunt saw it as society would see it, as the way to arrange her future, to find her a husband. A small but insistent voice within her cried

24

out that she wanted to go back to Shropshire, carry on just being Papa's daughter.

'Does it shock you, my dear? It is, alas, the great problem when one has not a mama to guide one. One has to be pragmatic. When a young lady makes her curtsey to society, it is also her chief opportunity to secure her future, and a future means being married, having an establishment of one's own. In the next few months you will meet many gentlemen, and it is almost certain that one amongst them will find you just to his taste, and he to yours. The days when marriages were arranged without either party having any knowledge of the other are thankfully consigned to the past, in most cases. Neither I nor your papa would expect you to marry a man you could not respect, nor hold in less than a firm regard. You are a beautiful girl, and if your manners and character are equally appealing, you will do very well, very well indeed, and we may expect an excellent match.' Lady Elstead regarded the round gown with disfavour. 'Of course, in order to show you at your best, it will be necessary to get you to a decent dressmaker before anyone sees just how . . . but it is not your fault, my dear, not at all, and your hair, well, my maid can arrange it before we go out shopping. You are no longer a child in the schoolroom. We will have you quite presentable before you have to go abroad in public.'

Henrietta felt rather flattened by all this. She had realised that her wardrobe was not up to London standards, but this sounded as if she was dressed so abysmally that being seen with her would be an embarrassment.

'I . . . I will be guided by you, ma'am, of course. I have brought my jewel casket with me, with such pieces as Mama left to me. I am not sure if there is a "fashion" for jewellery, but I can assure you that the quality is good.' She looked so downcast that Lady Elstead took pity upon her.

'If you inherited them from your mama, I know they will be beautiful. The art, with a girl in her first Season, is not to overdress with trumpery pieces, or large and gaudy stones. "Pearls are perfect, diamonds desirable", that is what I hold to, and so should you.'

'I have a pearl necklet, and drop earrings, and a diamond pendant and hair ornament, and a few brooches.'

'There. You have at least just what you need in that department. Now, where has Caroline got to, I wonder? Much of her wardrobe is complete, but I saw the most fetching hat yesterday, and we might as well visit milliners together, yes?'

Henrietta merely nodded. Lady Elstead rang to send a servant to ascertain if her daughter was awake, and shortly afterwards that damsel appeared, was introduced, and sent to prepare for an assault upon the emporia of the capital. This clearly appealed. By the time the trio returned for a late luncheon, Henrietta's mind was a whirl not just of chip straw and ruched linings, but, courtesy of several modistes, of sarsenet, spider gauze, vandyke and scalloped edgings, twills, satins and figured muslins.

Before dinner. Henrietta sat down to write to her papa, to reassure him of her safe arrival, and to warn him that she was undoubtedly making him poor.

. . . I am not sure that I have any say in the matter, my dear Papa, for I have no notion how many gowns one ought to have, nor of what stuffs. I shall not bore you with describing such things, for I know that it would tell you nothing, since you would have no image of what I meant, unless I were to send you the latest edition of La Belle Assemblée. *I confess my own understanding is rather jumbled at present, but I will be learning very fast, about as fast as the guineas disappear from your account! My aunt has also declared my hair to be dressed so badly that she had to have her maid attend to it before I went out in public, even wearing a hat. I have returned this afternoon already the proud possessor of no less than four hats, an opera cloak, a merino spencer, a pair of long kid evening gloves, three pairs of gloves for day wear, a spangled shawl and half a dozen pairs of silk stockings. The dressmakers are attending to*

the gowns, which must be adjusted to make them fit perfectly. If you were to see me next week, dear Papa, you might not recognise your own daughter.

I cannot say as yet that I like London, for I have not attended any parties, or visited any important sights, but I have been continually busy. I slept most soundly the first night through tiredness, but it is noisy here until very late, and I am unused to voices outside, and the constant sound of hooves upon the cobbles.

I have met my cousins, who are both very friendly. Cousin James is about to enjoy his first Season, having graduated last summer. You must tell Charles that he was quite correct, and young gentlemen embarking upon life in the Ton are definitely 'pups'. He will know what I mean and explain it to you. What surprises me is that Cousin James seems so tongue-tied with me, since he has sisters. Charles was never so awkward, and he has no siblings whatsoever. Cousin Caroline is very pretty, and has a soft voice. My first thought was that she is shy, but it turns out that she is not, but merely possessed of the soft tone of voice. We have discovered that we share the same tastes in poetry (which will make Charles shake his head, since he hates Lord Byron's poems) and look *awful in anything pink. I think we shall be the best of friends. My Uncle Elstead will be franking this for me, but he is going back to his estates for several weeks Tuesday next, so I may have to send letters crossed, Papa, though I know you find them difficult to decipher.*

I miss you terribly, but I am trying not to mope, and indeed, I am sure that once I am engaged at parties and not sat about thinking, I shall be happy enough. Tell Charles that I hope to write to him also in the near future.

Do send me all the news from home, especially when Mr Preston brings Dido to you. She was the sweetest puppy, Papa, and so bold and interested.

I must close now and dress for dinner. If I give this to my uncle it may be on its way to you in the morning.

I remain, dearest Papa,
Your devoted daughter,
Henrietta

As she addressed the letter she wiped away a tear and sniffed, but had regained her composure by the time she joined her relations before dinner. It was the first time that she had met Lord Elstead, and although her first impression of him was that he was a trifle severe in demeanour, he went out of his way to be amiable, and by the time the ladies withdrew, she was much more at her ease with him, and thought him very sensible.

It could not be said that the pace of Henrietta's life became any less hectic over the next week. Lady Elstead engaged a dancing master to ensure that the two young ladies would not disgrace themselves with the waltz, should they be given leave to dance it, and to improve their other dance steps so that they might complete the figures without concentrating upon them. She was only very slightly irritated that Henrietta turned out to be the better of the two. She had to remind herself that Henrietta had little French, by her own admission, and had never essayed the harp at all. There were dress fittings, and for shoes, morning calls which left Henrietta wondering how many new acquaintances she had made, and 'lessons' from Lady Elstead, who reminded both girls that they needed to know the relationships between the most important society figures, since it was so easy to praise a lady's sworn foe in an attempt to be polite, and thereby raise the auditor's hackles.

'One has to be not just polite, my dears, but politic, and that is rather different. Avoiding embarrassment is far easier than trying to brazen out a faux pas.'

Henrietta and Caroline nodded obediently. There were, it seemed, pitfalls of which they had been entirely ignorant. Lady Elstead was, of course, planning her campaign with the grim determination of a general in the field, as was every other matchmaking mama. Even friends, if bringing out daughters, might be classed as 'enemy' this Season, and, having surveyed quite a few of the 'opposition' during the reconnaissance that was the morning call, Lady Elstead had already identified several 'allies', ladies with girls who were either patently less attractive and would be honoured to form part of the Elstead circle, or such contrasts that each would show off the other. If a gentleman was only attracted to fair damsels, there was nothing that a brunette might do, and vice versa. Placing one's pretty brunette next to an equally attractive golden-haired maiden could show off both.

Lady Elstead did not, of course, reveal her plan to Henrietta and Caroline, and her 'lists' were kept even more closely to her matronly bosom. That Lady Elstead was a 'list maker' was known to her entire family and household staff. Lists were, to her, wondrous things, the writing of which gave substance to aims, form to formless ideas. She made lists for everything, from the contents of her jewel casket, with an additional one noting when each item was last cleaned or repaired, to those who had sent invitations over the last two Seasons, annotated as 'accepted', 'declined' and 'unable'. The 'unables' were those where some unforeseen event had prevented attendance at a function she had graciously accepted. Of course, some lists were mundane, but the

girl would not suffer, since she would live as well as she had previously, and the gentleman would see his family fortunes boosted, perhaps restored. Not that she would advocate a wastrel, an inveterate gambler, but some men had fathers who had squandered riches, mamas who had proved 'expensive in the extreme'. Some of these gentlemen were even reduced to marrying nobodies, tainted by commerce and trade. How much better would be a beautiful bride, of impeccable background. Yes, this brought some interesting names onto the list, and such gentlemen would be eager to secure such a prize, which would mean them applying for her hand quite early in the Season. Lady Elstead spent a happy half hour imagining the cachet that would attend her having found a match for her niece before the Season was half over, to be followed by a brilliant match for her daughter. The following half hour she permitted herself the luxury of drawing up a putative wedding invitation list designed to pay off many old scores.

In blissful ignorance, the two girls formed a very cousinly friendship. To Henrietta, as an only child, and with no close female friends, this was quite a novel situation, and she put out the feelers of friendship almost tentatively. She was used to fitting in with a male world, and being 'girlish' was almost something she needed to learn. Caroline was a little taken aback by Henrietta's almost 'boyish' attitude, since she was rather more forthright than most girls, but her mama reminded her that her 'poor cousin' had lacked the guiding hand of a mama since the age of ten, and had been brought up in a household with only her papa, and visits from his male acquaintance.

'I do not say that Henrietta is fatally rustic, you understand, for she is remarkably well behaved, but she is unused to the company of ladies, and has, perforce, copied a slightly more "mannish" way of going on. I am trusting you, my child, to show her how a delicately brought up female comports herself in conversation.'

As far as Cousin Caroline could see, the only problem with Henrietta's manner was that she clearly thought that 'beating about the bush' was sometimes ridiculous, if not verging on the dishonest.

'Do you expect me to tell lies, Caroline?'

'No, no, it is just . . . think of it like the dance, cousin. One could walk across the dance floor in a few paces, but that would not show off one's abilities, nor be entertaining. By using the steps, following what is expected, we show ourselves at our best. So if someone were to ask your opinion of a new book, or picture, saying "I thought it mediocre" is too blunt. One must try and say a few nice things about it, without overpraising.'

'What if I cannot think of anything?' Henrietta had a smile on her lips but a frown between her brows.

'Make something up.'

'But that is the lie, Caroline.'

'I think you are going to discover there are a lot of lies in the London Season, my dear cousin.'

CHAPTER THREE

SIR JOHN RECEIVED HIS BELOVED DAUGHTER'S FIRST letter, thankfully not crossed, within a week of her departure from his gate. It both cheered him, knowing that she was safe and well, and left him dispirited, because the house felt empty without her youthful and optimistic presence. It was illogical, he told himself, to think that the absence of one person rendered his house 'empty', but he could not remark to the servants about the small things he noted on his daily walk, nor invite the butler to play chess with him. Lord Henfield came over several times, and one afternoon they went out to shoot rabbits, but it had to be said that Charles was not his usual self either, and although he put a brave enough face upon it, he appeared a trifle low spirited.

The letter was read to him when he came for dinner, was dissected and smiled over, and both gentlemen reminisced about their very mildly misspent youths whilst considering 'pups'.

'At least I think we can be sure Henrietta will not be bowled over by her cousin,' declared Sir John.

'Most definitely not,' agreed Lord Henfield, gazing at the contents of his brandy glass as if it might produce some unexpected augury.

'One wants to see her settled and happy, of course, but, you know, Charles, the thought of her gone, perhaps residing at the other end of the country, quite fills me with gloom.' Sir Charles was watching his godson quite closely.

'Mm.' It was clear that Lord Henfield found the thought equally unappealing.

'She is not an angel. I never pretended she was, because at times she can drive a man of sense to distraction, wilful miss that she can be, but . . . she has a spark. Her mother had it, God rest her, and . . . I miss her damnably, and she has only been away a week.'

'Mm.' This time the 'mm' was more distant.

'Are you listening, Charles?'

'Mm. I mean, I am sorry, thoughts drifted off for a moment, must be your devilish good brandy.' It was a lie, but a soft one. Lord Henfield was imagining Henrietta, eyes sparkling, on the arm of some faceless man whom he hated for merely existing.

'I was saying how much I missed her.'

'Perfectly natural that you do, sir. Be a good thing when Preston brings over that puppy. Give you something to write about to Henry, and something to talk to.'

'As long as it does not answer back, eh?'

'Absolutely.' Lord Henfield poured them both another brandy.

Lord Henfield received his own letter from Henrietta a week later. He looked at her neat, still rather schoolgirl hand, and it brought back another letter from her adolescence, one he had kept, and in which she had been so upset and apologetic at angering him. There were no tear stains on this missive.

My dear Charles,

You never warned me that London does not sleep! Of course we are likely to be abroad in the early hours, but there is bustling about from dawn, and what with vendors in the streets, and link boys and horses, it makes one wish so much for the peace of the country. I have been forced to take to my bed for an hour some afternoons, which I would never do at home unless ill. I do not wish you to think, however, that I am not enjoying myself tremendously, even before attending any

*of the Ton parties. I never have to wonder what
to do with myself, and Green Park and Hyde
Park provide welcome places where one might
walk. Taking one of the maids with me means
dawdling, alas, so I prefer to take one of the
footmen. They always seem glad to be obliging,
which must mean that they enjoy fresh air too.*

Lord Henfield groaned. Trust Henry not to see that
footmen were as impressionable as other men.

*My cousins are delightful, although Cousin James
speaks too often in half sentences. His papa is
very proud that he obtained a 'very sound' degree
from Cambridge, but sometimes I wonder if his
wits are lacking. Of course it might be that he
is actually thinking very important thoughts,
and not paying attention to what he is saying to
me. You were so very right about 'pups', and he
counts as one. Now, I wonder if I threw a stick
in the park, would he fetch it for me? Am I not
wicked?*

*We attended the opera last night. I very much
enjoyed the singing, but was so glad my uncle had
procured us a box. I do not think the gentlemen
in the stalls were attending properly during the
arias. I did not mention this to my aunt because I*

have now been in Town nearly a week, and I am learning things. Gentlemen, when together and without ladies present, are inclined to drink rather too much. James looked very 'unwell' yesterday, and his mama was not at all sympathetic. I was at first shocked, since I thought she would be most concerned, but she simply told me that his disorder was self-inflicted, and that we should ignore it, and indeed him, for the rest of the day.

I have had fittings for new gowns, and my hair has been cut and is being dressed differently, so I do not think you would recognise me at first glance. I am definitely not a 'schoolroom miss' any more, and you will have to treat me like a real lady when next we meet, or at least try to do so.

Has Dido come to The Court yet? I do so hope Papa likes her, and that you are looking after Papa too.

Yours always,
Henry

At least she still signed herself that, he thought. He had always called her 'Henry'. The trouble was he was realising why, and that was because it kept up the lie that she was not actually a girl, just 'Henry'. He had known it for a lie these two years past, increasingly so, but had kept up the pretence to himself. At the same time, because he was the only person who used the name, it implied their closeness, and special bond. Now she was gone, and he was faced with the harsh truth that when she came back it might be only briefly, and as a prelude to becoming another man's wife. 'Yours always' would be meaningless then. He sent his reply to catch the mail coach from Ludlow.

My dear Henry,

Or is that appellation unsuited to your new 'grown-up' status? I was not sure that you would have believed me if I had told you how tiring the capital can be. I do not think you feeble for taking a rest in the afternoons, and indeed would advocate that you do so, so that the pace may not tell upon your constitution. I recall some young ladies looking positively wan by the time they were presented at court.

You are quite correct that gentlemen are inclined to drink too much, but not in general when there are ladies present. However, by the end of an evening, even at a ball, I would not trust to many being entirely sober. Thankfully, most gentlemen

learn to hold their drink. It sounds as if your
cousin, especially if he has been a good student,
has yet to acquire that ability. Do not tease him
over it, but do as your aunt says, and pretend not
to see.

He frowned. Was he sounding too avuncular, giving advice? He changed the subject.

Dido arrived yesterday, and has already chewed
one of the slippers you made for your papa last
Christmas and tipped up a three-parts-empty coal
scuttle, at which point she became a very black
puppy. Your papa appears delighted, but then it
was not he who had to bath the animal. I believe
Thomas was not so happy.

I have been a most frequent visitor but I cannot
replace you, my dear Henry. Your papa does very
well, but we both miss you very much.

You may have changed the styling of your hair,
and your gowns, but I trust you to remain the girl
we both hold in such deep affection.

Yours,
Charles

For a moment he wondered if he had said too much. No, she would take it to mean fraternal affection.

Whilst the Season was still comparatively quiet, Lady Elstead brought her daughter and niece gently into society, first by attending an evening party hosted by old friends, friends who had known Caroline as she grew up. This meant that Caroline was less overawed. It was, however, an important occasion, and both she and Henrietta were excessively excited to be dressing for their first 'grown-up' party, and inclined to be wide-eyed. Lady Elstead watched, but said nothing. This, after all, was why she was introducing them at a comparatively small social event, so that they might get the novelty of it out of their systems. After three or four evenings out, they should have gained a little poise. She recalled her own first party, and did not think them foolish. If tonight they stammered their responses for the first hour, and blushed, then they would be forgiven.

'You know, Maria, I am so glad I am not eighteen, are not you?' their hostess remarked quietly, partway through the evening. 'We managed it then, but it all looks so perfectly exhausting now.'

'Oh yes, and yet . . . The first time a gentleman sent one flowers . . .' Maria Elstead sighed. 'Being young is wonderful . . . once. I fear chaperoning the young is also going to be exhausting, though, and without the bouquets.'

42

'Ah yes, but you will have far greater prizes, seeing them safely betrothed.'

'Very true, Charlotte.'

'And two such pretty girls too. Your niece is set to inherit her father's entire estate, you say?'

'She is.' Lady Elstead saw her opportunity. 'One would not describe her as a great heiress of course . . . but . . . None of the estate is entailed.' Thus were sown the seeds, without her ever telling anything other than the truth. Knowing her hostess, this information would spread swiftly enough, and with just a little gilding. Nobody would be so mercenary or impolite as to ask the exact size of the estate, or the figure of its worth, and by not claiming too much, which would be found out by some busybody, just sufficient interest would be raised to give Henrietta's chances a little boost. She had beauty, birth and now bounty.

Henrietta herself was in total ignorance of such machinations, and was simply enjoying being part of a new and overwhelmingly exciting world. Her host introduced her to his nephew, Lord Netheravon, who possessed a head of golden curls, and a fine figure. His fair lashes blinked over startlingly blue eyes, and, although Caroline later suggested that he was an Adonis, Henrietta was more inclined to see him as a remarkably athletic cherub. He was patently impressed with her own looks, and made every effort to entertain her. He was droll, self-deprecating and had sufficiently

43

outgrown the 'pup' stage that condemned her cousin James to being treated as a younger, rather than older, relative.

'So, Miss Gaydon, this is your introduction to the Season. I hope you are not already bored?'

'Bored, my lord? How could one be bored?'

'But my dear young lady, cultivating at least the appearance of being bored is half the "act" of the damsel at her come-out. Mark my words, in three weeks you will be complaining at "such awful squeezes"' – he pitched his voice unnaturally high – 'and "positively interminable suppers". You all do it, every year, upon my honour, even if you would not swap these entertainments for a casket of rubies.'

'I shall not, my lord,' she assured him, dimpling, which he found entrancing.

'But you have to be, lest you be pointed out as "idiosyncratic". "There is Miss Gaydon," they would say, "who is so original. She loves every bruised toe, every worn heel, every syllabub and syllable of the Season".'

'But why not enjoy it?'

'Fashion, Miss Gaydon, fashion.'

'Then I think I may choose to be unfashionable, my lord.'

'Daring, ma'am, very daring, but I wish you well. I shall of course ensure that I am on hand to warn you if you begin to look the least jaded with it all.' His eyes twinkled, and his smile was, for a cherub, infectious. She found him very amusing.

'You mock me, my lord, which is most unfair, since this is indeed my first party.' Quite unconsciously, she looked at him from under her curling lashes, and he was hooked.

'Mock? You misunderstand entirely, Miss Gaydon. I am merely being supportive. You wish to be unfashionable in your enjoyment of the Season, and I say "bravo" to it. Behold me eager to serve you in any way to keep you to your intent.' His eyes still danced.

'Your words are good, but your eyes mock, sir.'

'Then I should shut them.' He did so, screwing them up tight. 'Except that now, ma'am, I am like to be accounted a danger, for I will walk into people, and fall down steps and . . . you would not wish to see me break a leg, or crush some unsuspecting matron, now, would you?'

'My lord' – Henrietta could not contain the giggle, however mature she had been trying to appear – 'do open your eyes, I beg. We attract attention.'

'I think, Miss Gaydon, you attract attention, and I am fortunate to have spent such an enjoyable five minutes in your close proximity,' murmured Lord Netheravon, opening his eyes, and bowing over her hand. She blushed, and he, thinking her charming, withdrew, not wishing to monopolise her. He was later seen making Miss Felbridge lower her eyes and laugh behind her fan. Lady Elstead was not displeased, for his was a name found upon both her lists. She had been less pleased to see Lord Martley presented to Caroline, although to all intents and purposes, he was a perfectly acceptable young man. For Henrietta, yes, she would countenance him as a suitor, but Lady Elstead had a very deep-seated and long-standing reason why Viscount Martley was almost the last man in London she would have considering Caroline as a wife.

The young man himself, ignorant of the light in which he was viewed, had spoken to both Caroline and Henrietta, and had told them they were the prettiest sight he had seen in a month.

'Which leads us to believe, sir, that you have spent the month hunting, or shooting, and not seen any member of the fairer sex other than housekeepers, cooks or maids,' Henrietta had countered.

'Now, Miss Gaydon, do I look like the sort of fellow to bamboozle young ladies?'

'Let me see . . . What do you think, cousin?' Henrietta raised her eyebrows at Caroline.

'Alas, I fear we are too much the novices to make a judgement,' she replied softly, but lifted her eyes briefly and smiled at the viscount, who was thus rendered speechless for a full half minute.

'I can only assure you both, on my honour, that I failed the bamboozling exam at Eton quite appallingly. The only problem is that I also achieved only mediocre marks in compliments, as has been proven.' He feigned dejection.

'Is that what is taught at Eton, my lord? How odd. My brother James used to write of mathematics and Greek.' Caroline quizzed him, but he had an instant answer.

'Ah, that was for the clever ones. I was never scholarly.'

'At what did you excel, sir, if academe and flattery were not your strong suits?' Henrietta pressed him.

'Well, Miss Gaydon, I was good on local geography. I knew the best place to purchase buns and cakes. I have kept up my skills, and thus am able to direct you, without any fear of getting lost, to where there is a selection of ices and delicacies set out for this evening.'

'You are saying that you are the ideal escort if one wants to be first to find the supper, my lord?'

'Every time, Miss Felbridge, every time. So if you would permit me to guide you . . .'

The Elstead party returned in the small hours, pleasantly tired, and feeling that the evening had been a success. It was late in the morning when Caroline came to Henrietta's bedchamber to discuss the people they had met, what had been said, and how others looked.

'Do you know, cousin, I was so very nervous, about being introduced to gentlemen, that is, but they were so funny, I forgot my nerves, except with Lord

Thirlmere, whose manner I found rather odious. His compliments were not to my taste' – Caroline frowned her displeasure – 'and there was a peculiar scent of snuff about him. I know Papa takes snuff, but he does not reek of it.' She shuddered.

'I was spared that, but a gentleman whose name I forget spent ten minutes describing his new horse to me.'

'He did not!'

'I promise you that he did. I can tell you all its good points, if you wish.' Henrietta laughed. 'He had not even the excuse of being a "pup".'

'A pup?'

'It is what Charles says young men are when they first come to London to make their mark.'

'What is he like?'

'Who? Charles?' Henrietta considered the matter. 'Well, he is quite tall, and he is a good shot.'

Caroline collapsed with laughter, which made Henrietta slightly huffy.

'I . . . I should recognise him . . . instantly,' gasped Caroline, hugging a tasselled cushion.

'But what am I meant to say? He is broad chested, his eyes are blue, or perhaps grey, his hair is dark chestnut colour but not "bay", and he has good teeth.'

'You might be describing your horse!'

'Oh, no, my horse cannot shoot at all.'

'Henrietta, you said you grew up with him.'

'Yes, but . . . how well can you describe your brother James, or your younger brother and sisters? When one sees someone, if not every day then several times a week, from infancy, details become blurred.'

'But he is not your brother.'

There was a pause.

'No.'

If Lord Netheravon's prediction did not prove true, it had to be admitted that after the first week of being at a party every evening, and having made a first appearance at Almack's, both Henrietta and Caroline had found their feet. Almack's was definitely a 'rite of passage', and provided a small reminder that there were very many pretty girls making their debut. Lady Elstead was careful to stress this, rather than to say that her two charges could be accounted among the top rank of beauties. Vanity, in her books, was a swift path to failure, for it made the most beautiful of face diminished by character. Both girls were expanding their circle of friends among the other maidens, but had a tendency to stick together as a pair, which more than a few gentlemen found awkward, since they would have preferred to dally with one particular girl, and a third party was not conducive to romance. However, there were none who remarked upon any other fault with them.

Lady Elstead crossed a couple of names from the lists, having seen those gentlemen focusing upon golden-haired damsels, but was able to add several names she had not previously considered, most notably Mr Robert Newbold. Mr Newbold found Henrietta a breath of fresh air. He was rather older than most of her followers, being some six and thirty, and was known to prefer older and more 'experienced' ladies. Girls in their first Season were too insipid for his tastes. Henrietta Gaydon, however, was different. Perhaps it was that slightly forthright, masculine approach deplored by her aunt and discomfiting to her cousin, but she had a spark he found most entertaining, and he began to abandon the card room for the dance floor much more than previously.

Henrietta's first thought was not that he was in any way interested in her in particular, because had it been so, then surely her aunt would have 'warned' her, for he possessed no title. It was only in the third week, when he had danced with her at three different balls in as many days, that Lady Elstead asked, nonchalantly, what Henrietta thought of him.

'Oh, he is very dry, wickedly so I think, and very entertaining. He does not put me to the blush, but his animadversions upon others are almost cruel, though accurate.'

'He seems quite taken with you, my dear Henrietta.'

'Me? Oh, but I am sure you need not worry, ma'am.'

'Worry? Why on earth ought I to worry, my dear. Goodness! Robert Newbold has had caps set at him these twelve years past and shown not the slightest interest. Not that I would ever suggest you did such a thing.'

'But why, dear ma'am? He is simply " Mr Newbold".'

'Mr Newbold, yes, but not 'simply'. His maternal grandsire was a duke, he owns untold acres in the north somewhere, and beneath them are layers, or whatever they are termed, of coal. He is enormously wealthy.'

'Oh. He does not strike one as rich.'

'That, Henrietta, is because he has no need to flaunt it.'

Her aunt's words gave Henrietta pause for thought. Mr Newbold was an entertaining companion, and she liked him, but could not imagine a romantic relationship with him. He had also not paid her the sort of compliments, funning or otherwise, that her newly acknowledged swains, such as Lord Martley and Lord Netheravon to name but two, had done. Even Cousin James, whom she discounted upon the grounds of his youth, paid her better compliments. No, Aunt Maria must be wrong.

Had she asked the gentleman himself, it is unlikely that she would have got an honest answer, but then again he was not sure in himself whether he was serious about the chit or not. She was refreshing, even to such a jaded spirit as he had become, and combined a youthful naïvety with some surprisingly mature attitudes. She was also patently not making any attempt to have him at her feet, a position Mr Newbold eschewed, and he was caught between vague irritation that his natural charms did not cause her heart to flutter in her delectable maidenly bosom, and curiosity as to why she was immune. He had avoided praising her, because he saw that she thought it a 'game', and not to be taken seriously, so it was not that which kept her friendly, but not entranced. Then again, he asked himself, did he want her entranced, turned from witty young woman into sighing maid, and was he, even for a moment, considering giving up his much-valued single state to woo and win her?

Mr Newbold himself might be confused, but among Henrietta's younger followers, he was seen as a dangerous threat. Discounting him as 'old' was only available to James Felbridge. The others saw him as 'experienced' and capable of playing a very deep game. Sir Desmond Corney bemoaned that it was dashed unfair of Newbold, who did not need the readies, to cast his eye over a chit who would solve many a gentleman's financial worries. If others thought that sounded too mercenary to be said out loud, they silently agreed.

'I suppose it is unfair to ask what he sees in Miss Gaydon,' sighed Lord Netheravon, as he played billiards with Lord Gorleston, 'since she is a dazzling girl.'

'"The Glorious Gaydon"? I know Shelsley prefers Lady Julia Somercotes, because only fair chits appeal to him, but even he admits she is one of the highlights of the Season. Dash it, my mama even asked me if I was going to make a push for her.'

'And are you?'

'With the likes of you before me? No. Above my touch, Miss Gaydon. My tongue would tie itself into knots, and my feet too, if I were dancing with her.'

'I do not think she takes what any of us say to heart, flattery or "knots". Very quick-witted, she is, but do you know what, I get the feeling she is playing with us all, Newbold included.'

'That's a dashed unpleasant thing to suggest.' Lord Gorleston looked quite shocked.

'Oh no, no, not in an intentional way. I cannot really explain. I do not think her heartless, only . . . none of us seem to have found her heart. She is amusing and amused, but . . . No, I cannot explain.' He pulled a face as his shot went awry. 'See, thinking about it has made me miss that cannon!'

CHAPTER FOUR

Lady Elstead had arranged for the two girls to make their curtsey at a drawing room at the beginning of April. Both young ladies were quite shocked at the required dress, which was so outmoded, with its hoops and ostrich feathers, and actually laughed, until they tried curtseying whilst wearing them.

'You make too much fuss, the both of you. Why, I can assure you your grandmama had panniers that stuck out well over an arm's length either side of her and managed perfectly well. The portrait that hangs on the turn of the stairs at Selmarsh shows it. Do you not recall it, Caroline, from when you last visited your Uncle Rustington?'

'I . . . oh yes, the lady with the tall white wig. I cannot decide which looked more awkward to wear, having such a thing on one's head, or having to walk sideways through doorways. Henrietta, she really did have skirts that made her look as if there were planks of wood inside them, and the bodice and skirt were entirely separate. Did you not say that ladies sometimes found mice in their wigs, Mama?'

'I believe they did, so be thankful you have but ostrich plumes in your hair.'

'And not an ostrich?' Henrietta giggled. She did not giggle, however, when she found out the cost of the ensemble, and went quite pale.

'For a gown I will wear but once? Oh, Aunt, what will Papa think?'

'Your papa is well aware of the cost of being presented, my dear, and whilst I agree it is a pity that the money cannot go towards more useful apparel, this is the way it is done, and everyone has the same expense. Now, I want to see you lower than that in the curtsey, and no wobbling, not even a tremor to make the plumes move, do you hear?'

It was clear that her ladyship was not going to bemoan what could not be avoided, and was far more concerned that it should all pass off without any mishap that might provide other matrons with an opportunity to make snide comments, however much of a charade it might be. It meant that for several days running Caroline and Henrietta had to be dressed in their unwanted finery and practise walking forwards, and backwards, curtseying and bowing their heads with the nodding plumes. On the first day, one of Caroline's dislodged itself from the headdress and flopped forwards over her face. Caroline laughed, but her mama evinced every sign of panic, and thereafter clenched her hands together as if in prayer whenever either girl bowed their head.

The preparations for the presentation took some of the pleasure out of it, confided Caroline to Henrietta, in the privacy of her bedchamber.

'I confess it is feeling more like a challenge to be faced, even though it does mean seeing the Queen. I would far prefer it was just another party, for Mama is becoming more nervous by the day, which makes me more nervous too.'

'I am still concerned at the cost.' Henrietta bit her lip. 'Papa may have expected it, but I feel it is a burden.'

'And it is not even as though the gowns are pretty.' Caroline pulled a face.

'Well, I have been thinking about it. There is plenty of material in the skirts, so one might have a bodice and a half slip made from it, if it is not too stiff, or perhaps an underskirt, but I am not convinced it will simply be too thick a fabric.'

'You mean have it cut up?'

'Yes, why not. It will be of no use otherwise.' She grinned. 'Unless we have curtains made from them.'

'Do not suggest that to Mama.'

'Well, no, I will not, but I think the ostrich feathers might be curled more, and dyed, and added to hats. I refuse to ever wear them as hair ornaments ever again.'

'They have caused us enough trouble.' Caroline sighed.

'Is that sigh over the feathers, or something else, Caroline?' Henrietta's eyes narrowed.

'I . . . oh, it is nothing.' There was a pause. 'What do you think of Marianne Dean?'

'I cannot say that I have spent much time in her company, but she appears to be very . . . industrious. She told me her mama is very keen for her to form an attachment in her first Season, because her younger sister ought to make her come-out next year. Apparently she is only fifteen months Miss Dean's junior. There is, I think, a lot of pressure on her. I rather pity her.'

'Yes, I can see it is not pleasant. Thankfully, Lydia and Amelia are some years from all this.' Caroline twisted a ring about her finger. 'Lord Martley danced with her twice last night, because he was her partner in one of the country dances as well.'

'Did he? Well, he waltzed with me earlier in the evening, remember, and I am sure he was going to ask you, except that your mama wanted to introduce you to old Lady Tretower.'

'And I have no idea why. Her ladyship seemed quite surprised when Mama came up with me. It is not as though she were some connection; at least, I do not think she is.' Caroline shook her head. 'I am perfectly sure I never had so many distant relatives until I came to London.'

'Such as myself?' Henrietta giggled.

'Oh! Oh no, of course not you, silly. You are not a "distant" relative except in how far away you live.'

Both girls now giggled, and Caroline described a paternal relation so awful that no distance could be far away enough, which made them both laugh. Eventually Henrietta shook her head, and returned to practical matters.

'Now, are you wearing your figured muslin with the silver thread for Lady St Athan's rout party, or the ivory half dress with the satin petticoat?'

Mr Newbold found Miss Gaydon in a pensive mood when he met her at Lady St Athan's, fanning herself gently.

'You must tell me, Miss Gaydon, are you frowning in contemplation of some puzzle, or have you decided, as I have, that the combination of puce and grey stripes that Lady Ditchling is wearing is an offence to the eye?'

'Mr Newbold! I would not be so rude.' Henrietta glanced at his profile, with its very slightly aquiline nose.

'Which thereby implies that I am. I see.' He raised one eyebrow.

'You see nothing of the kind, sir. It would, however,

be the height of impertinence for me to pass judgement on the dress of a lady as . . .'

'Old?'

'No! I was going to say "as senior, compared to myself", which is quite different.'

'What a pity we do not have you in the diplomatic service, Miss Gaydon.' His lips twitched, and Henrietta went so far as to rap his knuckles with her fan.

'I wish you would behave, sir.'

'Oh no, Miss Gaydon. Think how boring that would be. Now, will you tell me the reason for you being in deep thought, or is it some young lady's secret?'

'It is no secret at all, sir. Miss Felbridge and I are being presented on Tuesday, and . . . Do you think it treasonable to think it a waste of time and money?' She looked at him in perfect seriousness.

'You do not anticipate the event with eagerness? I thought every young lady wanted to be presented.'

'Have you seen what we have to wear? One looks a positive fright, it costs a huge amount that would buy at least four other, and far nicer, gowns, and . . .'

'So you would mind less if the cost were for some garment you felt flattering? Is that not vanity, Miss Gaydon?' He looked at her, laughter in his grey eyes.

'No, because it is a garment one may wear only the once and then it is set aside. One may wear other gowns time and again, as long as they are not worn every evening of the week.'

'So you complain upon grounds of economy.'

'Do you ever think of economy, Mr Newbold?' She looked at him squarely, and he was, for a moment, taken aback, but she was clearly in earnest.

'Not as such. I mean I do not concern myself at the cost of running my establishments, or how much a coat will cost from my tailor. I therefore do not think of "economising" but I do, though you would be surprised to hear it, think of "the economy" of the nation.'

'You do?' Henrietta did not conceal her surprise.

'Yes. You see, if one is very wealthy, and I make no pretence that I am not, it is wise to observe, and ensure that one's funds do not diminish. I am quite prepared to sit down with my man of business and discuss both the state of the country and its implications for my coal mines. Does that shock you?'

'No . . . yes, a little, sir.'

'Because you think my existence one of idleness, or that discussing such matters smacks of trade?'

'I think' – and Henrietta's brows drew together – 'because I assumed that wealth naturally breeds wealth, and that as long as one does not squander it upon gambling, it is self-perpetuating. However, I know my papa takes an interest in how the wool clip has sold on the Home Farm, and the price of wheat and wool, to ensure his tenants pay a rent that is fair, neither so high it reduces them to giving up their tenancy, nor so little as to hand them all the profit. That is much the same thing on a smaller scale.'

'And your papa is not a poor man.'

'No, but . . .' There was something in the statement that made Henrietta put her head on one side. 'You make it sound as if he too were rich.'

'Is he not?'

'He is not impoverished. At least he was not until he had to pay for my court dress.'

Mr Newbold, who had gathered from report in the clubs that Sir John Gaydon was a man of some substance in the Marches, refrained from pressing the matter, and returned to the forthcoming presentation. After all, it mattered not a jot to him whether the man was wealthy, rich as Croesus, or mortgaged up to the hilt.

The presentation was made. Neither young lady embarrassed themselves by tripping, wobbling, or in any way showing up Lady Elstead, who told them she was very pleased with them both, and permitted them to go to the Pantheon Bazaar next day to spend their pin money on ribands and embroidery silks. They returned to find Mr Newbold had sent flowers to them both, with congratulations, which made Henrietta laugh, Caroline blush and Lady Elstead ponder.

Henrietta could not resist writing to her papa and to Lord Henfield after the great event.

My dearest Papa,

I have seen the Queen! She is a very elderly lady with a rather long face, but very regal. Caroline and I were very nervous, since the court dress is so unlike anything else we wear, and most unnatural. We also had to have ostrich feathers in our hair, which Lady Elstead said was once the rage, but I confess I dislike. The actual drawing room was very grand but in a tired way, and there was much waiting and doing little. I understand it is taken as an important event even now, but it was more of a trial than a treat, my dearest. Your daughter looked a fright, but then so did every other young lady present, which will have to console you.

I am now very much settled into the routine of the Season, and have worn through two pairs of silk stockings just from dancing. There are a couple of young ladies for whom I do not much care, but everyone else is very nice, and the gentlemen are charming. Ought I to tell you that I am 'beset by beaux', Papa? Perhaps that is the wrong word, but the alliteration is good. I mean that I am never lacking in a dancing partner, nor does any hostess have to find a gentleman to lead me into supper. Several gentlemen have sent me flowers, and one wrote me a poem, but it was very poorly written, and he was struggling to find things that rhymed. How could one be impressed by having 'adoration' rhymed with 'inspiration'?

The spring flowers are out in the parks, and yesterday I needed but a spencer and was still perfectly warm upon my walk.

I am enjoying my Season, Papa, and am not at all bored by it all, despite the prediction of Lord Netheravon, but do not think that I have forgotten you, for you are daily in my thoughts and prayers.

I fear you are perhaps being too lenient with Dido. If she is wilful, you must make it clear that the behaviour is not to be borne, and if she upsets Cook much more you will have to placate her, Cook that is, by employing another kitchen maid.

Your loving daughter,
Henrietta

Sir John wondered who Lord Netheravon might be, and what exactly his prediction had been.

The letter that Lord Henfield received was crossed, and took rather more deciphering.

Dear Charles,

What a lot I have to tell you about! I have now been presented, which sounds a wonderful thing, but in truth it was not as exciting as I had dreamed. Her Majesty is old and looks quite frail. Have you ever seen the King or Queen? I feel very sorry for the poor King.

You would have laughed to see me, and Cousin Caroline, in our court dress, for it is most outmoded and unbecoming, but it does mean that all the girls who are presented look equally awful. My Aunt Elstead was as nervous as we were in case we made some terrible mistake, but all went very smoothly, except for one poor girl whose heel caught in her hem as she made her curtsey. The rending sound was very audible, and unless Her Majesty is very deaf, she must have heard it, but she remained perfectly impassive. The other girls felt sorry for her, but the lady presenting her, and I do not know if it was her mama, looked exceedingly put out. It is a good job that the gentlemen do not come and watch the proceedings, or they would remain in their clubs and not come to any of the parties to see us again. Can you imagine me with ostrich feathers sticking from the top of my head? I hope that your answer is 'no'.

I am trying to do as you suggested in your first letter, dear Charles, and rest in the afternoons, but there is so much going on I often do not get the chance. However, I do not think that I am in danger of becoming wan as yet; at least, my mirror does not tell me so. I think that eventually one must tire of the social life, but at present I have not, as Lord Netheravon predicted, come to find it boring, and being popular is most enjoyable and I have not yet had to sit out a dance at Almack's, which makes some other young ladies jealous. I am a little less fortunate in having an admirer who attempts poetry, very badly, but he is very much of the 'pup' variety, and so not serious. He also tends to sigh in my presence, which is remarkably disconcerting, and he appears a trifle disordered of dress. My cousin Caroline says he is trying to ape Lord Byron, but I think he is merely feckless, or has a very inept valet.

Lord Henfield smiled at this. So she was not so immersed in the Season that her eye had become uncritical.

It has become apparent that my cousin James's odd behaviour is because, for some reason, he fancies himself to be enamoured of me, which makes things very embarrassing. He is a very nice young man, but I do not like being regarded the way a good dog regards its master, and it renders it most difficult to converse with him. Treating him with disdain feels cruel, like kicking the loyal hound, but even smiling at him is taken as encouragement. What should I do? I am a guest in his parents' house, his cousin. I keep hoping that he will swiftly recover from this foolish attachment, which I have done nothing to deepen, rather as one recovers from mumps. Oh dear! I am become a disease! Thank goodness you at least are immune to me.

His lordship's smile twisted into a grimace, even as he turned the paper to read the crossed sheet.

We have tickets to see Mr Kean at the Theatre Royal a week Thursday playing Othello, but I have it from Lord Martley that Mr Kean did not appear for two performances this last week, so perhaps he is unwell. It would be a shame to have to see an understudy.

I have worn your mama's brooch upon several occasions, and it has been remarked upon most favourably. My aunt says that it is exceedingly pretty, and I have worn it with my own mama's pearls, and a locket that my uncle bought for me as a gift. There are some young ladies in their first Season who deck themselves out with a large assortment of jewels, but my aunt is very condemning of the mamas who permit their daughters to show such lack of taste. I am sure you will be pleased to hear that she is perfectly strict with my cousin and with me also, and we do not, like 'pups', get into scrapes. The worst thing that has happened is that the lace of my boot broke when I was walking the other morning, and I had to hide behind some shrubbery in order to tie off the remnants without showing my ankle in public. It was good, thick shrubbery, Charles, I promise, and I had the footman stand guard in front of it. I think the poor man must have been quite embarrassed, standing there in front of a bush.

I trust you to be looking after Papa.

Ever yours,
Henry

Lord Henfield sat very still for several minutes, the letter on his knee before him. She thought him 'immune', did she? The implication was that she would not wish it otherwise. If only she knew, if only he had been honest with himself, let alone with her. He had suppressed his feelings, for honourable enough reasons, but they had not dwindled, but rather burgeoned once she had left home, and he was no longer struggling to hide them. Perhaps, if he had revealed them to her, she would have recoiled, 'run away' to her London Season to find a worthier lover. He recalled Netheravon, dimly, as a fair youth, a year his junior, but Lord Martley was unknown to him, and if the appalling poet was not 'serious', then who was? He wondered, with disquiet, what information Sir John had received, and resolved to visit his godfather upon the morrow.

CHAPTER FIVE

'I HAVE HAD ANOTHER LETTER FROM HENRIETTA. In view of the social vortex in which she appears to find herself the centre, I am remarkably touched that she is so good a correspondent.' Sir John smiled. 'I fear my responses must seem dull in comparison.'

'I had a letter also. She is certainly having a good time.' Charles sighed, looking glum, at which Sir John raised an eyebrow, and spoke his mind.

'Tell me, Charles, why on earth did you let Henrietta go to London without saying anything?'

'Sir?'

'You have been moping about here like a spaniel whose master has gone away. If you love the girl, why did you do nothing? Why are you still here?'

'But one simply cannot love a girl one has known

from an infant . . . like a sister. It is not right . . . I mean . . .'

'You did not love her "as an infant". As I recall, you frequently thought her very silly, and a perfect nuisance, and, I might add, you were a stripling. A few years makes a huge difference when very young, and a lad of fourteen would look down upon a little girl of five as an encumbrance that might sometimes be tolerated. Well, now you are a man grown, and Henrietta is not a child, except perhaps to me, and to a father a daughter will always be "their child".'

'It would horrify her to know my feelings for her. I will be eight and twenty next birthday. I am too old, and she thinks of me as she would her older brother,' declared Charles gloomily.

'I know to a day how old you are, my boy, since I am your godfather, and ask yourself this. If you did not act like her older brother, would she still see you in that light?' Sir John was brisk. 'I cannot give you an answer, but I am prepared to say that she may well not do so. She is dashed fond of you, I know that. When she disobeyed you, at sixteen, and went into the stall of that brute of a bay hunter you had, after you had told her it was dangerous, you said you never wanted to speak to her again.'

'I was mad as fire, sir, you know that. I was perfectly right, the beast was dangerous, broke a stable lad's leg the next week.'

'Yes, but what you don't know is that it was not the trimming that I gave her that kept her in her room for two days thereafter. She was desolate. She wrote you a letter.'

'I still have it,' admitted Charles, in an embarrassed mumble. 'She said that even if I never spoke to her again she hoped I would at least read her apology, because she could not face the thought that I would think so badly of her.'

'As I said, she is dashed fond of you. But if you leave her among all the sprigs in Town, what was it again, ah yes, "beset by beaux", she may make a decision she will live to regret.'

'And I take it you would have no objection to my paying my addresses, sir?'

'Don't be a damned fool. I would welcome you with open arms, as you ought to know full well. There's none to follow me, the title goes to some second cousin, but the estate is not entailed, and it goes to Henrietta. Not that her inheritance is of importance to you, but it would please me to know it would be in good hands, as she would . . . in fact the best. I think you would rub along very well indeed, so go home, pack your bags, and go up to Town, post.'

'Yes, sir, and . . . thank you.' Charles rose, and shook his friend and mentor by the hand.

In the end it was some five days later that Lord Henfield arrived in the metropolis, a trifle travel-weary, and wondering if he had done the right thing. How might he compare to polished London beaux, and would it be possible for Henrietta to regard him in any other light than as a dear family friend? The answers in his head were negative.

He took a room in Grillon's, and went to his club for dinner, not that he visited it more than a dozen times in the year. He sat, preoccupied, wondering whether he ought to make an appearance in South Audley Street and leave his card, since he had no invitations to the sort of parties to which the year's young ladies were going, evening after evening.

'Henfield! Good gracious, old fellow, I had no idea you were up in Town.'

Lord Henfield looked up, and beheld a face wreathed in smiles.

'Gorleston, how are you?'

'In excellent health, but I thought you only came up to Town twice a year, and when it is a dashed sight quieter.'

'Yes, but . . .' Lord Henfield did not feel he could simply blurt out that he was coming to make a push for the affections of a young lady who lived but a mile from his own door in Shropshire. He therefore told a half truth. 'I have come in part on my godfather's behalf. His daughter is making her come-out this year, with Lady Elstead, and . . . Fathers of only daughters . . . You know the sort of thing.'

'Lady Elstead. Oh, you must mean "the Glorious Gaydon". Stunning-looking girl, I must say.' Lord Gorleston was so taken with the image in his mind he did not see Lord Henfield's hands clench into fists, and rattled on regardless. 'Above my touch, not that I am looking to set up my nursery just yet. Not often you find a beauty with wits and a sweetness of temper too. Always thought the "diamonds" were as they were named, hard, very hard. She is the exception, but you must know that, if she is your godfather's daughter.'

'Er, yes, yes I do,' acknowledged Lord Henfield, whilst wondering how he could indeed have known it so long and blinkered himself from its truth. 'I cannot pretend to be pleased to hear she has gained a soubriquet, however.'

'Well, it is only among the gentlemen, and the young lady has done nothing, absolutely nothing, of which her papa might disapprove. It is just that she has everything, and a tidy little inheritance to boot, if rumour is true. Such a girl is bound to be "discussed". She even has confirmed bachelors eager to join her entourage.'

'Entourage?' Things were sounding worse and worse.

'Well, if she accepted all the offers to procure her a glass of champagne she would be unable to stand up for any of the dances.' Gorleston paused, and his mind changed track. 'I say, where are you putting up?'

'Grillon's.'

'Well, pay your shot there, and come and stay with us. Mama wanted to come up for this Season to prepare her own "plan of campaign" for next year, when my sister, Charlotte, is presented, and so the house is opened up. We rattle a bit, especially now my father has bolted back to Norfolk over some local crisis, and I would lay odds will remain there.'

'Are you sure Lady Vernham would not object?'

'Why would she? Besides, if you want to get to all the squeezes where Miss Gaydon will be belle of the ball, she is the person to get you invitations.' Lord Gorleston's open, friendly face showed that he foresaw no difficulties.

'It is very kind . . . If I do not intrude . . .'

'Dash it, we have known each other since Oxford, and my mama always refers to you as "that nice Lord Henfield". She may even swoon with delight, though I have to say she is not the "swoonish" sort.'

'I sincerely hope not.' Lord Henfield smiled. 'You persuade me. Remind me of the address, and I will be upon your doorstep by noon tomorrow.'

'Excellent. Now, have you dined?'

It was two evenings later when, having arranged to be Lady Vernham's escort for the evening to Almack's, Lord Henfield espied his reason for coming to London, although her hair was dressed so modishly that he had, as she had foreseen, to look twice to confirm it was indeed her. He threaded his way through the throng and approached her from an angle that gave a fine view of her profile.

'Good evening, Miss Gaydon.'

Henrietta spun around, her expression one of stunned surprise.

'Charles! But you are in Shropshire.'

'Patently, I am not. Behold me here, and' – he swept her a graceful bow, whose formality was slightly diminished by his grin – 'your devoted servant to command.'

'That sounds silly, coming from you.' Her lips twitched, but her eyes were a little sad. 'And I do not like you calling me "Miss Gaydon".'

'It is presumably what every other gentleman calls you in London, and I still count as a gentleman, you know.'

'But I would rather be just your "Henry".' She looked at him very seriously, and for a moment he could not reply. He could not tell her that he wanted her to be "just his", that anything else was too ghastly to contemplate, and that she looked so beautiful she made his head swim.

'I cannot say it out loud in Almack's, but you may be certain it is how I wish to think of you. Will you dance with me?'

'Let me see. I cannot give you the next dance, for I am promised to Lord Martley, nor the boulanger, because I have offered that to Cousin James, and I do not suppose you can waltz . . .'

'I can waltz.' He felt vaguely stung by the suggestion that he was either so old, or so unfashionable, that he could not do so.

'Oh.' Henrietta actually blushed.

'Show me your dance card.' She held it out to him, and he took it, his fingers touching hers. 'I am fortunate, I see, to find you have any dances free. Do your feet ache after an evening here?'

'A little, I confess, but it is worth it.' She dimpled. 'I found out early on it is far better to have sore feet than be a wallflower, and spend the evening watching others dance.'

'And have you promised yourself to anyone?' There was the merest hint of a pause. 'To go into supper, I mean.'

'Yes, but I wish I had not, for I would far rather be with you.' His heart leapt, but her next words dashed him. 'For you can tell me how everyone is at home.' Her smile was bright.

'If you are not engaged tomorrow morning, I might come to South Audley Street, and give you all the news.'

'Oh yes. That would be wonderful . . .' She waited a moment and stressed, 'my lord.' Her eyes danced, and her voice dropped a little. 'I have missed home, and Papa, so much. You sort of bring them with you. Thank you.'

He wished she had said that she had missed him. He bowed as Lord Martley came to claim her, and watched them as they took their places in the set. They made a good couple. Martley, of whom he knew little other than what he had managed to learn from Lord Gorleston, was tall, but only the most critical would have called him 'gangly', and he was young, and fresh-faced. He could not know what Henrietta was thinking at that moment, which was that suddenly, Lord Martley looked 'too young'.

Henrietta was a good dancer, with natural musicality, and she had attended the dancing master engaged by her aunt most attentively. It enabled her to indeed dance without having to think of the steps, which was, at this moment, very useful. Charles's unexpected arrival had thrown her mind into a whirl.

Her first emotion, after total surprise, was a great wave of homesickness. She missed Papa, and even the quietness and routine, though she had put such thoughts to the back of her mind since arriving in London. As she took Lord Martley's hand, however, she realised that it was not just what Charles represented that she had missed, but also his own person. He had always been there in her life, supporting, and even guiding, although she had railed against that often enough. Having him appear in London unsettled her, for she was both delighted to see him, and vaguely disquieted, in case he 'disapproved' of her gadding about.

'You look quite solemn, Miss Gaydon,' remarked Lord Martley, as the dance brought them together again.

'Oh, I am so sorry, my lord. It is just that Lord Henfield has come down from Shropshire, and reminded me of home.'

'You have not received any ill news, I hope.'

'Thankfully, no. But you see, howsoever much I am enjoying the Season, this is my first time away from my papa, from my own house, and at times it is . . .' She gave him a tremulous smile.

'You are fortunate, ma'am, that your home holds such a place in your heart. It shows that you have enjoyed an enviable upbringing.' He tried to make the comment sound light-hearted, but Henrietta thought she caught a hint of regret.

Lord Henfield, observing them closely, winced. A lady passing him exclaimed and apologised.

'I am so very sorry. Did I tread upon your toes? I am most awfully clumsy. Forgive me.' Her hand went to her cheek, and the zephyr gauze scarf draped asymmetrically about her elbows slipped to the floor.

'I assure you, ma'am, my toes are unscathed,' murmured Lord Henfield, bending to retrieve the scarf. She thanked him so fulsomely one might have assumed he had undertaken some quite heroic feat on her behalf.

'Dorothea.' The one word was an admonition. The 'clumsy lady' closed her eyes for a brief second. A matron of severe mien appeared at her elbow, and glared, for there was no other term for it, at Lord Henfield.

'We have not been introduced, sir.' It was a statement, and clearly a command that this fault be rectified.

'Lord Henfield, ma'am. Your very obedient . . .'

'Sarah Ottery's boy?'

'Er, yes, ma'am.'

'Hmm.' What 'Hmm' meant was uncertain. 'Well, you do not have her features.'

'I am considered to have taken after my father, ma'am.' His lordship was trying to keep calm, but was finding this fearsome woman perfectly terrifying.

'Hmm. I am Lady Leyburn. May I present to you my daughter, Miss Yate.' The announcement sounded half apology, half defiant. Miss Dorothea Yate turned an unbecoming scarlet, and made her curtsey. Her eyes pleaded that her parent's behaviour was not her fault. Lord Henfield took pity upon her.

'I am charmed to make your acquaintance, Miss Yate. Might I enquire as to whether your dance card has a vacancy for the next quadrille?'

'It does, my lord.'

'Then would you be so kind as to put me down for it.'

'With pleasure, my lord.' She made another curtsey, he bowed, and they parted, he to sustain himself with a glass of wine, and she to be harangued simultaneously for making a poor impression, and for speaking to a man before her mama had given her approval of said man.

By the time Lord Henfield had recovered his equilibrium, Lord Martley and Miss Gaydon had left the floor at the end of the dance, and it took some time to locate her again. She was talking to a man he recognised, although he did not know him well. Robert Newbold was some years Lord Henfield's senior, and had been one of the set of 'men of the world' to which he and his peers had aspired, on coming to London, although he himself had ceased to be awestruck after seeing the man treat several luckless 'average' ingenues with crushing disdain. He must be five and thirty or thereabouts, and was still unmarried. Perhaps Henry ought to be warned about him. It was with no small degree of displeasure that Lord Henfield watched him offer her his arm, and realised that it was he who had the honour of leading her into supper. What was more, Henry appeared delighted with the arrangement, for all that she had declared herself disappointed but a quarter hour previously.

It was an unsmiling Lord Henfield who led Henrietta onto the dance floor for their waltz, later in the evening. As he placed his hand lightly at her waist and looked down at her, he felt very confused. There was the trust in her eyes, but she seemed so much more grown-up in the six weeks since he had seen her last. He did not think it was simply her appearance.

'You do not seem very happy dancing with me, Charles,' she admonished him. 'I am accounted quite good, you know, so you could at least pretend.'

'I am sorry. It is just . . . I do not want you hurt.'

'By your treading on my toes? Oh no, I do not fear it, for you are able to waltz, sir, and very tidily.' She smiled up at him from under her lashes coquettishly.

'No. I meant by someone treading on your heart. Newbold is . . . has . . .'

'Warning me, Charles? I would rather you did not. You see, I am not quite as green as you imagine, and my Aunt Elstead has already informed me that I must not take the gentleman to heart, at least not yet.'

'Not yet?' Lord Henfield's voice rose, and the neighbouring couple glanced at them in surprise.

'Ssssh, Charles, please. You will have us stared at.' Henrietta frowned. 'I do hope you have not come to London just to be disapproving and cast a wet blanket over everything. Papa did not send you to do that, did he?'

'No. It is . . .'

'Then please, let us dance and be friends.'

'When have I not been your friend?' he asked, rather too earnestly.

'Oh,' laughed Henrietta, wishing he would be less serious, 'when you told me that new gown, the gown I had laboured over to make for myself, had too many knots of ribbon, and did not fit properly at the back. I was mortified.'

'You would have been more mortified if you had appeared in public in something that looked as if it had been made for a hunchback. That is what friends are for, to let you know the things you cannot see.'

'Which makes you also sound like some second conscience, Charles, and I really do not desire one.'

'You know that is not what I mean. Your papa did not send me to spy upon you, I swear it.'

'So is it simply that you had an urgent need that your shirtmaker in Ludlow could not supply, or was it' – she smiled – 'that you could not stay away from me?'

'Shirts are very important.' He dared not take the other option.

'Having them is important, but last time I looked, you were not going about Shropshire with frayed cuffs, nor had you grown so much as to burst forth from your linens.' She paused. 'Are you making a long sojourn in London?'

'You wish to be rid of me?'

'No. It was a "polite question". I have learned a whole list of "polite questions" that one may use in conversation and which indicate sufficient interest in the other person without being in any way personal.' She looked smug.

'You would have us reduced to that, Miss Gaydon?'

'Oh, do not look reproachful like that, please.' The violins ended with a long note. Henrietta made her curtsey and gave him her hand to lead her from the floor. 'We have been waltzing together at Almack's; what more could we want?'

It really did not help that he had a very long list.

CHAPTER SIX

L ADY ELSTEAD WAS NOT A GREAT PATRONESS
of the visual arts, but she knew where to be seen,
and from a variety of sources found out that which she
ought most to admire. The British Institution had opened
its Exhibition of British Artists in early February, and
now, at the beginning of April, she felt provided with
enough information to appear well-informed. James
Felbridge evinced a desire to accompany his mama
and sister, and, incidentally, Henrietta, and his mama,
resigned to the fact that the son and heir was in the
grips of infatuation, agreed. As she wrote to her lord,
still in the country, far better he get such things out of
his system with his cousin, who showed no likelihood
of being bowled over by his adoration, rather than some
foolish girl who might be equally smitten, or worse.

'Oh dear!' Henrietta put her hand to her cheek. 'But last night, Aunt, Lord Henfield said he would present himself here this morning, to give me all the news of Papa, and home.'

'Well, my dear, if he comes betimes he may accompany us, since I am sure there will be nothing quite so private that it needs four solid walls about it.'

Mr Felbridge was conscious of the mean-spirited wish that his lordship might prove tardy, but he was out of luck. Lady Elstead had been upon the point of departure when she checked her reticule for the vital list and found it missing.

'There now, I have left my list of pictures we really must admire on my desk in the green saloon. Henrietta dear, will you be so kind . . .'

'Of course, Aunt.' Henrietta, secretly thinking it very funny that one should take a list of things to admire without yet seeing any of them, went to obtain the forgotten paper. Upon the little desk in the green saloon, Lady Elstead had an assortment of her lists. Fortunately the top one was marked 'Pictures' and Henrietta picked it up with a smile, a smile that then froze. Revealed beneath was another list, partially concealed, one headed 'Caroline', and on it were three columns in a neat hand, of 'Ideal', 'Possible', and 'No'. Henrietta did not mean to pry, but the names were before her eyes, and it was perfectly obvious what the list meant. What attracted her attention was that at the top of the 'No' list was the name of Lord Martley, in capitals, and underlined twice. She frowned. Lady Elstead had not indicated in any way that she found Lord Martley unsuitable to her; indeed, she might be said to be looking favourably upon him. Why then was he clearly out of the question for Caroline? She ought not to be looking, she would not look further, except perhaps just a little? Then she saw it. At the bottom of the 'Possible' list a name had been added, in a slightly more rushed hand. Henrietta stared at 'Henfield' and felt a wave of something approaching nausea come over her. How could Lady Elstead consider Charles for Caroline? It was unthinkable, in the sense that Henrietta could not bear to even imagine it.

'Folly,' she declared at the piece of paper, and thrust it back under a list of guests for a dinner party. She took up the 'pictures' list and returned downstairs, outwardly calm, but this act was not helped by finding Lord Henfield, hat in hand, in the hall, and being told that he might accompany them if he chose.

He looked up at Henrietta as she came down the stairs, and smiled, though his eyes lacked their usual conspiratorial twinkle.

'It seems I must admire art, Miss Gaydon,' he said, making his bow.

'Well, it will probably do you good, sir. You may even find a painting you really like. Do you prefer landscape or portraiture?'

'Unless it is the likeness of a close family member, then landscape. A landscape gives rest to the spirit and does not stare back at one, nearly always accusingly.'

'You think that too, do you, my lord?' Mr Felbridge enquired tentatively. 'There is this picture of some ancestor in a ruff, halfway along the passage to my bedchamber at home, and I would swear he watches me as I pass by and is unimpressed by me.'

'What utter rubbish,' declared Lady Elstead bracingly. 'Shall we go, or are we to linger here all morning?'

The British Institution for Promoting the Fine Arts in the United Kingdom was a private society of connoisseurs, but they put on two exhibitions each year which were open to the public, with new works on show from February until May, just after the Royal Academy exhibition opened its doors. It stood in Pall Mall, so the journey from South Audley Street was delayed only by the amount of traffic along Piccadilly. Lady Elstead discovered that in including Lord Henfield she had worked things to her advantage, since that gentleman had very little knowledge of those artists whose work was, or was not, in vogue, and she could chatter away about Messrs Brokedon, Hilton and Shaw, whose names she scattered within her monologue. Lord Henfield listened, and nodded, but found her logic somewhat arbitrary and difficult to follow. He cast Henrietta several appealing looks, but she would not rescue him.

'You might have helped,' he whispered, as he alighted from the carriage.

'Why? Observing your discomfiture was far more fun.'

'Minx.'

'La, sir. I am "Miss Gaydon", remember, and you must be polite to me.' She cast him a sidelong glance under her lashes, and for one heart-stopping moment of surprise was sure that in his eyes was the look she had come to recognise in her beaux, but it was so transitory that she was forced to tell herself it was pure imagination.

The party dutifully each paid their shilling, Lady Elstead paying more attention to who else was present than what art might be displayed upon the walls. Unlike Lord Henfield, to her ladyship the landscapes and historical pictures, which were the more promoted by the Institution, were of less interest than the portraits of people she recognised. It gave her a certainty, since whether a likeness was indeed 'like' was far easier than recognising expert composition or delicate brushwork, and she did not need to surreptitiously consult the list from her reticule. Caroline simply enjoyed pretty pictures, but this caused minor embarrassment when she began to comment favourably upon a picture her mama was preparing to disparage. Lady Elstead found herself in a quandary, neither wanting to make her daughter look foolish, nor be heard by others to be praising a work declared inferior. She tried to make noncommittal comments, which ended up contradictory and muddled.

'And why, one asks, would anyone want to have a picture on their walls illustrating "Washing Sheep"? If the sheep were in pretty fields, with a vista . . . Mr Wilkie's previous work is better.'

'Are you familiar with the artist's work, ma'am?' The voice made her turn. Mr Newbold made her a bow, and smiled. Lord Henfield thought it the smile of a man who already knew the truth, regardless of the answer he might receive.

'Oh, Mr Newbold, what a start you gave me! Have you come to view the pictures?'

James Felbridge winced.

'Indeed, ma'am, but this is my second visit. I have come in company with my cousin, Lord William Dinsmore, for he is but recently come to Town.' Mr Newbold acknowledged the youthful Mr Felbridge and then looked at Lord Henfield as if dredging his face from distant memory.

'Henfield. You will not remember me,' provided his lordship helpfully, but a little gruffly.

'No, no, I am sure that I do,' replied Mr Newbold smoothly, already looking at Henrietta.

'Good morning, Miss Gaydon. Have, er, you a favoured picture?'

'Well, I am in admiration of all artists who can render a canvas that looks like the scene or person in the flesh, if a scene could be so described. I confess my watercolours were always decidedly insipid. I like the one of "The Duke of Wellington Entering Madrid" because of the horses. I can say they look very . . . equine.' She smiled, with a mixture of charm and self-mockery.

'I am so glad that you do, for it is the picture I have purchased.'

'Oh! Does that mean I have good taste, sir?' She raised one delicate eyebrow, and he laughed.

'Undoubtedly, Miss Gaydon, but I would not have doubted it had you chosen another.'

Lord Henfield stiffened. Henrietta was enjoying the flattery, and engaging in the sort of banter that had previously been solely between her and himself, except that now the term he would apply to it was 'flirtation'. It hurt. He knew it was illogical, but it did not make it any the easier to watch. Mr Newbold glanced at him, and made a very fair assessment that the man was jealous. He did not know how Henfield could be so if he had barely met the young lady, but the signals were there.

'And have you a favoured picture, Henfield?'

'I make no pretence to knowledge, but like pictures I could live with upon my wall. I find the historical pictures of interest, but, to be honest, the idea of having a large canvas of' – he consulted the catalogue for the full title – '"An Attempt to Represent Achilles Shouting from the Trench, as Described by Homer" before me every day is most unappealing. I could certainly live with that nice little "View of Tintern Abbey". In scale and subject, and in my uneducated view, execution, it is an admirable picture.' He sounded a little defensive.

'There is certainly a difference between works one might admire for their skill and evocation, and those one would, as you say, live with upon the walls of one's house.' Mr Newbold sounded conciliatory, but Lord Henfield felt there was a degree of patronising also.

'Well, you would not want this odd-looking lady staring at you every day, to be sure,' murmured Henrietta, who had turned to view a portrait subscribed, in gold lettering, 'Hermione'.

'Indeed, although Mrs Bartley, the actress, is most definitely not "odd-looking" in real life.'

'Oh, you mean . . .'

'Alas, yes, Miss Gaydon. Personally, I cannot understand how it passed for exhibiting. Its only advantage would seem to be a brevity of title.'

'My sister, Henrietta's mother, and I were painted by Romney as infants,' sighed Lady Elstead, as though she remembered it well, although in truth she had been but four years of age and had absolutely no recollection of it.

'His portraiture of children has rarely been surpassed, ma'am.'

'I do know that my mama was so entranced with it that I believe she had it hung in her bedchamber.'

Henrietta noted the uncertainty, and the implication that whilst Lady Elstead's mother was delighted to have a picture of her progeny in her private chamber, she had been less inclined to have them there in person. At this point, Lord William, who had been conversing with a gentleman at the far end of the gallery, approached, and was introduced. After a short interchange, he and Mr Newbold moved on. Both Mr Felbridge and Lord Henfield were glad of this. In an effort to engage his cousin in conversation and exclude Lord Henfield, Mr Felbridge deployed his classical learning to expand upon the scene with Achilles that Henfield considered unappealing. Never had studying Greek literature shown itself so useful in day-to-day life, and he warmed quickly to his theme. Henrietta was polite, but not encouraging, although once in his stride, her cousin appeared unstoppable, and at least he stopped talking in half sentences.

Lord Henfield, seeing Henrietta's lack of interest, hid a smile. It was her turn to be 'discomfited'. He applied himself to entertaining Miss Felbridge, which ought not to have been difficult, since they could both of them talk about the pictures without pretending any deep knowledge. However, with his experience of young ladies primarily through long contact with Henrietta, he found that she did not respond in the way that he had anticipated, and that conversation was a little ponderous.

Lady Elstead was congratulating herself on the 'success' of the expedition, when a voice behind her made her freeze.

'It is all very well, Martley, but I still say it is not a patch upon the "Rebecca at the Well" we have at Hazelton.'

'But Mama . . . Oh, here is Miss Gaydon, and Miss Felbridge and, of course, Lady Elstead. Good morning, ladies, Felbridge, Henfield.'

The gentlemen made their bows as Lady Elstead turned, her lips drawn in a smile that would fool nobody.

'Good morning.' Even the two words seemed to exclude the lady upon Lord Martley's arm. She was fair, and one of those ladies who, unlike Lady Elstead, inclined to the slender, if not slightly emaciated, with the approach of middle age. She was probably only a little over forty, and from the vestiges that clung to her as closely as did her gown, it was clear that in her youth she had been a considerable beauty, but now she was beauty's ghost. There was no trace of grey visible in her hair, but it had lost the lustre of pale gold it once possessed, and the fine bone structure of her face was rendered to gauntness. Her eyes, however, were large, and almost violet blue. Sighing suitors in their day had called them limpid pools, but as she stared at Lady Elstead they were hard as sapphire.

'Mama, I do not think you have been introduced to Miss Felbridge, and Miss Gaydon,' announced Lord

Martley, with the veriest hint of panic. 'Ladies, may I present you to my mama, Lady Pirbright.'

Both young ladies made their curtsies, and were acknowledged with a gracious inclination of the head.

'I knew your mama, Miss Gaydon. You have been blessed with the look of her.'

'I have been told the likeness is very pronounced, ma'am,' replied Henrietta quietly.

'Indeed. She was extremely pretty, as are you, my dear.'

Henrietta blushed, but wondered why the 'she' had been given such stress.

'Dear Honoria,' murmured Lady Elstead, shaking her head. 'It saddened me that she always felt she was in my shadow.'

'Yes, it must have seemed so looming, and black,' agreed Lady Pirbright, with an air of innocent corroboration.

Lord Martley cast glances at both the other gentlemen, glances of mute appeal and interrogation. Mr Felbridge looked as confused as the viscount himself, and Lord Henfield's expression was that of the male confronted by a situation involving the 'weaker sex' which he could neither comprehend nor control. It also contained a strong hint of relief that neither lady had anything to do with him, and he could play the innocent bystander indefinitely.

'Have you a favourite exhibit, ma'am?' enquired Caroline desperately, and earned a look of gratitude from Lord Martley.

'I have not as yet studied all of them,' answered Lady Pirbright, as she 'studied' Caroline critically. Caroline later admitted to Henrietta that it quite put her to the blush, and she could not decide whether the lady was looking for a fault in her person or her dress. 'One needs to spend some time with each, for it is easy to form an initial impression which later proves over-generous.' Her look became more of a glare, and Caroline subsided into silence.

'But all the paintings have been passed as good enough for exhibition, have they not, ma'am?' Henrietta suggested.

'They have, but that is in many ways deceptive. I make no pretence that I, or Martley here, could paint anything to match the least work on these walls. They are all professional creations, but some are merely the adequate results of learning, as an apprentice learns, how to draw and to mix and apply paint, and others are true artistry.'

'My mama attends all the exhibitions,' volunteered Lord Martley. 'She is accounted to have quite the eye for masterpieces.'

'That is perhaps going a little far, Martley, for there are very few paintings to which that term may be applied, and I have no especial talent with sculpture. However, I will admit to an unerring ability to detect inferior works dressed up with eye-catching frames and subjects which attract the attention to what is, underneath, poor quality,' Her ladyship's glance flicked for an instant to Lady Elstead's face, which wore a mask of disinterest, but whose eyes glittered, and she delivered the coup de grace: 'And of course I do not need to be "told" what I must admire.'

'Then one wonders at this being your first visit,' responded Lady Elstead.

'My first? Oh no. This is perhaps my fourth. You would not understand, of course, dear Lady Elstead, but to properly appreciate a picture, one must spend time with it, not parade in front of it.'

'I have always held that good taste is bred not taught, and a slavish attention to whether the brush strokes are akin to those of . . .' She waved her hand, as if that might conjure up a name. '. . . Torrigiano, is merely showing book learning.'

'Yes, you would find that difficult – indeed, impossible,' tittered Lady Pirbright, 'since Pietro Torrigiano was a sculptor.'

'I meant,' corrected Lady Elstead, 'Titian, of course. A mere slip of the tongue.'

'Ah yes, they do both begin with the same letter . . . so confusing.' Lady Pirbright smiled, and let the following silence say more than further comment. After this pause to enjoy her victory, she tapped her son upon the arm and said brightly, 'Now, Martley, we must leave Lady Elstead's party to their . . . perambulations. Good day to you all.' With which she smiled, bowed her head very slightly, and led him away.

The 'Elstead party' might have been posing for a sculptural group entitled 'The Bemused and the Belligerent', in which everyone bar Lady Elstead herself counted as 'the Bemused'. After a minute, Caroline gave a nervous smile, and asked Lord Henfield if he thought some cows in a background were not a little too like horses. It was a silly question, and she knew it, but nobody wanted to touch upon what had just passed, and so he launched into a most impressive reasoning as to why that may have appeared to be so.

James Felbridge, acutely embarrassed, offered Henrietta his arm, and suggested she might like to look again at a marble in the Grecian style, which would enable him to talk about what the Grecian style encompassed. Lady Elstead was, perforce, isolated, and had the opportunity to fume privately.

It was not long afterwards that her ladyship declared that they had seen all that was of interest, and suggested that they return to South Audley Street for a light luncheon, to which she graciously invited Lord Henfield, since his original motivation for visiting had been to speak with Henrietta about Shropshire, and he had not had the opportunity to do so.

Lord Henfield accepted the invitation, but only because Henrietta desired so particularly to hear of all that had happened at The Court since her departure. Her smile as he sat beside her would have had him remain and eat stale bread and water, had it been all that was available.

'How does Papa? Has he any slippers remaining? Has he truly missed me? Has Dido alienated all the servants? Has the rector's lumbago eased?' Her questions tumbled out, and the 'society miss' fell away for a while.

He answered her calmly, watching her every expression.

'Your papa was in excellent health when I left him, but that is not to say that he does not miss you exceedingly. I have been a frequent visitor, of course, but he misses the pleasures of conversation, and of course, the opportunity to win at chess every day.'

'But I do win, sometimes,' exclaimed Henrietta.

'Only on those rare occasions when you do not rush into a situation without thinking even one move ahead. How often have I said a "surprise move" is neither one that is made within seconds, nor one that is entirely unexpected because it is suicidal?'

'Far too often, Charles.'

'Perhaps he ought to try and teach Dido how to play chess.'

'You think a puppy would make fewer errors?' She pursed her lips.

'Possibly, but at least there is no fear that you will chew the pieces.'

'Even in frustration?'

'Even in frustration.' He smiled, and it was a reminiscent smile. 'I have to add that the aforementioned puppy lost a tug of war with the senior housemaid over a mop, a fight with the cat from the stables, and buried a bone in your esteemed sire's bed.'

'But she ought not to be allowed upstairs, Charles.'

'I never said that she was.'

'Oh.' She paused. 'I do hope I have not introduced a problem into the house, and without me there to take any blame.'

'It is not a matter of "blame". A puppy is always . . . a puppy. She is very affectionate, and has given your papa something to think about.'

'Yes, how he has lost his slippers and heaven knows what else.' She smiled, but he thought there was a sadness in the smile.

'He will be very relieved when you go home, and not because of Dido, you know that, Henry,' he said gently. It was the first time he had used her name since he came to London. Lady Elstead, who had been listening quite openly, since the conversation had hardly been deeply personal, snorted.

'Henrietta, that is my niece's name, and I am sure her father is well aware that if all goes well, "going home" will be transitory.' She did not speak angrily, but there was insistence in her tone.

Charles Henfield said no more, but looked solemn for the rest of the meal. For her part, Henrietta found that she had no appetite, and pushed what was upon her plate around until everyone else had finished eating. When Lord Henfield left, she went up to her bedchamber to change her gown.

Caroline came and sat upon Henrietta's bed, idly running a finger and thumb along a length of carmine satin ribbon.

'You never mentioned that Lord Henfield was so handsome. If only he were not also so very severe.'

Henrietta almost dropped her hairbrush, and looked at her cousin reflected in the mirror.

'Charles, severe? But he is the most . . .' She halted, thinking of him last night, and today. He had been 'Charles' , 'her Charles', only for a moment or two and then something had happened, and he had withdrawn into 'Lord Henfield' and had confused her, being alternately prickly and judgemental, and rather sad.

'Perhaps he finds London not to his taste,' mused Caroline. 'He does not look like a man who loves parties.'

'No, I think he is not. He enjoys the company of friends, but not hours making polite small talk.'

'I wonder why he came to Town, then.'

'So do I.'

'And yet,' continued Caroline, 'he does not look like those gentlemen from the Shires whose evening dress does not fit them well, and who tread on one's feet in the sets. There is no rustic awkwardness to him at all. I saw him waltz with you and he was very good.'

'Yes, I suppose he was.'

'And he danced later with Miss Yate, who was more likely to tread upon his toes than the other way round. Have you ever seen a girl so clumsy?'

'I . . . did not observe Miss Yate.' This was not true. Henrietta had watched them dancing, and he had seemed more relaxed than with herself, had even looked as if putting his partner at her ease. He had not been at ease dancing with her. And Caroline thought him handsome. Henrietta sighed, and ran a hand along her brow.

'Caroline, I am sorry, but I fear I have a headache coming on. I think I may lie quietly for an hour, so that I will feel better for this evening.'

'Oh, you poor thing! Shall I bring you some lavender water for your temples?' Caroline was all concern.

'No, no, I am sure a rest will suffice. It is not too bad, and if I am alone for a while and quiet . . .'

Caroline laid aside the riband, rose from the bed and gave her cousin a hug before departing. Henrietta did lay herself down upon her bed, but she did not close her eyes. The truth was that however exciting it was to be admired and courted, she did want to go back to Papa when it was over, and thus far could not imagine leaving him to become the wife of some young man in a distant shire. Yet if she returned without having accepted an offer, she would be seen as having failed, having wasted her Season, and she would not be offered another.

'But life was so comfortable,' she whispered to herself, 'and I was happy.'

CHAPTER SEVEN

LORD MARTLEY WAS NOT SCHOLARLY, but he was no fool. What had happened at the exhibition had been totally unexpected, and disturbing also. Whilst his relationship with neither of his parents was particularly close, he generally kept on good terms with them by dint of doing as he was told, and he would not normally have described his mother as the sort of woman who clawed in public at other ladies in society. If anything, she liked to appear bored by them, as if more active emotions would be wasted upon them, and confined her vituperative comments to her nearest and dearest. Yet something almost visceral lay at the bottom of this morning's exchanges, and it boded ill for his nascent romance. Not considered one for the muslin company, he had discovered that he was actually dwelling, in odd moments, on the thought of what it would be like to have an establishment of his own, a pretty and affectionate wife, and all the benefits that such a person brought. It had not occurred to him that there would be any parental opposition to this, in fact the reverse. He had imagined much hand-shaking, and basking in unaccustomed approval. Without knowing why on earth such a degree of animosity existed between his mama and Lady Elstead, he was working in the dark, but broaching the subject was not something to be undertaken lightly. His best bet might in fact be to ask his father, who might well have little detail, but could surely provide at least some information.

With this worthy aim in view, Lord Martley ascertained that his sire was dining at home, wrote a short note to the friend to whom he was vaguely promised for dinner, and cried off. He then turned up at the family residence, and girded his loins to raise the issue over the port.

'It's not a woman, is it?'

'Good grief, no, or rather, yes, but . . . it is Lady Elstead.'

'What!' exclaimed Lord Pirbright, spilling his port as he refilled his glass. 'You must be raving.'

'Raving? Oh, oh! I see! No, no, sir, enough to give a fellow nightmares, but . . . No, you see, I escorted Mama to see some dashed boring pictures this morning, and Lady Elstead was there with young Felbridge, and her daughter and niece, Miss Gaydon. I did the decent and introduced the two young ladies, et cetera, but it

102

was abundantly clear that I might as well have lit some enormous firework. Mama and Lady Elstead squared up like prize fighters, not literally of course and . . . I had no idea, sir. None at all.' Lord Martley looked both perplexed and rather hard done by.

'Best just leave well alone, my boy. Women . . . Odd creatures.' This was no help whatsoever.

'But have I missed something, sir? Or does this date from some distant past antipathy?'

'You were not to know, I grant you. I am not myself sure of the details, but I know that the pair of them have been at daggers drawn since their come-out, and everyone knows not to let them within spitting distance of each other.'

'Everyone except me,' sighed Lord Martley gloomily.

'Well, as I said, you were not to know, so there is no blame, and I am sure your mama will forgive you.' Lord Pirbright paused. 'The Gaydon chit is quite a hit this Season, so I perceive. Decent stock, and like to inherit a nice estate in Shropshire.' He went no further in approbation, but glanced at his heir's profile.

Lord Martley did not say anything, though the implication was that Miss Gaydon was not 'beyond the pale', at least in his father's view. What irked him was that if he was not to blame then no 'forgiveness' ought to be needed. He tossed off the end of his port, wished his father a pleasant evening and left, in pensive mood.

* * *

Henrietta had put the rather embarrassing incident out of mind, and was trying not to wallow in homesickness, which talking with Charles had brought on like the tide coming in. London was alive, full of exciting things, and people, but as to being at ease in it, no, Henrietta was putting on an act attempting to persuade herself as much as others. If it were just for these few months she felt that she could cope, no, better than cope. She would store up memories that would provide plenty to look back upon. The trouble lay in the fact that it was all preliminary to her leaving Papa for good, and running her own establishment. In itself this was not frightening, having been de facto mistress at The Court for over a year, since Mrs Claines, the housekeeper, had gently shifted the responsibility for the household decisions to her, and guided her to the point at which they were perfectly normal.

She dressed for the evening with a small frown between her neatly arched brows, and Sewell admonished her that if she kept the expression for too long she would encourage a permanent wrinkle.

'You mark what I says, Miss Henrietta. You keep looking like you've lost a guinea and found a farthing, and that pretty face of yours will set firm all miserable, and then what will the young gentlemen make of you?'

'Sometimes, Sewell, I wish they would make less anyway,' sighed Henrietta.

'No you do not, for being courted is what every young lady wants and aims for.'

'It would be helpful if one could limit the number and quality, though, and I have already rebuffed three strong hints of wishing to apply to my papa from a man who was himself old enough to be my papa, a shy baronet from Kent with a stammer, and my sighing poet. In none of them could I find anything to admire, and I am not at all certain any of them considered more than my face and figure, unless it was also my likely inheritance.'

'Is that what has put you in this mood, Miss Henrietta? Well, you just stop thinking of those gentlemen, and consider the ones you do like.'

'But I am not sure I like any of them enough to marry them, even if they asked, Sewell. Perhaps I am cold-hearted.'

'Don't think such silly thoughts. Now, you look perfect, so off you go and dance every dance.' Sewell fixed a final pin in Henrietta's hair, and beamed into the mirror at her. It was impossible not to smile back.

Her myriad suitors found Miss Gaydon even more emotionally elusive than usual. Mr Munsley danced a quadrille with her, and plied her with compliments which, he later lamented to his crony, Lord Chilwell, he had spent all afternoon devising.

'Perhaps that was the problem, Munsley. She might have thought you lacked spontaneity,' suggested his friend gently.

'But I had practised until they sounded perfectly natural, I would swear it.' Mr Munsley shook his head sadly. 'You know what, Chilwell, it was like trying to grab smoke.'

'Grab smoke? Never tried that, not even when foxed. Waste of time anyway.'

'Exactly. I am probably wasting my time with "the Glorious Gaydon", but dash it, she is a beautiful creature, and witty too.'

'You mean "too witty".'

'Chilwell, you may be right. Pity.'

Lord Netheravon, whose wits did not require him to prepare his speeches beforehand, nevertheless might have agreed with the unfortunate Mr Munsley. Having failed to secure the chance to lead her into supper, he won a waltz, and the opportunity to sit out a country dance and entertain her with the unfortunate tale of his latest bet upon a horse. She smiled, she laughed even, as he described his confidence and the disbelief when he heard how it had not even got beyond the starting line.

'Talk about "pride cometh before a fall", Miss Gaydon. Of all the unfortunate things to happen, to have the saddle girth break just as the jockey set him off. There will be those who suggest foul play and dark dealings, but myself, I think it is the dreaded Netheravon luck.'

'Or lack of it, my lord?'

'Absolutely. Would you be so kind as to remind me, when we meet, not to place bets on horses.'

'What about other animals?'

'Ah, now only the gamester bets upon geese, or pigs or . . . moles for all I know of it. I am not a gamester, I assure you.'

'What makes one of those, my lord?'

'Well, I cannot say what makes them bet, but they try to see the opportunity in all sorts of rum things, whether Monday next will see a hailstorm in Barnet, or whether they can walk the length of St James's without seeing more than three men they know at three in the afternoon. Laying a wager upon a horse is mere sporting interest.'

'But in your case, sir, also wasting your money, because of the "Netheravon luck".'

'Sadly, true, so true. I may have to drown my sorrows in a glass of champagne. May I procure one for you also, Miss Gaydon?'

'You may, sir, and thank you, but if you are able to drown them in so small an amount, may I suggest your sorrows do not amount to much?'

'That, Miss Gaydon, is because the majority of them have been cast aside by the pleasure of your company.'

'Vastly pretty, my lord, but I warn you, I am very sceptical of compliments. I have but recently endured listening to a gentleman flatter me throughout a dance, but in such a way it sounded as if he spent all day learning his lines as for a play.'

'Then do not give the fellow another thought, ma'am. He is clearly unworthy to lay his homage before you.'

'Was it homage you were laying? I thought you were looking for sympathy?' Her eyes danced.

'You are cruel, ma'am, very cruel.'

'Yes, but I am permitting you to bring me a glass of champagne.'

'You are, and I had best procure it forthwith.' He smiled, bowed and went upon his quest, leaving Henrietta smiling, and her smile brought Mr Newbold to her elbow, one eyebrow raised.

'Now, tell me, Miss Gaydon, are you smiling because you have found Netheravon entertaining, or, much more likely, because you are glad to be rid of such a rattle-pate?'

'That, Mr Newbold, is very uncharitable. I am of course smiling for the former reason, and because he has been so kind as to go to fetch me a glass of champagne.'

'But had you announced that you were in need of refreshment, ma'am, half the room would have been rushing to obtain a glass for you.'

'I am thus glad I only made my request quietly, sir. Think of how unpleasant would be the effects of so many glasses.'

'But you would not need to drink them all.'

'Ah yes, but I would, for to reject them would be terribly unkind to the gentlemen involved.'

'Your kind-heartedness does you great credit, Miss Gaydon. I would never have entertained such a thought.'

'No, Mr Newbold? But perhaps you have a very strong head for champagne.'

He laughed, and was still showing signs of merriment when Lord Netheravon returned.

'Now that is unfair, Newbold, pouncing upon Miss Gaydon when a fellow has gone to execute a deed upon her behalf.'

'It was not slaying dragons, Netheravon.'

'You think not, but if you had had to edge past the bulk of Duxford, and avoid an aunt and two cousins, then you would see that it equates with at least a small dragon.'

'The size of a cat, my lord, or a large dog?' Henrietta was enjoying herself.

'Oh, definitely a large dog-sized dragon, Miss Gaydon, and with dashed sharp teeth and breathing fire.'

'You will have to ignore Netheravon, Miss Gaydon, for he is clearly in the realms of fantasy.'

'Only in as much that it is a dream become true to be able to do Miss Gaydon a service. Your champagne, ma'am.' Lord Netheravon bowed, and handed her the glass, his eyes twinkling.

'Miss Gaydon, forgive me, but I must retire.' Mr Newbold could twinkle as well as his lordship, but his mouth was set in the pretence of seriousness. 'I cannot stomach such sugary utterances. Wit I can enjoy, but Netheravon here is, as I said, a rattle-pate.'

'So he has been traducing my character to you, Miss Gaydon. Shame upon him.' Lord Netheravon achieved a look of virtue.

'Rattle-pate,' said Mr Newbold again, his lips twitching as he bowed to Henrietta and withdrew. His idea was that she would tire of such light and frothy conversation and find his own more acerbic wit rather more entertaining in the long term.

'You do not castigate me as a gabster, do you, ma'am?' entreated Lord Netheravon, with a look that Dido was probably mastering in Shropshire, being a mixture of devotion and innocence.

'No, my lord, I just remember that you are very unlucky with horses,' she said consolingly.

'But since you have put me down for a waltz after supper, I shall account myself the luckiest of men with fair ladies.'

'I am so relieved that I have been able to set your mind at ease, my lord.' She brandished her dance card.

'My evening is thus made, Miss Gaydon.' Lord Netheravon finished his champagne, bowed and went away in anticipation of dances with 'the Glorious Gaydon'.

Lord Henfield had been more interested in the conversation at luncheon than the patent antipathy between two women he did not know. He was vaguely buoyed by Henry's missing her home so much, although part of him did fear it was her father and the house that she missed, rather than himself, and since he was currently before her, assessing if she had previously missed him was difficult in the extreme.

Meeting Martley had also been 'useful', and he could neither ignore the youthful viscount as inconsequential, nor yet see him as a dangerous rival for Henry's affections. He was pleasant in manner, possessed of good looks, and might just count as not being 'a pup'. Felbridge most certainly fell into that category, and Lord Henfield could see just why Henry would find the slightly earnest and bumbling devotion of the young man, who needed four or five years to mature, beneath taking seriously.

What was most worrying was Henry herself. At times the girl he had known all his life was there before him, but at others she had developed into a creature he could barely recognise, and not just from her modish appearance. In six short weeks she seemed to have developed an assurance that was more than her frankness at home, and a flirtatiousness he had never encountered before. She had never flirted with him, or at least it had not felt like flirting, just the friendly banter of . . . he sighed, brother and sister. How could he become the suitor now? Would she be horrified, or would she think it funny? She expected certain behaviour from him, and he did not want to slip into that, because it would reinforce her seeing him in a fraternal light. She might even want to tell him how her heart lay with regard to her beaux, and that would tear him apart, hearing her describe her love for another man.

It was a pensive and serious-looking Lord Henfield who presented himself at Lady Cowper's that evening, brought along in her son's stead by Lady Vernham. Lord Gorleston had regarded this as an escape, and actually thanked Henfield for freeing him to dine convivially with three friends.

'But you need not think that I will expect you at my elbow all evening, young man, I assure you.' Lady Vernham smiled at him. 'I am not slow-witted, and playing poodle for a lady old enough to be your mama would not make for entertainment. You make sure you go and dance with all the pretty young girls.'

This had sounded ideal, except that in practice her ladyship meant 'go and dance once you have been introduced by me to a number of "useful" people, and brought me an ice, and a glass of ratafia'. It left him champing at the bit, as he watched other men bow and smile at the Elstead party, and arrange for dances of their choosing. What was especially galling was seeing her in animated conversation with Lord Netheravon, who then proceeded to bring refreshment and remain for another full ten minutes at her side. Henry certainly had not exaggerated when she said that she was not lacking in partners. He almost ground his teeth, and it was at that point that Lady Vernham, observing his profile, realised that her escort was not simply out to espy possible partners for an enjoyable evening party. She took pity upon him, and tapped him gently upon the arm with her fan.

'You know, you are not going to impress her by looking like a mastiff about to launch itself at an intruder, Henfield. Be carefree of manner, and charm her, not dull and defensive.'

'I am not sure "charm" is my strong suit, ma'am,' responded Lord Henfield, his eyes upon Henry's dimpled countenance as she bent her head, and a dark-haired youth with high cheekbones and twinkling eyes murmured something that made her cheeks colour delicately.

'Then what is?'

'I . . . we have always just been supremely comfortable with each other, until now. Could say anything, not need to finish sentences . . .' He looked troubled. 'But that was back in Shropshire, and a world away from this. I am now classed with her papa as "family", and I am not her brother.'

'Ah.' It was a short answer, but Lady Vernham comprehended a lot. 'Well, my suggestion is that you declare as such.'

'But I cannot just . . .'

'Do not interrupt. Tell her, as though it were a game, that you do not wish to miss out on the pleasure you can see her admirers give and receive, and beg permission to join their company for the duration of your stay in London. Make it sound light-hearted at the outset and see what happens.'

'Would that work, ma'am?'

'It has a greater chance of success than glowering at the poor girl. Now, go.' She nearly pushed him from her, and in the direction of Miss Gaydon. He wove his way through the assembly.

'Are there any dances remaining for which you might accept me as a partner, O much-admired Miss Gaydon?' He felt a fool, but if Lady Vernham was so sure . . .

Henrietta turned, and her smile seemed to become more wary.

'That depends, my lord.'

'Upon what?'

'Whether you are here to scold me or not.' She looked very slightly mulish.

'Do I appear only as a scold?' He was rather taken aback, and attempted to appease her. 'Unless you have been doing something "terribly wicked", such as planning to throw sugar plums at your hostess, I . . .' He stopped, seeing the mulish look harden.

'I am not a child. Why do you have to keep trying to make me feel as if I were still a child to be looked down upon.'

'I did not mean . . . I only wanted to . . .' He looked both confused and despondent. 'When we were at home, it was not like this,' he said miserably.

'We are not at home.'

'No. Now you are the belle of the ball, and I cannot compete with those who are expert in dalliance, and are new and exciting. I am just . . . the same old me.'

'So it is my fault that I am entertained?' She was suddenly defensive. He was not scolding her, but he was making her feel guilty, and she disliked it. He ought to be an ally, one with whom she could laugh at the whirl in which she found herself, and instead he was distancing himself, and blaming her. It was not fair. 'I can assure you I am not being entertained at this minute. I regret that my dance card is full.'

'Even though you have not looked at it, and you did not say as much when I enquired. I see.' He paused. 'I hope that you enjoy your evening, Miss Gaydon.' He bowed, and withdrew, with a face fit for a funeral.

Lady Vernham, who had been watching, whilst apparently in conversation with a matron animadverting upon the difficulties of obtaining perfectly fresh lobsters, permitted her delicate brows to draw into a brief frown. Once she had disengaged from the lady, she went in search of the unhappy viscount, whom she found glaring at a marble bust of Circe as if she was responsible for all the faults of her gender.

'What happened?'

He turned. 'I made a mull of it.'

'That, I must say, was perfectly obvious. Tell me what happened.'

He obeyed the command. At the conclusion, he shook his head. 'If I were to try and be as at home, she would treat me like a relative, and if I try and woo her as she is, I get nowhere.'

'Oh, for goodness' sake.' Lady Vernham was not sympathetic. 'I am out of all patience with you, you foolish boy.'

No woman had called him a 'boy' since his mother died. He looked uncomfortable. Lady Vernham watched, assessed and came to a decision.

'Somebody needs to take you in hand, Henfield, and it is going to be me.'

CHAPTER EIGHT

For Henrietta, Lady Cowper's party had not been a success, although she had indeed managed to fill her dance card, had been paid many nice compliments and enjoyed the first half hour. Lady Elstead was even, unbeknownst to her, about to add another name to the list of possible suitors. Sir Lawrence Coleford was not a wealthy man, but his lineage was good, and he had not been classed as a 'fortune hunter' for he was not to be seen chasing every new heiress that appeared among the Ton. Had Lady Elstead asked Henrietta what she thought of the gentleman, she would have been shocked to find Henrietta having to cudgel her brains to bring him to mind. Her disagreement with Lord Henfield had cast a damper over the entire evening, and Henrietta was both upset and confused. Charles meant 'home' and being comfortable, and yet here he was making her feel unhappy. She was delighted to see him, but wished also that he would go away. What she could not see was that she was foisting all her own inner worries upon him as the cause.

Henrietta was struggling. She had become swiftly caught up in a world she only partially understood. Her mother had been a very present 'Mama' to the child, but her untimely death had meant that from before adolescence Henrietta had lacked a woman's guidance. She was shy with other young women, and in many ways socially out of her depth, yet her natural assurance with the male sex ensured that she did not simper or cower in their presence, like some of her peers, but could appear at ease and poised. What she thought of as mere friendliness could even be misconstrued as flirting, for she was used to banter with Charles Henfield, and discuss serious issues with her papa. She was using this mask of assurance to conceal her inner insecurity. Men flocked about her, and she liked being courted and praised. It made her feel 'grown-up', and the woman of the world that she knew, deep down, she was not. It was a performance, a charade, highly enjoyable but without any foundation, and without a foundation upon which to stand, Henrietta was 'wobbling'. She was also feeling the pressure of her many beaux.

Lady Elstead had not actually expressed the wish that there should by now be gentlemen posting into

Shropshire to obtain Sir John's permission to pay their addresses to his only daughter, but her questions about her niece's reactions to various suitors were becoming a burden to the young lady. The raison d'être of the Season, to see girls find husbands, hung over Henrietta like a Sword of Damocles. She did like several of the gentlemen who danced with her night after night and paid court to her, but none of them touched her heart; for none of them could she imagine leaving Papa and The Court. What frightened her was that she was sure that if she told her aunt this, she would be told off for being foolish. Her aunt expected her to like a prospective husband, but did not believe that she should only accept an offer if head over heels in love.

It was an unhappy Henrietta who tossed and turned in her bed, and awoke unrefreshed, and to Sewell's recommendation that she lie for an hour with slices of cucumber upon her eyelids to reduce the heaviness.

Lady Vernham slept well, and awoke at a suitably advanced time of the morning. She sat in bed, and pondered over her morning chocolate. Her decision the previous evening to take Lord Henfield 'in hand' had been made upon the spur of the moment. He was a decent and pleasant young man, who deserved to be happy, but was doing everything to prevent himself attaining that state. Lady Vernham had guided two daughters to successful marriages, which showed every sign of being 'comfortable'. She had not, thus far, attempted to steer a gentleman along the path to matrimony, and had anyone suggested that she do so with her son, she would have laughed at them. Gorleston was not yet letting his thoughts dwell on setting up his nursery, and even the idea of guiding him was both embarrassing and, she thought, pointless. Henfield, however, showed all the signs of a man 'needing' to be married, and it was perfectly evident that Miss Gaydon was the sole object of his affections. Lady Vernham sighed. She had seen it before, when a man was blind to the obvious until it was too late. Well, if he applied himself, it might not yet be too late for Henfield.

'I wonder if I am going to exert myself to no purpose,' murmured her ladyship into her cup.

Her maid, correctly assuming this was a rhetorical question, did not answer.

Lord Henfield barely slept at all. He could not rid his mind of his dismissal, and the more he tried to work out what he could have done differently, the more complicated everything appeared. He was also dreading what his hostess might say in the morning. His own mama had been a generally mild and amenable lady, but once, in his father's words, she got the bit between her teeth, she could be remarkably forceful. He remembered the very unpleasant exchange of letters with his school when Mama decided that the outbreak of measles, during which he had been very ill, had been exacerbated by the contagious boys being treated in their dormitories rather than moved to the school infirmary. Her spouse's suggestion that the virulence of the outbreak meant that there was probably insufficient room in the infirmary had fallen upon deaf ears.

Lady Vernham did not appear mild. She looked like a lady who smiled, spoke softly, and then made one squirm if one upset her. Failure to do exactly as instructed would definitely upset her. When he finally got to sleep, Lord Henfield's dreams were troubled with being made to write a hundred lines, each of the phrase 'Henry has come to hate me'. His valet, upon seeing him, did not, however, recommend cucumber.

When he went down to breakfast he found Lord Gorleston tucking into a fine York ham, and buttered eggs. He looked in a cheerful mood, and regarded his friend thoughtfully.

'You know, you really ought not to get top heavy if you are acting as my mama's escort for the evening, my dear fellow.'

'I did not drink too much. I wish I had, then I would have forgotten the entire evening.'

'Oh dear, that sounds bad. Here, come and drown your sorrows in ham and eggs. Not that you could actually drown in them, but you get my meaning. Food will make you feel better.'

'I do not think anything can make me feel better,'

bemoaned Lord Henfield, but sat down anyway.

'Not wishing to pry, of course, but . . . Anything I can do, you only have to ask.'

'Make me into someone else,' sighed Lord Henfield.

'Lord, you are feeling dismal. Not something you ate, is it? I know my father was as blue as megrim once after some soup with crab in it, or was it lobster?' He cut his friend a second slice of ham, since one looked insufficient.

'It is neither food, nor drink. It is me.'

'No. I am sorry, Henfield, but you have lost me there. I mean, you were happy enough being you a couple of days ago, and a man don't change how he sees himself overnight.'

'It is more that she does not see me as she used to.'

'Ah.' It was a percipient 'ah'. 'Now I think I understand, except, dash it, you have only been in Town a few days. You cannot have fallen under the spell of . . .' Lord Gorleston stopped, his fork still impaling a morsel of ham on his plate. 'Oh. Like that, is it? Not considered a downy one. My mama is the one for intuition, but . . . Miss Gaydon, I take it?'

'Yes.'

'Well, since you have not changed, as far as I can tell, since last we met, excepting this blue-devil you have today, and the chit was happy enough in your company in Shropshire, the situation cannot be hopeless.'

'I have not changed, but she has.'

'Are you sure?'

'Yes. I have known her from the cradle and . . .'

'But she was a baby then.'

'I know, I know but . . . Since she came to London she has not just changed her hair and her clothes, which I knew she must do, but she has become so . . .'

'Grown-up?'

'Yes, and yet no. She acts grown-up, she gives me set-downs like a grown-up, but . . . How can I explain that underneath she is still the girl I laughed at, and then with, the girl I . . . love, but she keeps her imprisoned behind the veneer.'

'Well, that is certainly a bit deep for me, but I think I understand most of it.' Lord Gorleston paused. 'Your character has not changed so why should hers, the real one? If what you say is true, then she is giving in to the excitement of the Season, and it will pass with the Season.'

'By the end of which Lady Elstead will expect to see her suitably betrothed.' Lord Henfield's gloom descended once more.

'That is not a problem as long as she is betrothed to you, my friend.'

'Which brings us full circle. Last night she would not even dance with me.'

'Might have been her feet.'

'What?'

'Dancing slippers pinching her toes. Makes one dashed crotchety, I can tell you. Had a new pair of

123

hessians once, and went for a saunter to the club, and by the time I was at the top of Piccadilly they were crushing my toes like the devil. Took 'em straight back. My father said it was my own fault for not going to Hoby, and I think he was right.' Lord Gorleston frowned, possibly contemplating the wisdom of his parent.

'It was not her slippers. I . . . she does not want me to be too formal with her, but when I tried to jest as we were wont to do, she cut up at me. It was irrational and . . .'

'They are.'

'Who are what, Gorleston?'

'Females. Illogical. Mind you, none of 'em ever had to learn rhetoric or logic at school so what can one expect. I have sort of decided already that I am not going to worry about whether the girl is logical, when I come to get leg-shackled. As long as I am comfortable with her . . . And she does not squint. Never could abide a squint.'

'I was comfortable with Henr . . . ietta, till she came to London.'

'Do not dwell upon it, dear fellow. Tell you what, perhaps she saw that long face coming on and she cannot bear to see you miserable.'

The butler entered the room.

'Excuse me, my lords. Her ladyship wishes Lord Henfield to know that she will be pleased to see him in the Rose Saloon at eleven of the clock, if you have no prior engagements, my lord.' He looked to Lord Henfield, but not by a single twitch of a muscle could it be seen that it was not Lady Vernham's habit to have private interviews with her guests before luncheon.

'Er, please convey my respects to her ladyship and assure her that I will, er, present myself promptly.'

'Thank you, my lord. I shall have that message sent up to her ladyship immediately.' The butler bowed, and withdrew.

'What the devil does my mama want to see you about at eleven, Henfield? Please do not say you got a set-down from her too.'

'Not exactly, but the day may yet come.' He explained what Lady Vernham had decided to do.

'Good grief!' Lord Gorleston could think of nothing more to say.

The Rose Saloon was decorated in a dusky pink-grey, to which Lord Henfield took instant dislike. Lady Vernham was sitting with her hands folded in her lap, looking calm and regal. The clock upon the mantelshelf chimed the hour with a tinkling of bells.

'I am glad to see that you are punctual, Henfield.'

'Good morning, ma'am.' He made her his bow, which she acknowledged with a gracious nod of her head. He then stood, feeling very self-conscious.

'Do not stand there as though a schoolboy about to receive a trimming, Henfield. Sit down, and tell me all about Miss Gaydon, the one you know, not just the one I see.'

She did, he thought, at least realise that there were two 'versions' of Henrietta Gaydon. He began, hesitantly at first, but once lost in the past happiness of the relationship, he almost forgot Lady Vernham's presence. When he reached the point that Henry left home, her ladyship raised her hand, and then her voice.

'Stop. You have painted a mighty pretty picture, but tell me two things.'

'Yes, ma'am.'

'When did it dawn upon you that you were actually in love with the girl, and how many other girls do you know?'

'I . . . I think I knew I loved her well over a year back, at heart, but you see, we had been so close, but like family, that it seemed wrong, and I recall her as a babe in arms.'

'The age gap is immaterial. Most men are considerably older than their wives, but since they marry adults, not "babes in arms", the years between are merely periods of time. Your disadvantage is that you know the process of her growing up. As a man, you now have to dismiss that. And my second question?'

'Er, well . . .' Lord Henfield blushed. 'Not really a ladies' man.'

'Hmm, so she is the first chit to make you act like a lovesick fool. You have also to admit, she has attracted you just because she has treated you more like a brother, and not fluttered her eyelashes at you, and scared you off.'

'I suppose that is true.'

'Then, forgive me, are you sure that no other young woman in London would please you?' Lady Vernham looked hard at him. 'You have not entertained that thought, have you. You came post-haste to win the girl you have decided you love, but find her altered from the confiding neighbour.' Her ladyship tapped a finger upon the arm of her chair, and said nothing for a full minute.

'Lady Vernham, I cannot deny I have never courted another young woman, have few among my acquaintance even, but Henrietta is my personal perfection, knowing as I do her "imperfections". I do not idolise her as some beautiful goddess, you see. I love her for what lies beneath, at least I think still lies beneath.'

'She dresses in the high kick of fashion, and is lapping up the adulation of being one of the hits of the Season. Is the new Miss Gaydon the butterfly from the chrysalis, or "your" Miss Gaydon acting on the stage that is the Season? No' – Lady Vernham admonished with a finger – 'do not answer me. I will say in favour of the latter that she is courted by a host of eligible fribbles, and, I note, Newbold, who is no fribble, but I have not seen any sign that she favours any above the rest. A maid on the catch would have been narrowing the field by now, if she had any sense, and Maria Elstead would be pushing her hard. So she is not mercenary, though with her inheritance . . .'

'Ma'am? Forgive me, but Henrietta is not some great heiress. My godfather's past investment in the Trent and Mersey Canal has paid good dividends, I know, and his estate is profitable and of some size, but it is hardly ducal, and he is in excellent health, so she may well not inherit, I hope, for another twenty years.'

'Is that so? Well, I have not heard any figures mentioned, but Lady Elstead has certainly not done anything to disabuse the Ton of the idea that the chit is heiress to a portion of Shropshire that would be a very pleasing addition to any man's estates.'

'So she is hunted by fortune-hunters too?' Lord Henfield sounded outraged, as well as shocked.

'Not the gazetted variety, no. They prefer short-term gain, and waiting is not their strong point. Let us just say, some would find that a life of moderate economy would be nice to leave behind at some stage in the future.'

Lord Henfield put his head in his hands and groaned.

'And that will do you no good at all, young man. There is no sign whatsoever that her head is being turned. It might simply be that she is enjoying spreading her wings.'

'That is essentially what Gorleston said at breakfast.'

'He did?' Lady Vernham looked genuinely surprised. 'Well, I never! I have always considered my son to be amiable but far from acute.'

'I think that sums up his view of himself too, ma'am, but he described you as "the downy one".'

'He ought not to describe me in such vulgar terminology,' declared her ladyship, secretly pleased. 'Now, back to the matter in hand. If you truly believe no other chit will make you happy then you have to work out what she wants from you.'

'But that is the problem, ma'am. She wants the friend, not the suitor, and last night even the friend put her out of sorts.'

'Can you not be both? There is no law of nature that says a lover may not be best friends with their beloved, nor that a friend may not entertain passion.'

'At present, Lady Vernham, I am proving unable to show any success at either one, let alone combine the two.'

'Having seen you last night, I can say, with some assurance, that you dither between the two, and thus are successful at neither.'

'But you just said . . .' Lord Henfield was confused as well as embarrassed.

'There is a difference between being indecisive and charming the girl from a basis of long-standing friendship.'

'Charming? Can I do charming?' He sounded very sceptical about this.

'If you put your mind to it. I have known some most charmless men who made enough effort and found themselves wives, and you do not lack charm, my boy, just confidence. You look at men like Netheravon and Newbold, and are defeatist. No doubt you say "I cannot be like them".'

'It would be an act.'

'And what is your Miss Gaydon doing at present? Acting, as are they. Act with her, not against her, and at the end of the Season the girl can sigh and say what a glorious time she had, whilst having the security and comfort of a husband who will cherish her and also be her friend. Such a position is enviable.'

'Do you think I can pull this off, ma'am?'

'I would not put it in such terms, but yes, I do. You are a good-looking enough man without looking "dangerously handsome", you have humour, when you are not lost in gloom, and you can dance well. I saw you last night and you even made the awful Leyburn's daughter look competent, poor child.'

'Miss Yate. She does appear very . . .'

'Downtrodden. That is the word you seek. Aurelia Leyburn is a bully. She probably bullied Leyburn to death, and she makes life a misery for the girl. Never going to do well, of course, but had a chance, until she had her mama criticising her every step, and then she became so self-conscious she grew clumsy and distrait. From what I have heard, there was even a young man of unimpeachable breeding but little prospects, a younger son in the army, or was it navy, back in Norfolk, but that was squashed because Aurelia wanted a better catch. She'll get none now, and although it is good to see Aurelia's desperation, it is a shame for the girl.'

'I believe her name is Dorothea.'

'Is it? Well, do not offer for her out of sympathy, that is all I . . . but on the other hand . . .'

'Ma'am?'

'I think showing just enough interest in Miss Yate might be advantageous. A little jealousy in your childhood companion might waken her to possibilities. Hmm.'

'But would not be fair to Miss Yate.'

'Nothing in life is fair to Miss Yate, so your attempts would be futile. Now, we have to plan your campaign.'

'This is not a battle, Lady Vernham.'

'No, Henfield, it has more strategy. It is a war.'

Charles Henfield gulped.

CHAPTER NINE

LORD MARTLEY WOULD NEVER HAVE BEEN DESCRIBED as scheming by any of his many friends and acquaintances, who generally put him down as the best of good fellows, and both open and honest. However, he was currently engaged in scheming that for him was of Machiavellian proportions. If Lady Vernham considered Lord Gorleston 'amiable but not acute', she at least spoke with maternal affection. Lady Pirbright, whose last moment of closeness with her eldest son had been just before the umbilical cord was cut, regarded him as a fool of a magnitude only marginally different from her lord, and that the slight improvement was only through his inheriting at least a few drops of her own, superior, blood. He certainly inherited her looks rather than those of his sire, but she was wont to tell her friends, few though they might be, that he took after his father in wits, and was therefore disobedient through failing to comprehend her simple commands.

Following the interview with his papa, Lord Martley had spent a convivial evening with some of his cronies, and returned home very nearly sober and at the remarkably early hour of one in the morning. When he broke his fast at barely past ten of the clock, he had no thought that he might find his mother in possession of the breakfast room, and it very nearly made him decide that starvation was a better course. She had espied him, however, and so escape proved impossible. He sat, awaiting the inevitable lash of her tongue, and found instead that he was being extolled, if not ordered, to 'make himself pleasant, if that is possible' to Miss Gaydon.

'The girl, despite residing with That Woman, seems polite, and is sole heiress to her father's property, which is apparently extensive in Cheshire.' Lord Martley did not think it wise to correct the geographical location. 'Whilst not convenient for the greater part of our estates, acres are not to be ignored, and they could always be sold off for something nearer Town. You cannot complain that the girl is ugly, for she is patently one of the successes this Season. It does mean, however, that you cannot simply meander along and hope she notices you. You must apply yourself, Martley, do you hear?'

'Yes, Mama.' He paused, as the cogs of his brain whirred silently. 'I shall make sure that I am in Miss Gaydon's vicinity as often as possible.'

'Good. At least you can obey basic instructions, which is more than your father appears able to do.'

Lord Martley thus took his sire to be in her bad books, which was a location with which he was also painfully familiar. He made a reasonable breakfast in the circumstances, which included being told what to eat, and how many times to chew it. He then withdrew, not, as his mama assumed, to prepare for 'lounging about' at his club, but to go out for a walk in the park. She would have regarded this activity with suspicion.

In fact, Lord Martley was going for a walk to think, and sitting in his bedchamber felt more like sulking. He dressed with care, despite his preoccupation, and left the house with only the smallest of frowns upon his brow. However, he completely failed to acknowledge a friend passing upon the opposite pavement, narrowly avoided being run over by a man driving a high-perch phaeton, and, upon entering Hyde Park, strolled in an aimless manner for the best part of three quarters of an hour. It was then that he was hailed by a soft feminine voice, and found himself before Miss Felbridge, Miss Gaydon and an accompanying maid, taking a constitutional. It might not be the hour for promenading, but the two young ladies had their heads together and were content in their own company. Miss Gaydon looked pensive, but Miss Felbridge appeared both bright and cheerful. He offered both ladies his escort for a turn about the shrubberies, where his failings as a botanist soon had Miss Felbridge stifling giggles.

'But are you sure, Miss Felbridge? Not that I am doubting your abilities, but it might be a dandelion in disguise.'

'I assure you, my lord, that whilst I could not give you the Latin for it, that is definitely a tulip.'

'That would account for the thrashing I got as a small boy, then. I saw the gardeners pulling up weeds, and so, being an egalitarian sort of little fellow, I thought I would help. What I pulled up were just like those, and my protestations of good intent fell upon deaf ears.'

'Were you frequently chastised, my lord, for "helping" with things?' Henrietta found his confessions droll.

'Lord, yes. You perceive me, the picture of eagerness to assist my fellows in their daily grind, but did they appreciate it? Not a jot. The cook banished me from her kitchen more often than I can recall for licking spoons, and think how much cleaner they are without jam or cream left upon them.'

'And were any of these spoons still in jars or bowls, my lord?' Miss Felbridge followed her cousin's lead.

'I . . . cannot deny that on occasion they were.' Lord Martley grinned. 'However, I was very useful in the kitchen. I once invented a whole new dish by adding sultanas to a bowl of peas.'

'Dare we ask what inspired this dish, Lord Martley?' Henrietta asked.

'Well, sultanas are sweet and rather nice, and I thought them a similar size to peas, which are just green and a bit boring.'

'How odd that "peas with sultanas" has not become a staple upon our dining table, cousin,' commented Henrietta, and bit her lip. Caroline was wiping her eyes, and was so overcome that she dropped her parasol.

Lord Martley picked it up, brushed any traces of dust from it and handed it back to her.

'Thus were the deeds of the knights of olde, ma'am.'

'Thank you, my lord, although in chivalric terms, would this not be accounted quite a trifling service?'

'Had there been a dragon in the park, Miss Felbridge, be sure that I should have slain it for you.' His eyes twinkled and met hers, and they smiled in unison. Henrietta wondered why young gentlemen seemed to portray tasks undertaken for ladies as 'quests'. Was it to make the ladies grateful, or did they secretly feel that modern life lacked the masculine glamour of being a knight in armour? She thought the realities of the past would have actually been rather uncomfortable.

His lordship continued to entertain the young ladies for a full quarter hour, and then, feeling that he had spent his time well, made to leave them. He strode away with a spring in his step, secure in the knowledge that he had obeyed his mama, given mild pleasure and advanced his own cause.

* * *

The cousins were still in light-hearted mood as they left Hyde Park, and had just crossed into Upper Grosvenor Street when they came face to face with Sir Lawrence Coleford, who made his bow, and seemed keen to change his own plans and provide them with an escort as far as the front door of the house in South Audley Street. Henrietta and Caroline exchanged the briefest of glances, but neither young lady felt confident that they could avoid his company without appearing grossly discourteous. Henrietta was also desperately trying to remember who he was, and it was only thanks to her cousin addressing him as 'Sir Lawrence' that she managed to place him. He was punctilious, and, in comparison with Lord Martley, incredibly dull. His conversation veered between a lecture and ponderous flattery. He also possessed a thick enough skin not to realise that the young ladies were not charmed, for which they initially gave thanks. However, it was made clear at his departure that he considered this 'delightful five minutes of perambulation', as he phrased it, paved the way for him seeking them out at the very next party and placing his name upon their dance cards.

'Oh dear,' murmured Caroline, as she removed her gloves. 'I do think we may be haunted hereafter by that gentleman.'

'Yes, he is the sort that sticks, like those little green seed-balls on cleavers that matt the dogs' coats and get into one's hems.' Henrietta pulled a face, and Caroline laughed.

'Now you have made things impossible for me, dear cousin. When next I see him I will be thinking botanically.'

'Unlike Lord Martley.'

At this Caroline coloured a little. 'I am not sure he is as wildly ignorant as he pretends, but he is always so cheerful and helpful.'

'He is, I will grant him that.'

'You sound as though begrudging, Henrietta.' Caroline frowned.

'Oh, not begrudging, just . . .' Henrietta could not voice the thought that had struck her, quite forcibly, that the one thing she would not, could not, grant Lord Martley, was her hand in marriage. She wondered why. He was sweet natured, good looking, optimistic and never overstepped the mark, unlike a certain young gentleman of whom her aunt was thankfully unaware, and who had, presumably in a state of alcohol-induced boldness, attempted to place his arm about Henrietta's waist as she left one of the small withdrawing rooms during a ball at Lansdowne House. Henrietta did not know his name, nor did she have any desire to ascertain it in the future, and the sharp slap she had delivered might well have served to both sober him sufficiently to become aware of his error, and put him off further encounters with a beautiful young lady possessed of a very firm palm. So why was she not able to imagine a life with Lord Martley? It was an unanswerable question.

'He is terribly good looking,' whispered Caroline, with the merest hint of a sigh.

'He is personable,' replied Henrietta, and then noticed the dreaming look upon her cousin's face. 'Do you prefer him to Lord Netheravon, or Sir Oliver Ryall? Sir Oliver has danced with you three times this week.'

'I . . . I do, but Henrietta, you saw how Mama was with Lady Pirbright. Can you conceive of either lady giving their blessing if – and I must stress that I have no proof that Lord Martley prefers me over any other young lady, and may indeed have his eyes upon yourself – he were to dare to offer for me?'

Henrietta was secretly taken aback that Caroline even mentioned the word 'offer'. If she had even begun to imagine such an eventuality, she must have quite a serious tendre for the gentleman.

'To be honest, Caroline, and you know that I am painfully so, it does sound a match unlikely to be greeted with delight upon either side, but if you were both sure of each other, would that not be set aside?'

'I wish that I thought so, but I do not.' Caroline paused. 'I am not in love with Lord Martley, you understand,' she averred with more determination than belief, 'it is just that . . . I could be, so very easily.'

Henrietta did not know whether to advise her cousin to let her feelings hold sway, or to keep them in check, and so said nothing, but squeezed her hand in a supportive manner. Support might be what she would need, since Henrietta had not forgotten the 'no' list.

Lord Henfield was not feeling up to a walk, brisk or otherwise. Whilst Lord Martley was formulating plans, however fuzzily, with a sense of optimism, Lord Henfield felt more beleaguered than confident. He eschewed a light luncheon, and at two o'clock forced himself into action, and set off to Bond Street, where he dithered for the better part of an hour before the windows of several jewellers', and then screwed up his courage, and entered the premises of one who had a good selection of pearl items in their window. He emerged some short while later, a little lighter of pocket and very slightly lighter of heart, and then went in search of Henrietta, to make his peace offering. When he reached the house in South Audley Street he was greeted with the information that the ladies were at home, which instantly presented Lord Henfield with a predicament he ought to have foreseen. He did not relish the idea of making an apology and giving Henry a present in front of her relations. There appeared to be, however, no alternative. He looked uncomfortable, though he did not take the coward's way and simply leave his card, but requested that it be taken up to Lady Elstead. He was rewarded a few minutes later by Barlow announcing him.

His card had in fact caused a degree of fluster on Henrietta's part, since she was conscious that, however much he had annoyed her, her behaviour the previous evening had been both rude and, though she hated to admit it, childish. It was a blushing Henrietta who made her curtsey when he entered the room, and Lady Elstead was swift to note the awkwardness between them. Lord Henfield made polite and general small talk for some minutes, but then rose, and approached where Henrietta sat, very straight-backed.

'I . . . last night, Miss Gaydon, I spoke as you said, as though you and I were still back in Shropshire. I wanted us to be upon the best of terms, and in attempting to regain the friendship we used to have, I . . . I made a mess of things, and then compounded my error by sulking, which made me far more of the "child" than you. I beg you will forgive me, and cast the evening from your mind, and' – he glanced at Lady Elstead – 'if Lady Elstead permits, I beg also that you will accept this small token as apology, and with my enduring affection.' He withdrew the small parcel from his pocket and held it out to Henrietta. Her fingers touched his as she took it from him, and he swallowed hard. She looked at her aunt, who nodded, and Henrietta proceeded to unwrap a small box in which a pearl ring nestled in blue velvet. A small 'flower' of pearls surrounded a little sparkling diamond, and the shoulders of the ring were set with delicate emeralds. Lord Henfield had a sudden panic that the ring would prove too large or too small for any of her fingers. He let out an audible sigh of relief when, after finding it a little tight upon the middle finger of her right hand, she slipped it, with the merest effort over the knuckle, onto the fourth finger. She raised her eyes to his, and they were misty.

'It is I who should apologise, my lord, and I am not deserving of such a gift, which is to reward behaviour of which I can assure you I am ashamed. I was both churlish and childish, and . . . I am sorry, Charles.' The last four words were blurted out, and had he been alone with her he would have taken both her hands and held them tightly, and used his pet name for her, but he knew her aunt disapproved of 'Henry'. He could but smile a little shakily at her.

'I am glad you like it.' He paused. He really could not ask what he had planned to ask, that she let him start afresh, not with others listening, but then he had an idea. 'It is not, of course, a bribe, Miss Gaydon, but might I be so very bold as to request a dance upon the next occasion we meet where there is dancing? Perhaps tonight, if you are to be at Almack's?' His tone was cajoling and sincere but not over-serious.

'You have my hand upon it, sir,' Henrietta managed, though her throat felt tight, and she extended the hand graced by the pearl ring, and clasped his, squeezing it very slightly. 'Friends,' she whispered, and for a moment Charles Henfield forgot the other ladies in the room.

'Yes,' he answered, as softly. It was, he thought, a step back in the right direction.

Anything more private was impossible, as Caroline waxed lyrical over the gift, and edged closer to her cousin, to enable her to turn Henrietta's hand one way and then the other to catch the light. For her own part, Henrietta was overcome, and rendered thereafter speechless for the rest of the visit.

When he left, shortly afterwards, having refused the offer of tea, he went to his club, where he took a brandy, and wandered a little aimlessly about the rooms, contemplating an evening at Almack's with a mixture of anticipation and dread. It was in the billiard room that he met Lords Gorleston and Netheravon, arguing good-naturedly over the rival merits of two horses entered for the Derby.

'Afternoon, Henfield. I have nearly beaten Gorleston all hollow here, so if you wish to take over . . .'

'I warn you, Netheravon has had the most amazing luck this afternoon.' Lord Gorleston smiled at his two friends. 'Of course, it could just be that I should not have had that Chablis.' Whether he had injudiciously imbibed or not, he was perfectly capable of noticing that Lord Henfield appeared in a better frame of mind. 'Drowning your sorrows or celebrating, my dear fellow?' He nodded at Lord Henfield's glass.

'Neither, though you do find me more hopeful than earlier.'

'Well, if it is because you have put money on Waterloo in a fit of patriotic fervour, do not get too hopeful; in fact, do not get hopeful at all,' commented Lord Netheravon. 'My money's on Manfred, though Gorleston here is still with The Student. Odds are too short for my liking on him.'

'Er, no.' Lord Henfield did not wish to reveal his thoughts, especially to Netheravon.

'Would have more interest in the runners for the Oaks,' remarked Lord Gorleston cryptically.

'Ah, now I never feel as sure about fillies.' Lord Netheravon shook his head. 'You simply cannot trust them to behave to form. I only once bet on the Oaks and the filly played up all the way to the start and threw the jockey the moment the starter dropped his flag.'

'Exactly Henfield's problem, eh, Henfield?' Lord Gorleston grinned, but then nodded at Lord Henfield's frown. He was not going to give the game away. However, Lord Netheravon had made the mental leap from four legs to two without further prompting.

'Whichever way you look at it, the female of the species, and it applies to all species most likely ... not just human beings but even tigers or ... squirrels ... anyway, the female of the species thinks differently and can career off in the most unlikely direction for no apparent reason. Do not get me wrong, the "fillies" trotted out at Almack's are delightful, but can one understand them? I am deuced sure that I cannot.'

'You see, there may lie your problem, Netheravon,' observed Lord Gorleston. 'You secretly hope that you will, and me, I just happily accept that I won't. I never understood my sisters, or my mama, and learned early that it is a waste of time worrying about it. Accept them for what they are, beautiful . . . endearing, but . . . er, not meaning my mama, you understand . . .'

'Quite so.' Lord Netheravon chuckled. 'That is remarkably frightening, thinking of our mamas as simpering misses.'

'Not sure mine ever mastered simpering. Giving set-downs is more in her line, but my father seems dashed fond of her, in his quiet way.' Lord Gorleston was in awe of his mother, but deeply attached to her.

'Do you have sisters, Henfield?' Lord Netheravon took his shot and looked up at the viscount.

'No, only child.' Lord Henfield felt a twinge, as if he had told a lie. That was the problem; Henry had been so much his sister when she was small that he felt he could understand the two men who did have sisters. It was, he thought, slightly heartening that even the full and legal possession of sisters did not provide a deeper insight into the female mind. 'I did have a very nice spaniel bitch, though, as a boy, and she seemed quite logical, for a dog.'

'Cocker?' The topic, as Lord Henfield had hoped, moved smoothly into gun dogs and shooting, and he relaxed. When he eventually left the club, with Lord Gorleston at his side, that gentleman apologised.

'Nearly came a cropper, and all my own silly fault. I

really ought not to try and be witty. Profound apologies, my dear fellow.' From these concise utterances Lord Henfield understood the whole.

'You are a good friend, Gorleston, and I know you would not try to put me to the blush for sport.'

'So, has my mama's advice given you hope?'

'It was not so much advice as a plan of campaign, really. You know, if Wellington had had Lady Vernham in the Peninsular, I am dashed sure the war would have been over a year earlier.'

'Oh, much more than a year, Henfield. Wellington would only have needed to send my mama out in front of the Frenchies to tell them that their behaviour was not what she expected of French manners, and that they put her out of all patience and should go home.' Lord Gorleston grinned widely.

The two gentlemen were still chuckling at the top of St James's.

CHAPTER TEN

Henrietta's mind was in a whirl of confused thoughts when Lord Henfield departed, and she paid little attention to Lady Elstead's approval of the nature and scale of the present, until that lady commented that his 'sin' must have been great.

'Oh no, ma'am, that is the awful part. Truly, he was not at fault and it was me, being . . . silly and fractious. It is such a beautiful ring, and I am so undeserving of it.'

Lady Elstead probed the exact nature of the contretemps more closely, but Henrietta just shook her head, and repeated 'undeserving'. Failing to learn anything more by these means, Lady Elstead gave up, but went away to rewrite her Henrietta list with Lord Henfield's name at the top.

'She could do better, of course,' she murmured to herself as she did so, 'but if it comes to pass it will not be set at my door. Everyone will assume that there was an understanding before she even came to London. Oh well.'

Henrietta dressed for the evening with uncharacteristic indecision, and surveyed three different gowns and tried on two of them before deciding which she would wear. Sewell chastised her for being 'feather-headed', and shook her head.

'And there was I thinking as you had got yourself all serene about parties and dancing and the like. Now, Miss Henrietta, keep still, or I will end up placing these flowers in your hair all awry and have to start again.' The maid fussed, and primped and surveyed, until such time as she felt her mistress passed muster. 'There now, fine as fivepence.' She stood back, and smiled.

'Thank you, Sewell. No need to wait . . .'

'As if I would go to bed, knowing that you will come in and leave your gown crumpled and your dancing slippers where any might fall over them. You just ring as always, and I will be up.'

'You are the best of maids. Thank you.' Henrietta rose and pressed her cheek to her old maid's, which caused Sewell to shoo her from the room in embarrassment.

Henrietta knocked upon her cousin's door, and found her eyeing a small, but very pretty, corsage.

'That is nice,' she remarked. 'Go on, Caroline, tell me who sent it.'

'That is the thing, cousin. I do not know. It was simply delivered, addressed to me most clearly, and with no message or indication as to the sender. I am wondering if I should wear it, in case I should encourage a gentleman I actually dislike.'

'Are there any?'

'Well, if it is Sir Lawrence Coleford . . .'

'Ah yes, but the flowers show a delicate touch and he would not do more than say "violets" or "lily of the valley".'

'Unless he was so vague that he left all to the florist? Oh, what shall I do?' Her hand went to her cheek.

'Do you know, I think you have to be prepared to be dishonest. If it is he, or some other man you do not care to bestow your best smile upon, look surprised, and thank him, and say, "and I thought . . ." without finishing the sentence and giving any other name.'

'Henrietta, that is positively devious. The flowers are pretty, and they do go with my gown.'

Henrietta nearly laughed. Since neither young lady favoured even the palest of pinks, and most of their gowns were in shades of white and ivory 'with a tint of', the cream and pale lemon flowers were never going to clash.

'Absolutely. I think you wear it and risk it, yes?'

'Yes!' Caroline beamed at her cousin, and Henrietta wondered if Caroline was quietly hoping that the sender was Lord Martley.

Almack's was exceedingly warm, and the ladies were fanning themselves for real rather than from any flirtatious reasons. At least, thought Henrietta, muslins were thin. What it must be like for the gentlemen she dared not imagine. Lady Elstead timed their arrival to be neither early, showing desperation, nor late, showing, as she said in the carriage, 'an inability to prepare oneself in good time, or a house where the staff do not wind the clocks regularly'. Henrietta scanned the room, wondering whom she might see, and most especially seeking Lord Henfield, since she was determined to both thank him once again for his present, and to be especially nice to him.

Whilst it was ridiculous to even consider that a gentleman would come to Almack's and only dance with one lady, she nevertheless felt a twinge of disappointment to find that he was already upon the dance floor, and with Miss Yate as his partner. He did dance, she thought dispassionately, very well for a man more at home with a shotgun in the crook of his arm, and the hope of a cosy dinner on the table rather than ices and feats of culinary artistry, not that Almack's provided either of those. As she watched him move up the set, she was conscious of both contentment and a strange melancholy. She had the oddest sensation of possessiveness, as though Miss Yate were dancing with 'her Charles' – as though she had borrowed him for the dance, but would be expected to return him afterwards.

The musicians held a long note, and the dance ended. Lord Henfield bowed to Miss Yate, and offered her his arm. She looked up at him with a smile, a smile of gratitude and pleasure. As they turned to leave the floor he looked in Henrietta's direction, and for a moment their eyes met, and held. Then Lady Elstead was introducing Henrietta to some old acquaintance and she had, perforce, to give her attention elsewhere.

'You know Miss Gaydon from before her Season, I take it, my lord?' Miss Yate had followed his gaze.

'We virtually grew up together.'

'Ah. The friends of one's youth are very precious' – Miss Yate sounded wistful – 'and should never be set aside.'

'Are you a country person, at heart, Miss Yate? I confess all this' – Lord Henfield indicated the throng about them with his hand – 'is very fine for a short time, but I am far more at home in Shropshire.'

'I . . . I prefer the fresh air and the space of the country, but of course I must go where my mama dictates.'

'But the time will come when you are married and . . .'

'I shall not marry, not now.' Miss Yate spoke hurriedly, and with some intensity. 'Whatever Mama may think, Season after Season, I shall not marry.'

'You know, I think you do yourself disservice, ma'am. Not all men are interested in merely the obvious. A lady's character is of more worth.' He bowed over her hand once more, and left her prey to conflicting emotions.

* * *

Lord Martley was a popular young man, and the lady patronesses were never troubled that he might leave lesser young ladies without partners, for he was willing to be introduced to any that they felt needed a chance, and did not complain. Until the arrival of the Elstead party he had placed himself very much at the Countess Lieven's disposal, and had, he felt, 'done his duty'. From the moment he saw that Miss Felbridge wore a corsage of creamy yellow flowers, his evening was a success, although he was denied the chance to secure his first dance with her by being detained by an acquaintance, and then saw Sir Lawrence Coleford making his bow, and also make Miss Felbridge look defensive. Whilst being a naturally non-belligerent sort of fellow, this made his lordship wish he could remove Sir Lawrence and offer to punch him on the nose. How dare he upset Miss Felbridge. A small sound not unlike a very repressed growl issued from his lordship's lips, and the gentleman with whom he was speaking blinked, and asked whether he was suffering from indigestion.

However, at this point Sir Lawrence evidently decided to address himself to charming Miss Gaydon, who appeared no more pleased to see him but who, in Lord Martley's opinion, was far more capable of fending for herself. It was, he thought, brave of her, but it was her cousin's sweet vulnerability which entranced him. Miss Gaydon was a delight as a dancing partner, and one with whom it was entertaining to engage in light-hearted conversation, but he was never filled with an almost overwhelming urge to protect her. Lord Martley was treated by his mother as little more than an idiot and a child, but Miss Felbridge made him feel like a man, in every possible way, just by looking shyly at him, and lifting the corners of her generous mouth in a smile.

Disengaging from the conversation, Lord Martley wove his way through the crowd to present himself before the two young ladies. Miss Felbridge gave a small 'oh' of delighted surprise, and if her cheeks were a little pink it was not from embarrassment.

'Miss Felbridge, Miss Gaydon, I trust that I find you in excellent health this evening, and ready to wear your dancing slippers into rags, or whatever one does with slippers, from dancing all evening.' He sounded bouncy, and fun, after Sir Lawrence's leaden overtures, and even Lady Elstead, who had been watching in a bemused way, could not deny that he appeared friendly and not at all intense and lover-like. Of course, she was not eighteen, and nor was she already three parts in love with him.

Sir Lawrence was not a man to understand subtle hints. He did not, therefore, make a request for a dance and then withdraw, but remained, just like the cleavers plant with which Henrietta had compared him.

'As I was saying, Miss Gaydon, it is rare that one finds a young lady who can conduct a conversation upon a sensible subject whilst dancing, and . . .'

'You must have been dancing with all the wrong young ladies, Coleford,' interrupted Lord Martley, beaming. 'My sisters used to chatter like jays, or was it jackdaws, when they were at their dancing lessons, and on the most erudite subjects, and a young lady with whom I danced earlier was telling me about the state of the road out to Knightsbridge. I could point her out to you, if you wish.'

Sir Lawrence looked rather taken aback by this.

'I, er . . .'

'If the state of the King's highway is not your subject, there is always Miss Daresbury, who has strong views upon the abolition of slavery in the Colonies, but I do warn you that she dances the right steps but never quite to the beat of the music. I think I saw her over by . . .'

'Thank you, Martley. That will not be necessary.'

'I have the second cotillion after supper free, Sir Lawrence,' offered Henrietta, keeping a straight face.

'Then please place my name beside it. I shall await it with unfathomable pleasure.' Sir Lawrence bowed, as Caroline bit her lip and Lord Martley suffered a twitching of the muscles in his cheeks. He then, with a great show of reluctance, moved away.

'"Unfathomable"?' managed Lord Martley. 'Well, I can safely say I find the greatest pleasure in dancing with both of you ladies, but I would never say that it was "unfathomable". Makes it sound a silly thing to be happy about.'

Caroline gave way to giggles behind her fan, and her

mama rebuked her.

'Dare we ask what "erudite" subjects your sisters discussed, my lord?' Henrietta had mastered her voice.

'Ah, well that is where I have to make a confession. My sisters never discussed anything other than hats, and trimmings on gowns from what I heard. Had to think of something, and . . .'

'It was a lie in a noble cause, my lord.'

'And I think an erudite conversation about hats entirely possible,' added Caroline.

'If you forgive me that deception, ladies, might I request that you find a place for me upon your dance cards?' Lord Martley thought this a cunning move, since Lady Elstead could hardly permit him to dance with her niece but demur at his dancing with her daughter.

'I have the last waltz before supper free, my lord,' offered Caroline, trying to sound casual.

'And I have a quadrille immediately afterwards,' announced Henrietta.

'Excellent. And since I am to be engaged with you around supper, might I have the pleasure of escorting you, Miss Gaydon?'

'I . . .' Henrietta saw Lord Henfield drawing close, and was inspired. 'I regret I am already engaged with Lord Henfield, but I am sure my cousin . . .'

'If you will accept a second choice, my lord?' Caroline sounded a little uncertain, with a niggling doubt that

Lord Martley really did prefer her cousin.

'Miss Felbridge, consider me honoured in the extreme. Until the waltz before supper.' He bowed. 'Evening, Henfield. Lucky fellow to have Miss Gaydon on your arm into supper.'

Lord Henfield did not bat an eyelid.

'Exceptionally so.' He looked straight at Henrietta, and she extended her hand. 'But you see, Martley, I have to resort to . . .' He changed his mind. '. . . playing the card of old acquaintanceship, since I do not possess the suavity of you London types.' He bowed over her hand.

'It would not fit over my glove,' she whispered, and he heard not an excuse but a plea that he should know the truth. He squeezed her fingers very slightly to show he had heard, and understood.

'Me, suave? Must have the wrong fellow, Henfield.' Lord Martley shook his head. 'Newbold can be suave, or Littlehampton, or Netheravon, but I am . . .'

'Entertaining, my lord, most entertaining, and without such as yourself the Season would become a terrible bore within weeks.' Henrietta gave him her brightest smile.

'If I may entertain, ma'am, I am not without use. Until the waltz before supper, Miss Felbridge.' He bowed to the three ladies, nodded at Lord Henfield, and threaded his way between the groups of people to speak to Lady Jersey.

'So, I am to take you in to supper, am I, Miss

Gaydon?' Lord Henfield permitted himself a wry smile. 'I wonder at the motive, since Lord Martley is, in your own words, "most entertaining".'

'You are, my lord,' declared Henrietta, and ignored the question of her motive. 'You are also down for the waltz before supper.'

'Is that in order for you to twirl about the floor and bump into Miss Felbridge and her partner?' Lord Henfield suddenly felt as if the last few days of misery had been but a dream. Here was Henry, his Henry, behaving like she always had with him. A warning voice within told he must not slip into Shropshire mode for the evening, since he had a 'war' to win.

'It most certainly is not, sir. It is by way of a thank you, for . . . forgiving me.' She looked quite shy, and then serious. 'I did not deserve . . .'

'We shall not speak of it now. I . . .' He turned to Caroline. 'I believe the next dance to be a country dance, Miss Felbridge. If you are not engaged, might I solicit you as a partner?'

Caroline thanked him and accepted, and Henrietta was left wondering.

When Lord Henfield appeared at her elbow to claim his dance, Henrietta looked up at him questioningly. He did not look as if he were about to scold her. She laid her hand on his arm and he led her onto the floor, where he placed his hand lightly at her waist, and smiled at her, with a trace of wistfulness.

'You said we would not talk of my . . . behaviour, but I think you do have something to say. Perhaps you ought to say it now, so that I know the worst.'

'There is no "worst". If you regret your words it takes the sting from them, and the gift was not to reward your behaviour but to atone for mine, for I said the wrong thing. I did not mean to do so, but ever since I came to London I have been confused.'

The music started, and they began to twirl like automatons about the dance floor.

'Confused?' Henrietta frowned. 'Why?'

'Because I knew you would look different, new gowns, a new way to dress your hair, but you seemed to have changed so very much, and I did not, do not, know how to act. If I try to be as we were at home, it can be taken that I am treating you as a child, though I have not thought of you as such for several years, I swear. Yet if I try and behave like the men I see flocking about you, then I look blockish and stiff and . . . I have drifted between the two and done nothing but annoy you, Mi . . . Henry. I want the chance, just the chance, to be as popular with you as Martley, or Netheravon or Coleford.'

'Hmm, Sir Lawrence is not popular with me.'

'Tell me what you want from me?' Lord Henfield's hold tightened a fraction, and his words, softly spoken, begged.

'I . . .' Henrietta looked up into his face and suddenly

felt a dizziness that owed nothing to their revolutions to the music. 'I do not know. I . . .' She was a little breathless. She had looked into that face a thousand times, and yet this was the first time. She was looking at him not as 'Charles', big brother substitute, dear friend. What she saw was a man with grey-blue eyes that drew one in, whose corners crinkled when he laughed, a man with a firm chin and a small white scar upon the jaw, which she remembered he got many years ago when he fell from a tree when trying to rescue her entangled kite. At which point the 'brother' blended in once more, and the stirring of emotion seemed all wrong. Her lips were parted, her bosom heaving.

'I just wish that I could please you.' Actually, he wished at that moment he could kiss her. 'I will try to be as the others are, if that is what you want. I am not some Bond Street beau, you know that, but beneath my clumsiness you know also that I only ever want your happiness.'

She just stared at him. They twirled about, and afterwards neither could explain how they did not cannon into other couples. When the music ceased, both looked as if they had suffered some sort of shock. Lord Henfield drew Henrietta's arm through his own, and led her back to where Lady Elstead was waiting, and watching. What she had seen had distracted her from Caroline, which was perhaps as well.

Lord Martley completely forgot about whether or not

Lady Elstead was watching, once he had Miss Felbridge in his hold. She looked up at him with just the degree of bashfulness and adoring hero worship that would be guaranteed to set a fellow's heart racing, and so Lord Martley's heart raced. For several revolutions he could say nothing, and then he successfully uttered the thought at the top of his mind.

'You wore it.'

'Oh, thank goodness,' exclaimed Caroline, which was not quite what he was expecting. 'I feared, since there was no note, that I might in error wear it and give some gentleman whom I do not like the impression that . . .'

'You . . . like me, Miss Felbridge?' Martley managed, and Caroline made an indeterminate gurgling noise, which was not intrinsically attractive, but in this instance conveyed a satisfying affirmative. 'I am so glad . . . that you wore the flowers.'

The pause was just long enough to let her know that was not all about which he was glad.

'They are perfect,' she breathed, and blushed.

'No, it is you who are . . .' He caught his breath. 'I ought not to be so bold, Miss Felbridge, but right now, and right here, I feel the boldest man in England.'

'I wish I too could be bold, my lord, for if I was I would say that this must be the best dream I have ever had.' She trembled slightly, and he felt it in the hand he held.

'It is not a dream.'

'It has to be, because when I awake there will be the

real world, a world where your mama and mine are in such enmity that what I might wish with all my heart must be impossible.'

'If you wish it with all your heart, then it must not be permitted to be impossible, Miss Felbridge.'

'Do you have a way to achieve it?' There was a trace of hope in her voice.

'At this moment, no, but if I have your wish, I will strive to find a way.'

'You have my wish, and you have my heart, my lord.' It was daring, beyond daring, but the pair of them were behaving entirely from instinct.

'Then somehow, Miss Felbridge, my dear, dear Miss Felbridge, I will find a way.' He had always sounded light-hearted, but now he exuded determination.

Caroline blinked away a tear. Had Lady Elstead been watching them she might have wondered at the seriousness of their expressions for the remainder of the dance, and been heartened by both that and their silence, although had she read their thoughts, or known the frisson that existed between them, she would have been horrified. They returned, exchanging slightly tense 'nothings'. Had Henrietta not been as self-absorbed, she might have come to exactly the right conclusion. A more astute viewer than Lady Elstead would have remarked upon the similarity between both couples, but her ladyship's understanding was moderate, rather than good, and focused upon her niece.

'Well, I am mightily pleased that I am not of an age to waltz. It strikes me that having such a dance before supper will disrupt the digestion so much that there will be an awful lot left upon the tables, even with the poor fare one gets here.'

Henrietta and Caroline looked at her as if food were an unknown substance.

'I think, ma'am, that the "disruption", as you term it, is quite transitory, and that the passage of a few minutes will restore the appetite.' Lord Henfield spoke carefully, forming the words one at a time in his head, which was muzzy. It was like being foxed, but without the physical disorientation.

'Though I doubt that it means we ought to let those who have not waltzed eat before us,' added Lord Martley, playing to his 'amiable fribble' persona. There was just a hint of desperation in his voice, and it wove its way into Henrietta's head.

'I do not think running for the supper room would be the done thing, Lord Martley.'

'No, Miss Gaydon, you are, as always, entirely right.' He threw her a grateful look.

Henrietta felt as though her mind and body were divorced, and only those aspects of her brain which controlled movement and simple tasks were working. She was struggling with a concept so important that it threw everything else into the vague distance. What she really needed was not sustenance, but somewhere to think, and think alone. She let Lord Henfield lead her to supper, but could not recall afterwards having taken a single mouthful, or placing anything upon her plate. She was preternaturally conscious of his proximity, and both excited and, in a peculiar way, appalled.

For her part, Caroline had no appetite at all, and Lord Martley had to coax her to eat anything.

'You must, for otherwise you will fall in a dead faint during some dance with another fellow, and I could not bear to think of you in another man's arms,' he whispered.

'Oh, how beautiful!'

'Not at all. How awful.' He managed a grin in his more normal mode, and she smiled, although she felt she would far prefer to cry with a mixture of happiness, relief that her affections were returned, and fear that, for all his brave talk, the dream would remain the dream.

The advantage Lord Martley had over Lord Henfield was that he was dancing with Miss Gaydon immediately after supper, and his lack of repartee was not noticed. Lord Henfield withdrew into a brown study, from which he was reluctantly drawn by Lady Jersey, to dance with a nervous young lady with a slight stammer, who found his footwork excellent but his manner rather cool and strangely forbidding. Lord Martley, rather more accustomed to the social whirl, managed to make a recovery to the point where he could entertain three partners who were presented to him, but then quietly left, not, as most would have assumed, to end the night carousing with gentlemen in less refined surroundings than Almack's, but to go to bed, where he lay for some time veering between elation and trying to solve a seemingly insoluble problem. Miss Felbridge favoured him, had declared she loved him, and it made him inexpressibly happy. Yet at the same time the desired consequence of their mutual affection was no closer to being a reality. He had to think of something. 'Thinking of something' was not an occupation that had taken up much of his lordship's time, until now. Falling in love, he told himself, as the arms of Morpheus finally claimed him, presented huge challenges. He dreamt of slaying dragons that kept telling him he was a ninny.

CHAPTER ELEVEN

UNLIKE LORD MARTLEY, AND TO A LESSER EXTENT Lord Henfield, the two young ladies were not in a position to do other than try and act as if nothing had occurred that was out of the ordinary. If Miss Felbridge's smile was a little dreamy, the gentlemen favoured with their names on her dance card saw little difference in the diffidence of her comments. Henrietta, being more noted for her sharp wits, was, thought Lord Netheravon, 'a trifle out of sorts', which he put down to the heat, and she did not disabuse him. Her dance with Sir Lawrence Coleford tried her patience, since he was a dancer of only moderate capabilities, and spent every moment where the dance brought them together in describing the location and advantages of his country seat in Lincolnshire. She only wished he might retire there in the immediate future.

It was quite late in the evening when Mr Newbold spoke with Henrietta. He was curious. He knew very little of Henfield, other than he was accounted a solid enough fellow, one of the 'gentlemen of the shires' who did not come up to Town more than was necessary for a decent tailor and to meet old acquaintances. He had ascertained that he was some family friend of Miss Gaydon's, but tonight what he observed was not two friends dancing. What further surprised him was that he had not viewed what he saw dispassionately. What stirred within him was a very rare emotion, one of slight resentment. He might even go so far as to term it jealousy, and that annoyed and perplexed him.

'I shall not ask if I might have the honour of a dance, Miss Gaydon, for your expression is one of having tired feet upon a warm evening. Might I procure you a glass of lemonade and receive the alternative honour of a little conversation? I have even discovered an unoccupied sofa where one might be seated, with Lady Elstead's permission.'

Her ladyship smiled.

'Then I am in your debt, Mr Newbold. I would adore a glass of lemonade.' Henrietta sighed. 'Never have I found Almack's so oppressively hot. I believe two young ladies have had to be revived a little after supper. I can only suppose that you gentlemen are made of sterner mettle.'

'It is, I confess, uncomfortable, and London is not at its best in the heat. Let me show you to that seat, and

166

then fetch the lemonade, as long as you do not give up the place beside you to some other daring fellow in my absence.'

'I would not be so cruel or unfair, sir.'

'Good.' He did as he said, and she fanned herself whilst he was gone. In truth, her head really was beginning to throb, and she rubbed her temple with her free hand. He returned within a couple of minutes, and smiled at her.

'Poor Miss Gaydon. I think this evening has tested your stamina.'

'That makes me sound a very weak creature, sir, and I do not think that is true.'

'And you have only flagged after supper, not before.'

'Indeed, I was perfectly well then.'

'And particularly happy.' Mr Newbold was watching her.

'I . . . was not at all unhappy.'

'Is Lord Henfield a frequent visitor at your home in Shropshire?'

'Lord Henfield?' Henrietta's voice rose half an octave. 'He . . . his estate is within walking distance of our house, and he is my papa's godson.'

'Ah, that would explain it.'

'Explain what, Mr Newbold?'

'The natural ease between you. Except that this evening it was a trifle strained, I thought.'

'We have not argued, sir.'

'Oh, I do not suggest that you have,' he replied cryptically. Henrietta was fanning herself more agitatedly. 'I think, Miss Gaydon, that I am being less than fair to you this evening. What you should do now is to persuade Lady Elstead that you are in need of your bed, and perhaps a tisane for the headache.'

'Yes, that does sound the best course.'

He wondered why he had let her escape his questions so easily. Seeing her unwell, and she did look genuinely rather frayed, brought out the chivalric in him, he decided.

'Drink your lemonade, Miss Gaydon, and I shall return you to her side and support your cause.'

'Thank you, Mr Newbold. I should have guessed that I could rely upon you.'

'At any time, ma'am.'

The tisane helped, but not as much as she had hoped. Of course it did nothing for her muddled thoughts. Henrietta was in a state of shock, as much as anything. There had been hints before, of course, easily dismissed, but tonight Charles Henfield had, whilst being the 'Charles' bound into the fibres of her life, been also a man in an entirely different sense, and that amazed her, thrilled her, scared her. It was as if a curtain were pulled away, and there he was, not brother, not friend, but . . . she dared not even think the word. She had danced with his arm about her, and although she had done so on other nights, this was different. He had asked what she wanted from him, and in such a voice. The answer that had sprung into her head had been 'everything'. She had wanted, in that moment, to be drawn even closer, to be kissed. She had never wanted to be kissed by any of the other men who paid her court. She had tried to imagine it, and failed, but her imagination now was all too successful. She tingled at the thought of it, and yet was ashamed.

She wanted Charles to kiss her, the Charles who had been a scrubby schoolboy when she had been a baby, an adolescent when she was a little girl, always there, often complaining at her being in his way, yet also somehow always prepared to give up his time. The incident with the kite, when he had cut his chin, had been one such. Looking at it from his perspective she could only wonder at his patience. What youth of fifteen would want to help a six-year-old fly a kite? He had not, but she had pestered him and he had given in, and stood behind her and helped her. Then there had been a wasp flying about her face, and she had panicked, and it had stung her nose and she had pulled so hard upon the kite strings that it had crashed into a tree. She had been screaming, and while her nursemaid fussed over her, Charles had climbed the tree to rescue her blue kite to cheer her up, and had slipped on his way down and tumbled the last few feet. A branch had caught the side of his chin and gashed it, and so the nursemaid had ended up screaming too, at the sight of the blood. Henrietta vaguely recalled there being quite a lot of it for what ended up a small white scar. It felt odd, wrong, to be wanting that same 'brotherly Charles' to kiss her.

Admittedly, in the last few years he had not seemed much older than herself, but . . . to want his kisses? She sighed. What if she let herself think of a future with him? There would be leaving home, but only just, and the same neighbours and Papa able to see them every day if he wished and . . . No. That would make her think she wanted to marry Charles as a means of solving her marriage problem and yet not leave her own familiar surroundings, and that must not influence her. But what was she thinking? To consider him as a husband at all was . . . the unthinkable being thought. She had plenty of men who liked her, perfectly nice men.

A small but insistent voice in her head said 'yes, but you love none of them'.

She hid under the bedclothes, but the thought did not go away, and when she slept, she was aware of a loneliness, because Charles Henfield was not anywhere in the world of the dream.

Caroline, equally glad to retreat into the seclusion of her bedchamber, let her maid help her prepare for bed in near silence, which the tirewoman put down to exhaustion. Her only sign of animation was when she objected to the removal of the very slightly wilting flowers of her corsage. After the woman had left, Caroline carefully extracted the blooms. She then tore a piece of tissue paper that encased her best gown in her linen press, and gently wrapped the flowers and pressed them between the pages of a book of poetry, which was rather thin, and weighed it down further with two romances on loan from Hookham's Library. She would keep those flowers, and they would always be a reminder of tonight, whatever befell. She sniffed, and climbed back into bed and covered her face with her hands. She wept. She wept from a mixture of supreme happiness, disbelief and a desperate fear that all her hopes would be blighted and her life ruined.

Lord Martley was the nicest of men, the best of men. He was not perfect, she told herself, but did not believe it, for he was perfect – perfect for her. He was happy and non-judgemental, not some man who would forever be correcting a 'little fault' or mistakes in her; he made her feel safe, and alive and . . . He was good looking, no, handsome. He stood straight and not so tall as to be lanky and his eyes were full of kindness and laughter. When she was with him the world was bright, and life was exciting.

He had as good as declared himself, been daring and yet circumspect, darling man that he was. He was going to find a way that they could be together, and she hoped, prayed, that he would but . . . Fate would keep them apart, or rather Mama and Lady Pirbright would do so. He would make every effort, but she could see herself being torn from his arms and forced into marriage with some unnamed but obviously old and tyrannical brute. The fact that she had not encountered anyone even vaguely matching that description did not matter. His aim seemed like some impossible quest. She took a deep breath, which was half sob. He was going to do this for her, so she too must be brave, and help him. At first she could think of no way in which she might assist, but then realised that if Mama guessed their attachment, all would be lost. She must therefore behave as if Lord Martley meant no more to her than any other gentleman. This would be exceptionally difficult, but a Test of Love. She must also, of course, let her Love know that her outward appearance of disinterest was in fact a cloak about a heart that beat only for him. Deception was not something that came easily to Caroline Felbridge, but she resolved to try her very best.

She then attempted sleep, but her pillow was damp, and her heart full, and her mind occupied with delicious fantasies.

Lord Henfield was perhaps less confused than Henrietta, having faced the 'brother and sister' problem, but he was certainly subject to conflicting emotions. Henry's manner towards him tonight had been not just approachable, but as though she had seen a revelation.

His instinct, for he had no experience upon which to build, was that she had looked at him, at last, as she did her beaux. Was he vain to think that she had liked what she saw? There had been a moment, transient but real, when her expression invited much more than he could give her, in public, and at Almack's. Had she looked like that and they had been alone in the gardens at The Court he would not have been able to stop himself. He would have kissed her, and declared his passion for her. It was passion, it was ridiculous to deny it, and tonight it had been, if not let off its leash, permitted to come out of the shadows. It was liberating, and yet also dangerous. He tried to be calm. They had danced together, and she had, perhaps, cast the 'fraternal' from her mind. To assume anything more was to let dreams hold sway. Lady Vernham had described his course as a war, and if it was, then this was only a first battle won.

Supper had been a vague period involving foodstuffs, and making an attempt to be normal. From choice he would have left immediately thereafter, but to do so would have occasioned possible remark, and besides, he could sometimes watch Henry. She looked rather warm and disorientated, and had he not feared she would see it as a slight upon her constitution, and interfering, he would have suggested that she have Lady Elstead take her home. She danced, and she smiled, but the smiles were forced, and her steps not as light as usual. He did not see Mr Newbold fetch her lemonade but did catch

cautious and circumspect. 'Do you look forward to running your own house? I mean, does it frighten you at all?'

'What?' Henrietta opened her eyes, and frowned. 'Frighten me? No, why ought it to do so? I have been running much of the day-to-day affairs at home for ages. Papa does not want to be bothered with preserves and sheets and whether the scullery maid needs a tooth drawn.'

'Of course, your position is different. I . . . I have not had to deal with anything like that, yet. And of course, it does depend upon the size of the establishment.'

'Were you thinking of a palace, cousin?'

'No.' Caroline's thoughtful expression changed into a grin. 'I can think of nothing worse than living in anything so huge and formal.'

'I do not think the maids would have to wear feathers in their hair as we did for presentation, though.'

'Goodness, no.' She paused. 'I do not think it is the size of the house that is important, but rather the happiness in it.'

'Is that going to be your profound statement of the day?' Henrietta stretched.

'Do you know, I think it shall be.' Caroline slid her feet back into her slippers, and stood up. 'Are we not engaged to walk in the park with the Misses Fairburn this afternoon?'

'Yes, but they said that they would not knock until half past four o'clock at the very earliest.'

'Might we go to Hookham's before luncheon, then? I have a book to take back, and Jane Trusham was telling me about *The Prisoner of Chillon*, and I still have not read it.'

'Yes, that will not take us long. I confess I do not seek a very active day' – Henrietta sounded languorous – 'and I think we are dining with the Soughtons, which I am not looking forward to, because "Young Gerald" is a perfect bore, but thinks himself so amusing, and his mama agrees with him.'

'It is a great pity she and Mama are such close friends. I fear the others at dinner will not be . . . vibrant, and if we finish late, I do not think we will go on to Lady Donnington's, which is a pity, because there will be dancing and our friends will all be there.' Caroline sighed. She was thinking of one friend very particularly.

'When I first came to London, I wondered if I might find life a little flat afterwards, since our time is so filled with events, but I am starting to think it may yet be a blessed relief, at least to my feet. I am a great walker at home, but standing for hours, and dancing almost every evening, does take its toll.' Henrietta rang the bell at her bedside. 'Now, Caroline, I am going to cast you out and get up and dressed. I think I will write a letter to my papa after luncheon, since I have been very remiss and have not sent him any news for over a week. He will be wondering what has happened to me.'

'Or will think you so busy gadding about that you have not had time, dear Cousin.'

'I will always have time for Papa.'

There was a knock at the door, and Sewell entered.

'There now.' She bobbed a curtsey, but addressed both young ladies firmly. 'Here are you both, and her ladyship rung for her maid this half hour since. It is the young as is meant to be able to stay up to all hours, but I am not so sure.'

'Her ladyship did not dance all evening, Sewell.' Henrietta pushed her cousin from the edge of the bed, and threw back the covers. 'But behold me now ready to face the day.'

'What is left of it,' muttered Sewell, and shook her head.

Caroline departed, laughing.

CHAPTER TWELVE

THE TWO COUSINS SET OFF UPON THE SHORT WALK to Hookham's Library a little after noon, defying the gloomy prediction of Barlow the butler that they would get very wet. He eyed the skies with a sense of foreboding and ensured that the footman carried an umbrella, but the young ladies were more interested in chatter than meteorology. Both kept from the subjects closest to their hearts, but there was plenty to discuss that had nothing to do with the Lords Martley or Henfield, and they arrived in Bond Street still perfectly dry. The main object of their visit proved unattainable, since the volume in question was out upon loan, but they did meet two other young ladies, exchanged views upon Mrs Edgeworth's latest book, and emerged a half hour later to a black sky, and a rolling rumble of thunder.

'Oh dear, and I so dislike thunderstorms,' bemoaned Caroline, as the first heavy droplets spattered onto the pavement. The footman unfurled the umbrella, and opened it, unfortunately with such force that one of the arms snapped completely and the fabric flapped like a wounded crow. Amidst his loud and profuse apologies, another voice was heard.

'I say, you will be soaked to the skin in no time if you stand there, ladies.'

Caroline turned, and her face lit up. Lord Martley, safe beneath an umbrella so taut that the rain was beating a tattoo upon it, sketched a bow.

'We appear to have a broken umbrella, my lord.'

'Then permit me to stand between you as a thorn between roses, rather than the other way about, and offer you my escort as far as South Audley Street.'

'But were you going in that direction, sir?' asked Caroline.

'It is an excellent thoroughfare, and I have an urgent desire to see it,' he declared, grinning. 'Now, ladies, no time to dither.'

He stepped between them and, in order to remain as close as possible and keep dry, they both drew close and slipped an arm through his. The unfortunate footman trailed behind them with his 'wounded' umbrella. A flash lit the sky, closely followed a few seconds later by a crack of thunder, and Lord Martley felt Miss Felbridge grip his arm more tightly.

'Do not be afraid, Miss Felbridge. Lightning strikes the tallest thing about, and, whilst I am not short, I am not as tall as a building. You are more at risk from catching a chill if you get too wet.'

So keen was he that they should not get wet that they had almost to run to keep up with him, and it was two slightly breathless young ladies who thanked him profusely upon the steps of the house and begged him to enter at least until the storm had passed. He showed suitable reluctance, but since Barlow was holding open the door and staring at him, he submitted to their entreaties. The trio entered, followed by the footman, who earned a frown from his superior. Lord Martley handed his wet umbrella to Barlow, followed by his hat and gloves. Lady Elstead was just coming out of the morning room, with a list in her hand, and heard the laughter. She looked over the banister, down into the hallway.

'Dear ma'am, we were caught in the storm and the umbrella broke, and Lord Martley saw us and offered us his escort, and his umbrella.' Henrietta unbuttoned her pelisse.

'Hateful things,' declared Lady Elstead.

'Umbrellas, ma'am?' Lord Martley looked surprised.

'No, thunderstorms. Do both of you girls go upstairs and change your shoes, for your feet will surely be very wet.'

'I fear that is true, Mama. There were puddles forming upon every step of the way. We have offered

Lord Martley shelter until it pass . . .' There was little natural light in the vestibule, except that which came from the fanlight above the pedimented doorway, but at this moment the room brightened very suddenly, and was followed almost immediately by a great crash. Lady Elstead gave a screech and covered her ears. Henrietta and Caroline both jumped and exclaimed.

'Shall I show his lordship up to the Green Saloon, my lady?' enquired Barlow, with admirable sangfroid. Her ladyship nodded, her hands still over her ears. 'If you would care to follow me, my lord.'

Lord Martley followed Barlow up the stairs, where he was parted from the younger ladies, who went to change their footwear and tidy themselves. Lady Elstead, her hands now clasped together as if in prayer, having given Barlow instructions to inform Lord Elstead that they had a visitor, followed him into the room.

'I am sorry, ma'am, if I too look a trifle dampish.' He looked down at his hessians, and hoped that he had wiped his feet well.

'Not at all, my lord. I am sure that my niece, and my daughter too, of course, were most grateful for your timely escort.' Lady Elstead was wondering what to say. Discussing the weather was unnecessary, to say the least, and enquiring after his mama . . . She made a few bland statements to which responses were superfluous, and to which Lord Martley therefore made vague sounds of agreement. It was with great relief that she looked to the door as it opened, and her lord entered, accompanied by a bright flash and another clap of thunder, with timing which would have done credit to a theatrical production of *Doctor Faustus*. Lady Elstead squeaked.

'Good afternoon, Martley. Quite a storm, eh.' Lord Elstead, whose appearance was far from diabolical, advanced, hand outstretched, and spared his wife a swift glance and encouraging smile. 'Her ladyship abhors the things, but for myself, I love the freshness to the air that they leave in their wake.' He looked perfectly calm.

'Indeed, sir, very fresh.' Lord Martley shook the extended hand, and tried to look intelligent and capable. He half succeeded. 'Ladies are never happy with loud noises, and the flashes can be so bright one can even detect them with one's eyes shut tight. My sister, Lady Fylde, used to run and hide in the housekeeper's cupboard, where there were no windows, until my mama found out she did so, and made her go and stand in the orangery every time there was a clap of thunder. It did not cure her of a fear of thunderstorms, but it did give her a dislike of oranges, which she now associates with them.'

At this point Caroline and Henrietta entered the room together, and it was therefore impossible to tell that Lord Martley's seraphic smile was directed at one and not the other. Caroline, under no illusions whatsoever, fought down the rising blush.

'I trust no toes were too wet, ladies?' Lord Martley looked happiness personified.

'Thanks to you, my lord, only to the smallest degr— Oooh!' Caroline jumped. The storm made one final effort to upset the ladies in London. Lady Elstead grabbed a cushion and held it in front of her face. Her husband gave Lord Martley a shake of his head and an embarrassed smile.

'We would have been soaked, without a doubt, my lord, but for your umbrella.' Henrietta tried to look as if the storm did not affect her so very much. She felt that she at least ought not to be frightened, even though she was, just a little bit.

'I . . . We are very grateful for your assistance, sir. It was fortuitous that you happened to be passing at the time.' Caroline's voice shook very slightly, and it might have been the effect of the thunder. 'I hope it is dry again this afternoon, when we are going to walk in the park with friends.' She looked at him under her lashes, and he comprehended it in a moment.

'They tend to pass quite quickly overhead, Miss Felbridge, thunderstorms, not friends, so I would expect that you will be able to enjoy your outing, as long as it is not too early.'

'Oh no, it will be about the promenading hour,' said Caroline blithely. She felt very clever.

'Then I would hope that your perambulation takes place under blue skies.' Lord Martley looked out of the window. 'The black clouds are certainly moving away, and as Lord Elstead was saying, such storms do make the air wonderfully fresh and keep down the dust.'

'Yes, my lord, but that is because the dust becomes muddy water that splashes on hems, and it is more difficult to remove than from boots.' Henrietta smiled wryly.

'I shall remind my valet of that when he "tut tuts" over mine, Miss Gaydon.'

'My dear, I think you may put down the cushion.' Lord Elstead looked at his wife, who was now clasping the cushion to her bosom, as though wild horses would not part her from it.

'But has it gone, my lord?'

'That last crack was more distant. It has passed over us and gone on so . . .' As if to prove this there was a flash, which made her ladyship flinch, but then a gap of some moments before the rumble, which was a more rolling sound. 'You see, you may be easy.'

Lady Elstead heaved a deep sigh, and placed the cushion back in its place, smoothing the fabric.

'And its passage is my cue to depart, my lord, ladies.' Lord Martley made his bow, and left, with a single brief glance that Caroline knew was all hers.

After luncheon it was clear that the gentlemen had been correct. A watery sunshine bathed the damp capital, and there was steam rising from some of the thoroughfares along which Sir Lawrence Coleford walked purposefully. Caroline went to practise upon her harp, which she said she had neglected of late, and Henrietta sat quietly in the small parlour, composing a letter to her papa. It was a difficult letter, because she was not used to concealing anything from him, and this time she was ignoring a very important topic. The beginning was not too awkward, since she could tell him that they were going to watch a balloon ascent the following week, and that she and Caroline had been saved a soaking, that very morning, by the timely appearance of Lord Martley.

I do not blame the poor footman, for he was merely attempting to get the umbrella up swiftly to prevent us getting wet, but it was the most unfortunate circumstance, and Lord Martley's coming upon us at that moment undoubtedly saved the day, or at least our bonnets, which I am convinced would have been utterly ruined. I did not say anything, since Caroline is most discomposed by thunderstorms, but what was in my head all the way back to South Audley Street was that poor heifer of Farmer Leigh that was struck by lightning. I shall never forget seeing the beast dead in the field. I have to report also that whilst Caroline very much dislikes thunder and lightning, my aunt is perfectly terrified by them. It was almost funny to see, though one does of course have sympathy with her nerves.

Having exhausted the thunderstorm, the letter became complicated. She was sitting, staring out of the window, but seeing nothing beyond what was in her head when Lady Elstead peered round the door. It was most unlike her ladyship to peer.

'Ah, there you are, my dear. I wish to speak with you, upon a matter of some importance.' Lady Elstead came in and sat upon a rather uncomfortable sofa. She then patted the seat next to her, rather self-consciously. Henrietta set down her pen and dutifully came to sit down.

'My dear, Lord Elstead has had . . . representations made to him, by a gentleman.'

Henrietta's heart sank. 'He has, ma'am?'

'Yes, but before he would give an answer which might send Sir Lawrence all the way to Shropshire, he . . .'

'Sir Lawrence? Sir Lawrence Coleford? But, dear aunt, I have only known him a few weeks, to speak with, and we have not engaged in private conversation more than half a dozen times.'

'Well, he seems very sure. I . . . I do wonder if he might be so ardent because he fears some other man might pre-empt him, and be seen as a better match, which is of course not impossible. You are a very pretty girl, my dear, and very popular.' Lady Elstead patted Henrietta's hand. 'You have some admirers who might ask permission to pay their addresses whom I would advocate most strongly that you, and indeed your papa, consider seriously. I am rather disappointed in Sir Lawrence, who has been, in my view, rather too swift, but if you felt anything for him, and' – she now held up her hand to forestall interruption – 'I can tell that it is not the case, I would not discount him as a husband.'

'I can only say that I had not, for a moment, even thought of Sir Lawrence in that light. Indeed, among my "admirers", as you call them, and of which I sometimes feel I have too many, an "embarras de richesse" even, he is almost the least likely to appeal to me.' Henrietta looked worried. 'What happens if my uncle tells him that his suit is not . . . I mean . . . How do I face him?'

'Goodness, my dear, do not worry about that. He is a sensible man and, for all his protestations that you are "his ideal", I hardly think his heart will be shattered. He has been terribly precipitate, and so cannot be altogether surprised if he is refused.' Lady Elstead looked vaguely irritated that Sir Lawrence had been found wanting. 'You will smile sweetly, let him dance with you, and at all times remain cool and calm.'

'That sounds easier than it may prove to be in practice, ma'am.'

'Nonsense, Henrietta. Needless to say, you do not boast of having refused an offer, and never name the gentleman, but I could trust you to behave well.' Henrietta still looked troubled. 'Oh, do not look so downcast. It is a feather, however secret, in your cap, and one day, when you are a matron like myself, it will be wonderful to be able to say, "Ah yes, several offers were made for my hand".'

Henrietta looked shyly at her aunt.

'I . . . what if none of the gentlemen make me feel . . . what if . . .'

'Hmm.' Lady Elstead's eyes narrowed. 'You must be realistic, my child. Perhaps you have, inadvertently, too romantic an aspiration. There is nothing, I repeat, nothing, worse than being left a spinster. A spinster at best becomes a quirky old maid pitied and frequently mocked. At worst she is a drain upon her family, though in your case, with no siblings, that is not the problem. Marriage gives you status and command, and marks you as successful.'

'But an unhappy marriage, ma'am . . .'

'I do not suggest you rush into the street and grab the first single man you meet, regardless of his character, Henrietta. It is most advisable that both parties like each other, to some degree. Antipathy from the outset is, I agree, a recipe for misery. Many couples who do merely respect and have a fondness for each other at betrothal come to feel something of the more tender emotions as their life together progresses. Indeed, "passion" as a basis for a union is a very poor reason, since such an emotion is most often transient.' She looked closely at her niece. 'Now, I have given you much to think about, I can tell, and I must return to your uncle and give him your answer.' Lady Elstead rose, and smoothed the skirts of her gown.

'Aunt, may I tell Caroline?' Henrietta burst out.

'You may tell your cousin, but privily, mind you.'

'Yes, ma'am.'

Henrietta sat for some time before she felt that she could write without her hand shaking. It was, as her aunt had said, 'a feather in her cap' to have received an offer, but of all the gentlemen of her closer acquaintance, and Sir Lawrence just about qualified in that category, he was the most unsuitable to her feelings. She took a deep breath. Of course in some ways that made it easier. Refusing him required no hand-wringing or dithering of thought. Better by far it was him than a gentleman whom she could only refuse upon the grounds that they were not . . . She tried to insert 'someone she might love' but her treacherous heart provided something, or rather someone, far more specific.

'No,' she admonished herself, out loud. 'I am deluding myself. This must stop.'

She picked up the pen with an air of determination, and dipped it in the ink.

I have, dearest Papa, just had a great surprise. My aunt came into the room where I am writing this, and told me that Sir Lawrence Coleford is closeted with my uncle, trying to ascertain whether he might be permitted to pay me his addresses. Lest you think that the gentleman will arrive upon your doorstep in the next few days, let me assure you that I have made it clear that I would most certainly not wish to receive such addresses. I think my aunt feels that he has been so precipitate, upon but a short acquaintance, that he does not deserve a positive response, so she has put no pressure upon me to accept. He is not a bad person, but his manner is leaden, and he lives in Lincolnshire.

Henrietta chewed thoughtfully at her lip. Papa was the best papa in the world, and very understanding.

I know that one is meant to find a husband in the course of the Season, but in truth, Papa, I find the thought weighs heavily upon me. I do not wish to leave the people I love, the places I know best, for anyone who has been introduced to me in London. The gentlemen who pay court to me are generally nice, some witty, some clever, some kind, but I have formed no attachment to any of them beyond a light friendship, and none have touched my heart. Yet if I return to you unbetrothed I know that my aunt will be sorely disappointed in me, and society will mark me as a failure. You may say that the latter is of no consequence, since I do not intend to return to society, but I know that my aunt has put considerable effort into making this Season a success for me as much as for Cousin Caroline, and it is not easy to contemplate disobeying her. Sir Lawrence did not meet with her approval, but it is not at all inconceivable that another gentleman whom she sees as a 'catch' may wish to offer for me, and then I am not sure how I can answer her.

Please do not think that I am miserable, darling Papa, for I am enjoying all the 'gadding about' as Caroline termed it this morning, but I long to be sat opposite you at home, telling you of all the things that have happened.

Your loving daughter,
Henrietta

She folded the letter and wrote his direction upon it. She wondered whether he might respond with advice, or simply with sympathy. She thought that in some ways it was a difficult situation for a man to understand, and, what was worse, the only man who would truly understand, and yet must not know, was Charles.

CHAPTER THIRTEEN

LORD MARTLEY WAS IN EBULLIENT MOOD. Miss Felbridge, his Miss Felbridge, had been clever, and given him useful information without anybody realising it. Not only did this show her wits, but that she was collaborating with him, not just waiting for him to do things. 'Collaboration' meant doing things together, and being together with her in thought or physical presence was very important to the viscount. All he needed now was a reason to be in the park at five of the afternoon, without looking as though he was just there to happen to meet Miss Felbridge and Miss Gaydon. He coloured. He suddenly felt rather bad about Miss Gaydon. It was possible, since she was in her first Season and unused to society, that she might think the interest he had been showing really was in her, when it was actually to enable him to be near Miss Felbridge. That was a bad thing, not gentlemanly, and verging upon the dishonourable. What he ought to do was make a clean breast of it to her, and reveal his attachment. He thought, hoped, that she would not think too badly of him. How he was to make this confession, which had to be private, he was not entirely sure. Lagging behind in the park would not only be obvious but might upset his beloved. His ebullience faded, and it was a thoughtful man who entered his club and ordered sustenance.

In the post-storm brightness, Hyde Park was quite crowded at the hour when society promenaded, gossip was exchanged and the occasional secret imparted. The Misses Fairburn were pleasant young women, only eighteen months apart in age, with a habit of finishing each other's sentences in the manner of twins. They were full of very mild gossip, of the sort that the young ladies might know, rather than the more dangerous variety that circulated among the matrons and mamas. Theirs was the gossip of impending betrothals, comments upon the gowns of friends and rivals, and a general interest in the Season, and both Henrietta and Caroline were able to take part without having to divert all their thoughts from the subject uppermost in the head of each.

Caroline was on tenterhooks, wondering if, and indeed how, Lord Martley might 'casually' encounter them. Of course, since the Misses Fairburn were unaware of the umbrella incident, they would not be suspicious, but Henrietta must be. In fact, when, after about ten minutes, they met his lordship sauntering along in company with Lord Chilwell, Henrietta was so caught up in her own thoughts that she did not think it engineered in any way. Lord Martley made his bow to the ladies, and, for the briefest moment, his eyes met Caroline's and sparkled with amusement at a secret shared. He was, however, circumspect, and ensured that he included the other young ladies in his lightweight conversation, and then, whilst Lord Chilwell sought to speak to Henrietta for a few minutes, he managed to have a precious interchange with his love.

'You were so clever, Miss Felbridge,' he murmured.

'Ah, but your comprehension was so swift, my lord.' She blushed a little. 'And you found us so easily.'

'You may think that, but in fact I have nearly worn out the soles of my boots upon these pathways.' He grinned, and then added, more seriously, 'I would walk barefoot to be able to meet with you.'

'Oh, how romantic.'

'I mean it, Miss Felbridge. Now you must attend to me. I shall continue to make your cousin as much my focus of attention as your dear self, to preclude gossip, but I must ensure that she does not feel that I have led her to expect . . . In short, I must arrange to speak privately with her, and confess my feelings, not for her, but for you. I am sure that she will not betray us. I am right in this?'

'I am sure that you are, but would you not prefer me to approach her?'

'It is my responsibility, and I am not a shirker.'

'I do not think it. I admire your honesty . . . as I do the rest of you, my lord.' She glanced shyly, but very tenderly, at him, and his heart thumped.

'Not worthy,' he mumbled, and then spoke in a more normal and bantering tone, addressing his friend and Miss Gaydon. 'You do not want to attend to anything that Chilwell says, ma'am, for he is a notorious bumble-head.'

'See how the man I account, or at least accounted, as my friend traduces me, Miss Gaydon. Ought I to call him out?'

'Oh, I do not think so, my lord, for Lord Martley is known to be always funning.'

'Deadly serious, I assure you, Miss Gaydon.' Lord Martley placed his hand over his heart.

'You see, he covers his heart lest I choose it as my point of aim,' declared Lord Chilwell.

'Not at all, my dear fellow, since if you were to aim at it, I could at least be safe in the knowledge that you would not hit me there.' Lord Martley was laughing, and the Misses Fairburn giggled as one.

'Miss Felbridge, come to my aid,' requested Lord Chilwell, feigning misery.

'Come, come, my lord, you should not be asking for protection from ladies.' Caroline wagged a finger at him. 'But if it gives you solace, tell me all about how terrible Lord Martley is, and I will listen very closely.' She cast Lord Martley a look that bordered upon saucy.

'Now who will be traduced? Miss Gaydon, I shall not listen to cruel words but beg you will tell me, will you be at the Donningtons' tonight?' asked Lord Martley.

'Why yes, my lord, I believe we are engaged to attend, but I fear quite late in the evening, for we dine first at Lady Soughton's.'

'Good . . . that you are going, not that you will arrive late, of course.' He paused, checked that the other ladies were listening to Lord Chilwell, frowned, and then spoke, his eyes not quite meeting hers. 'Miss Gaydon, might I try and have a few words with you, upon an important matter. I cannot do so here, but if we were to sit out a dance . . .'

Henrietta blinked. He sounded very serious, which was unusual for Lord Martley. 'If you wish, sir.'

'Thank you.'

It dawned upon her that his reason for wanting to speak with her might be to tell her that he wanted to know if his addresses would be acceptable to her. He was such a nice young man it would be awful having to say that they would not, but . . . and poor Caroline! Her heart did seem rather set upon Lord Martley, and it would be quite awful for her to discover it was her cousin whose hand he sought.

* * *

Lord Elstead, who was an old friend of Sir Humphrey Soughton, accompanied the ladies to dinner. It was, as Henrietta had feared, seen as an opportunity by Lady Soughton to let her 'pride and joy' work his magic upon Henrietta, whom she saw as a good match. She therefore placed him next to Henrietta. Rather to Henrietta's surprise, Mr Newbold was also invited, although he was seated on the opposite side of the table next to Lady Elstead.

Gerald Soughton was a young man secure in his own worth, and totally incapable of reading the boredom he induced in others. He was knowledgeable upon an eclectic selection of subjects, none of which were of the slightest interest to Henrietta, or Miss Clifton, who was seated upon his other side. The only entertainment for Henrietta was that Miss Clifton's answer to subjects that bored her was to focus upon a word and change the subject, upon which Mr Soughton simply brought it back to his favoured topic. It sounded like some bizarre parlour game, and made for a most surreal conversation. When Henrietta glanced across the table, she could see that Mr Newbold was extracting every ounce of pleasure from it.

Mr Soughton commenced with some 'very interesting observations' he had been reading about on the subject of Mr Davy's safety lamp and firedamp in mines. Mr Newbold's eyebrows instantly rose, since this was a most unusual topic to discuss with ladies, although he himself, as the owner of mines, was well aware of the invention and its uses.

'Apparently the metal gauze or mesh has to be of a certain specific size to prevent the firedamp igniting when in contact with the flame.'

'I am not, myself, much in favour of diaphanous fabrics,' responded Miss Clifton, in a repressive tone. 'My cousin Lucilla has a gown of spider gauze over satin, but it is so prone to catching upon the slightest splinter of wood or damaged fingernail that it had to be darned quite obviously after being worn but twice. It is also used far too much by ladies, and I use the term loosely, who choose to dampen their skirts in order to make them cling in a most unseemly fashion.'

'Firedamp is of course not the only concern when underground. There is also the danger of a lack of air, or bad air. Many deaths have been occasioned by it, but unless one can provide good air, it is impossible to prevent or predict.'

'I am never happy having a fire in my bedchamber for that very reason,' Miss Clifton declared.

Henrietta blinked, and inadvertently stared at Mr Newbold, who looked as stunned, but was struggling not to laugh. Miss Clifton then continued.

'One can never trust menial servants to ensure that the coal is not damp, and thus gives off billows of smoke, which, however frequently one has the chimneys swept, eddies into the chamber and is both unpleasant to the nose and leaves deposits upon fabrics.'

'It is quite remarkable how the industry of man has enabled him to reach deposits, not only of coal, but tin, and other ores, and also of precious stones, but I find it interesting that we in, as Shakespeare called it, "this sceptr'ed isle", do not have the frippery of gems but solid worth of ores and coal.'

'I do not believe in such things, myself.'

This brought Mr Soughton up with a start, and interrupted his own train of thought. 'You do not believe in geology, ma'am?'

'I said nothing about geometry. I said I do not believe in spectres, or anything of a supernatural nature. It stems from ignorance, and indeed is unchristian. Those who do believe are creating thoughts in their own heads.'

Mr Soughton was, for a moment, speechless. Finding it difficult to return to his own discourse, he turned to Henrietta, who was attempting to eat whilst controlling the urge to giggle.

'Miss Gaydon, you live in the Marches, I believe.'

Henrietta nodded, and affirmed that she did.

'I have walked upon parts of the great dyke created by Offa, a king in England, but not of England. It is a remarkable structure, of great length, and where I was walking above the valley of the River Wye, it is most commanding. When one considers the size of the available population to construct such an earthwork it becomes an even greater feat.'

'I am sure that is true, Mr Soughton. I confess that I have never seen it.'

This was an error, in that it meant Mr Soughton, confident that nothing he said might be challenged, gave a monologue for the next ten minutes, and Henrietta was only saved by Miss Clifton, who overheard the words 'Tintern Abbey' and asserted that Mr Wordsworth's poem upon it was 'very good and metrical', but that she preferred it when he utilised rhyme. Henrietta escaped, seeing that the gentleman on her other side was addressing his plate, not his neighbour, and enquired whether he had attended any of the plays in Drury Lane recently.

When the ladies withdrew, Henrietta did so with no small degree of relief. Caroline, who had observed from a safe distance along the table, whispered her own thankfulness that she had not suffered from 'an excess of Gerald'.

'He is quite inexhaustible, I must say. Oh dear, and here comes Lady Soughton, who will not doubt tell me how fortunate I am to have been able to hear his words of wisdom.'

Caroline stepped back, in what Henrietta later described as a very cowardly manner, and Lady Soughton delivered gushing praise of her son's intellectual powers. Henrietta feared she was to be singled out by him when the gentlemen rejoined the ladies, but she was fortunate, in that Mr Newbold managed to reach her first, and Mr

Soughton had to seek an audience elsewhere.

'I applaud you, Miss Gaydon.'

'You do, Mr Newbold? Why so?'

'Because you kept a straight face so that all but the keenest observers would not have noticed how difficult that was to achieve.'

'Which implies, sir, that you are one such "keen observer".' Henrietta raised an eyebrow.

'Of course, ma'am.' He did not say whether in general, or of her, but she blushed slightly, nevertheless.

'I am not sure which was worse, sir, having to be the auditor-in-chief, or trying not to laugh when he was boring Miss Clifton.'

'Indeed. I came to the conclusion that she is either one of those young ladies who, if they secure a husband, will become a formidable matron whom none dare defy, or she is slightly hard of hearing, and strong in opinion.'

'I always think "securing a husband" sounds rather desperate, as though one had captured and tied the man, like a horse at pasture, and is a most depressing phrase.'

'Then I apologise for using it, Miss Gaydon. Not that you will have to "secure" a partner.'

'I will not?'

'Of course not. You, Miss Gaydon, do not, as I confess most young ladies have to do, "trot up and down" and see which gentlemen might be persuaded to see if you are "up to their weight", keeping a form of the equine analogy. It is you who may do the choosing, and your only difficulty has to be whether to go for some untried colt or . . .' Mr Newbold did a very rare thing, and flushed. He had spoken upon the spur of the moment, without his customary thought, and could not continue, since to do so would mean implying he was a 'stallion'. That had far too indelicate connotations for Lady Soughton's withdrawing room.

'I am not sure that is any better, sir. It seems so . . . calculating.' Henrietta frowned.

'You are a romantic, Miss Gaydon?'

'Oh, not in the "Where is my hero?" theatrical mode, I assure you, but . . . there ought surely to be a feeling of tenderness when one looks upon, or thinks about, one's partner for life. One can, after all, sell a horse if it does not suit.'

At this Mr Newbold laughed, but it made him think. Perhaps Miss Gaydon did need more wooing than entertaining after all.

Henrietta, having forgotten Lord Martley for much of the dinner, made her curtsey to Lady Donnington with growing trepidation. Why had she not simply said that any private talk would be impossible, and put off the disappointment she must give to a young man she liked, but in no way loved? She hoped that he might not meet her until her dance card was full, but he had evidently been looking out for the Elsteads' arrival, and presented himself before her when only one dance had been secured, and by a fresh-faced young man who looked rather overawed at his own success in securing a cotillion.

'You look charming, Miss Gaydon, as always. Might I have the pleasure of this next dance, if it is available?' He made his bow.

'I . . .' Henrietta decided she could not run away from truth. 'I would prefer it if you were to find me a glass of champagne, my lord.'

'Then consider it done.' He disappeared for far too short a time, and returned, glasses in hand. 'I believe I have found a seat where you may rest yourself before dancing the rest of the night away, ma'am.' He led her into a smaller chamber, which, this early in the evening, was not much filled with people choosing to sit out the dancing.

Henrietta sat, rather primly, and he seated himself beside her, but not too close.

'My lord, should not such matters be discussed with my uncle, in the first instance?'

'Yes, well, not in this case, Miss Gaydon. I, er . . . I mean, I was not about to make a declaration.'

'Not a declaration, my lord?'

'Er, actually, no, Miss Gaydon, not a declaration but a confession.'

'Confession?' Henrietta was taken aback.

'I fear I have led you to assume, led everyone to assume . . .' Lord Martley looked thoroughly uncomfortable. 'But you see, my parents consider you a very good match and . . .'

'You do not, my lord?' After her moment's astonishment, Henrietta found that she could face the situation not just calmly, but with a degree of amusement. This young man was not in love with her, and nor was she in love with him. He was nice, and he was friendly, but, when she looked at him, she knew not a pang of regret. In fact, she was exceedingly relieved.

'No, yes, of course you are, and a delightful . . . beautiful . . . It's just that . . .'

'You would far rather pay your addresses to Another.' She gave the appellation weight, and nearly giggled at sounding so melodramatic.

'Yes. I am sorry, but yes.' His words came out in a rush. 'You see, while my parents have thought I was trying to fix my interest with you, I have been . . . falling in love with your cousin, whom my parents do not think a good match at all.'

'Whilst I do not fault your taste, my lord, may I ask why my cousin Caroline is not a good match?'

'Never understood it myself, Miss Gaydon, but it seems to be something to do with Lady Elstead from way back when she and my mama were brought out.'

'I see. So what has made you confess to me now?'

'I . . . it would be wrong to let you think that I . . .

and you are a beautiful, sparkling young lady, who is deserving of admiration and . . .'

'Guilt, then, my lord.'

He nodded, shamefaced, and fidgeted with his neckcloth, to its great detriment.

'I see.' Henrietta was repeating herself, but there was little else she could say. She paused for a moment. 'Has it occurred to you, my lord, that if your parents hold Lady Elstead in such violent dislike, the sentiment might be mutual? To the point where Lady Elstead, and thus my uncle, refuse your offer for Caroline's hand?'

'But . . . they never prevented you from dancing with me or anything.' Lord Martley looked rather panicked. Henrietta felt a twinge of guilt, but the poor boy really needed to consider things carefully. 'Poor boy' she called him in her head, though he must be at least six years her senior. It dawned upon Henrietta that at the outset of the Season she had thought all her swains glamorous men of the world, and now, after only two months, she had grown up a lot herself, and come to the realisation that when it came to the male of the species, the number of birthdays was not a good marker of maturity. She ought to have thought about it before, she decided, since Charles was actually nearly ten years her senior, and she had never thought of that span as very much at all. He was simply the 'older brother' she had never had. She frowned, as her inner voice reminded her yet again that Charles Henfield was not, and could most definitely never be, her 'older brother'.

'Miss Gaydon?' Lord Martley had been running on, but had become aware she was not attending to him.

'Oh! Oh, I am so terribly sorry, my lord. A thought occurred to me.'

'About my predicament?' He sounded eager to be reassured.

'Yes,' she lied, thinking rapidly, and thrusting Charles from her head with determination. 'You must be honest with your parents, and prove you are an independent man, not their immature son. If you are to marry my cousin, you will make her life the happier if it does not come as a total surprise to your parents, and they can appreciate her for her own qualities, and not judge her upon what happened many years past.'

'I tell them?' He looked unconvinced. 'Miss Gaydon, you have met my mama.'

'I have, and I tell you that if you love my cousin, you will be able to face her, and Lord Pirbright. You tell them the truth, and you ask, openly, what makes Lord Elstead's lineage and position insufficient to them.'

'But it is Lady Elstead who . . .'

'Yes. So they must therefore admit there is nothing on Lord Elstead's side, and either have to reveal what caused the rift decades ago, which may seem foolish now, or pretend there is nothing, and agree that your desire to wed Miss Caroline Felbridge is perfectly reasonable.'

'But they still will not like her mama.'

'My lord, they will not have to live with her mama, nor even meet her often. If you suddenly announce your engagement without your parents having any idea that it is not I who am your chosen partner in life, they would be most reasonably indignant. Think of it.'

'Yes, well, I see that is so, Miss Gaydon, but what if their reason for disliking Lady Elstead is . . . too great?'

Henrietta had no perfect answer to this, but could only state that as a daughter of the Earl of Prestwich, Lady Elstead's lineage was unblemished, 'otherwise they would have to have objected to me also. It can only be her, her person, and if her other relatives are not tainted by it, why should her daughter?'

'All of which does not guarantee me any success with Miss Felbridge's parents.'

'Very true, but one obstacle must be overcome at a time. I shall consider what to do. Might I ask if my cousin is aware of your feelings?'

'I . . . she is aware that I have a great . . . fondness.' He took a deep breath, and he looked at Henrietta boldly. 'No, not true. She knows that I love her. She is terribly kind to me, and understanding, and . . .'

Henrietta could feel a long list of Caroline's qualities were about to be placed before her, and was conscious that having them enumerated by the young man who found her own person not quite his ideal was lowering.

'Yes, yes. Do permit me to think upon this, and if I

may assist in the . . .' She nearly said 'plot', but altered it in time to 'plan', 'I shall do my very best.' In truth, she was not sure there was anything she might do.

Lord Martley thanked her and withdrew, feeling that things had gone remarkably well. Miss Gaydon had not been outraged, nor had she burst into tears at rejection. In fact, upon reflection, she had taken the news almost too well.

It was more than a little unfortunate that Lord Henfield, having seen Miss Felbridge upon the dance floor, and being rather blithely informed by Lady Elstead that she rather thought her niece was with Lord Martley, had gone on the hunt for her. Failing to find them in the supper room, he was coming along the passage when he saw Martley emerge from a withdrawing room, and looking rather pleased with himself. This gave Charles Henfield a feeling of foreboding. He himself entered the room to find Henrietta rising from a seat in one corner. There were no more than a dozen persons in the room, and none of them near Henrietta in age. When he caught her eye he thought she started, and he put it, uncharitably, down to guilt, not being able to see that it might be surprised pleasure. He felt aggrieved and rather hurt, after the previous night, but recalled the words of wisdom, or were they commands, from Lady Vernham. She had told him that sulking would never do any good, and that he must prove himself a match for his rivals, rather than presenting Henrietta always with 'choose me, or them'. So he bit back the regretful words that formed, and advanced with a smile, even if it was a slightly tired one.

'Now, do not tell me you are wearied, Miss Gaydon of the worn dancing slippers, because I know for a fact that you have been here less than an hour. It is I who ought to have that seat. Do you know I have danced with four young ladies, four, and if you begged me to waltz with you now I would simply have to decline through decrepitude.' He sat with an ostentatious collapse next to her on the sofa.

'Ah, well, if you are so "decrepit", Charles, perhaps I ought to offer to go and find you something restorative.'

'Such as a glass of burgundy?'

'I was thinking more a mustard plaster.' She giggled.

'I thought that was for colds and agues, or is that a mustard footbath?'

'Do not look at me, Charles. It is not I who is aged and worn out.'

'Then why hide yourself away when there are dances to be danced, and partners unlimited?' He wanted to know if she would lie outright, tell him a half truth, or the whole.

'Well, someone had something very particular to say to me, and . . .' Henrietta saw Charles Henfield's cheeks pale.

'Did you accept?' he managed, in a dry whisper.

'Accept? You . . . oh, you think . . . It was not that sort of "particular".' She looked a little disappointed, and again, he made the incorrect assumption, which was that she wished it had been, rather than the correct one, which was that she was unhappy that he felt she would accept an offer from . . . someone.

'You are the sort of girl for whom many men would wish to offer, Henry.' He said it softly, and she wondered, sadly, if there was a silent 'but not me' at the end.

'Well, I have, apparently, had one, but thankfully my aunt was happy for me to decline. It was rather sobering, and not exciting in the least.' Henrietta pulled a face.

'I do not think you want me to say "poor Henry", so I shall not. It is strange,' he said, in a philosophical tone, 'but of course the male perspective is so different, since we have the advantage of the positive, doing the asking, and yet also the greater risk, that of being refused. From the moment the offer is made, the choice is the lady's.'

'I am not sure that "choice" is quite the right word.'

'But you can say no.' He frowned.

'Oh Charles, be realistic. That is where the balance falls to the man. How often is a man forced to offer for a woman?'

'Well, I suppose if one were severely in debt or . . . There is no "or", is there.'

'No, there is not. We have not just the "it is a good match" but the fear that if we do not accept then there will be no other offers, and one ends as my Aunt Elstead fears, pitied, despised and alone.'

'That is certainly not a very appealing future' – his frown deepened – 'and I think I may say not "poor you" specifically, but "poor ladies" in general, without you objecting.'

'Granted.' Henrietta sighed. 'This is not a very cheerful conversation, Lord Henfield. At the risk of flouting convention, and sounding terribly forward, will you please ask me to dance with you?'

'I think, in the circumstances, it might be the only way to lift our spirits, Miss Gaydon. Will you do me the honour of granting me the next dance, if my aged bones have sufficiently recovered, of course?'

'Why, sir, what a charming idea. Let me see, oh yes, it is free.' Henrietta smiled, and placed her hand in his. The evening improved, for both of them.

CHAPTER FOURTEEN

HENRIETTA SLEPT MUCH BETTER, AND ROSE EARLIER. It was she who went to her cousin's chamber, and sat in the window seat, looking at Caroline, night cap askew and rubbing her eyes, and said the one word.

'Well?'

'Oh.' Caroline paused, then a slow smile spread across her face. 'He told you, then.'

'He did.' Henrietta pressed the back of her hand to her forehead, in a manner worthy of a Siddons, and declared, 'My own hopes dashed, Caroline! How could you?' She then ruined the effect by laughing. 'Sweet cousin, I wish you every happiness.'

'Thank you. Henrietta, he is the most . . . I am so fortunate to . . . yet I am still afraid that . . .'

'Love has robbed you of the ability to complete a sentence? Yes, it is rather worrying.'

'I wish it were but that.' Caroline's smile faded. 'I am so happy, and yet I fear that our mutual affection will not be able to overcome parental prejudice.'

'Lord Martley told me of that, although that encounter at the exhibition showed the state of affairs between Lady Pirbright and your mama. But Caroline, would she persuade my uncle to withhold his permission, if your happiness were at stake?'

'If I had not seen the depth of their antipathy, I would say she would not, Henrietta, but . . . whatever lies between them is an unbridgeable gulf.'

'If it is as it looks, one wonders what on earth could occasion such long-standing loathing. I have not been told to keep my distance; in fact, his name is probably on the List.'

'The List?' Caroline looked bemused, and Henrietta coloured.

'Er, you know your mama loves her lists, Caroline. I am sure she has lists for us too, lists of acceptable suitors, and such.' Henrietta did not want to actually admit to having seen such a list, and tried to sound vague.

'Well, if she has one, every other name must be crossed off, because I cannot, cannot imagine marrying anyone else. If they keep us apart I shall rather end an old maid.' Caroline sounded defiant.

'We must hope it will not come to that, and indeed work towards your goal. Caroline, could you not speak with your papa, and explain your situation? He is not unreasonable, and . . .'

'He will say that he will consult Mama, I am sure of it.'

'You do not know until you have tried, dear cousin.'

'Then I must be brave.'

With this resolve, Caroline rang for her maid, but, having screwed up her courage, found that her father had gone to his club, and wandered so listlessly about the house that Lady Elstead asked her if she felt quite well, and as the day wore on the courage dwindled to nothing.

In the cold light of day, or, more accurately, the cool dark of a very early summer morning, Lord Martley's optimistic attitude dimmed. What Miss Gaydon said made sense, and yet, facing Mama was not something done lightly, not without summoning up one's courage to an almost Shakespearean level. Lord Martley would have been the first to admit he was no Henry V. The obvious answer would be to approach his sire first, since that gentleman did not appear to have his own strong feelings upon the Elsteads. However, Lord Martley was well aware that his father's attitude was always 'Do nothing that upsets your mother'. This was guaranteed to do so, and therefore his news was unlikely to see his sire wreathed in smiles. As for Mama, well, Wellington's soldiers at Waterloo must have faced the Imperial Guard with less trepidation.

At least, he consoled himself, he was no longer deceiving Miss Gaydon. That had been starting to make him feel very guilty indeed, and having her on their side would mean his Beloved would have a confidante, and everyone knew young ladies needed one of those. He took to his bed both relieved and in a quake, which made for interesting dreams.

Being rather more au fait with his father's morning habits than Miss Felbridge was with hers, Lord Martley did not visit the parental home until after noon, and found Lord Pirbright in pleasant seclusion in the book room. His lordship looked up as his heir entered.

'Good afternoon, sir. Wondered if I might speak with you.'

'Again, Martley? This is getting serious.' Lord Pirbright smiled, but the smile faded as his son continued.

'Well, in some ways it is. I . . . I am going to offer for a young lady. At least, I am going to try to do so.'

'Good Lord. Is it the Gaydon girl? That would make y—'

'No, sir. And that is the problem. I want to offer for Miss Felbridge.' It came out in a rush, and was followed by a long and ominous silence. Lord Pirbright sat down heavily.

'You do not know what you are doing, my boy.'

'Sir, tell me truly, have you anything against Lord Elstead, or heard aught of Miss Felbridge that would make her a bad match?'

'No, but that is not the point, and you know it as well as I do. It would not matter if she were an angel with her wings hidden. Your mother will not permit it.'

'Can she stop me, though, sir? I am of age.'

'Legally, of course not, and it would be me who would have had that right when you were younger, but think, Martley. I will almost certainly be forced to cancel your allowance. How could you support a wife, especially a wife you value?'

'So you are saying that I have to marry as Mama dictates?'

'No, but not in direct opposition to her wishes.'

'I think that is clear, sir.' Lord Martley's face set into an unnatural grimness. 'I am forced to ask, were I to disobey her, and thus you, would you disown me, bequeath Hazelton House to one of my sisters' husbands?'

'When you inherit, you inherit title and lands, whether you are in favour or not.' Lord Pirbright looked equally severe. He was, beneath a less than effusive exterior, mildly fond of his son, and he could see that relations were about to become extremely strained.

'Thank you.' Lord Martley paused. 'I do not disobey from wilfulness, but if I can somehow win Miss Felbridge's hand I will do so, Mama's disapproval notwithstanding, sir.'

'It is your choice, my boy, and your future. I say no more.'

'Good day, sir. Give my . . . respects to my mother.' Lord Martley bowed, and left, feeling both more the man and less the son.

Mr Newbold had not made serious overtures to a lady since his first Season, when, greenhorn that he was, he had been smitten by a golden-haired damsel who epitomised all that he then thought he would desire in a wife. In the end she had become the wife of an earl with acres, presented him with four sons, and died in giving birth to the fifth. He had been very cast down when his suit was rejected, and even vowed never to permit his heart to be trampled in such a manner again, but it had not been a bruised heart that kept him from the altar thereafter. Once recovered from his youthful infatuation, he discovered that amusement was best found among the older ladies, who had the confidence of the married state, and were not inhibited by instructions to simper, or look the ingenue. He developed a reputation, which he enjoyed, of being dangerously witty and also a confirmed bachelor. Watching the lures cast out at him, the caps set at him, amused him, and his rare liaisons were conducted with discretion. It occurred to him that, were he to marry, he would simply become another husband and lose his singularity among the Ton, and the longer he maintained it, the less inclined was he to set it aside for a pretty face.

He had certainly found Miss Gaydon's to be a pretty face, and behind the beauty was a swift comprehension, so lacking in many of the girls brought out into society. It was both unusual and appealing, and also entertaining. Mr Newbold had thus conducted one of his more cerebral flirtations with Miss Gaydon, and only gradually realised that he was interested in more. He had seen the banter of youth make her smile, but not affect her heart. He did not play that game, nor try to 'storm her' with the wooing of a man of experience, rightly thinking she was not ready for such. Yet what she had said at the Soughtons' dinner gave him pause. She accounted him a friend, but was not going to wed just for friendship. If he wanted her, and he was coming to the conclusion that he did, he must reveal more of his own feelings. This was difficult, because he had spent years concealing them to great effect, and, if he were honest, he was only half sure of them. When he was with her he felt a degree of pleasure that made him contemplate a future with her as lady of his house, the woman he would live with upon a daily basis, and yet when apart he did not pine for her, think constantly of her. He wondered if he had become, at heart, a bit of a cold fish, incapable of deep passion.

So Mr Newbold arose in the morning pensive, and broke his fast in a brown study such that afterwards he could not say what had been placed before him.

* * *

Henrietta was not focused upon herself. This made life much the easier, since she was still in a muddle, torn between what she was increasingly sure she wanted, and a deep-seated belief that it was unthinkable, and also probably unthought by Charles Henfield. By setting herself the task of promoting the romance of her cousin and 'nice Lord Martley', she could put her own thoughts to one side, and be guilt free. That she was going against the wishes of her aunt was irrelevant, because whatever stood in the way was old and dusty, and no doubt inflated beyond all proportion. After all, what could one girl do that would set another at loggerheads with her for life? Snatching a dancing partner from under one's nose, spilling cherry compote over a favourite gown – these were not worth decades of animosity.

Then it dawned upon her that she was closer to a reason than she could have imagined. What if both young ladies had sought the attention of the same man? It was difficult for Henrietta, looking at two women over twice her age, and gentlemen as old as Papa, to imagine them young, let alone passionate and in the throes of love. She tried to be logical. Lord Pirbright was the older man, and had a weariness about him, as far as Henrietta could judge on having seen him but on three occasions. He looked in no way the type of man to have maidens swooning over him, even when his hair was not greying, and his face falling into lines of permanent stoicism. Then she remembered that in the book room was a portrait that might well be of Lord Elstead as a young man. She had entered the room but once, on her second day, being a little lost, and seen it, or at least a portrait of a young man in the fashions of thirty years ago. She abandoned the book whose pages she had been turning idly, and went to the book room, knocking in case her uncle was within. She had not thought far enough ahead to imagine what she would do if he were, and so when he called 'Come in' she was a little at a loss. She entered, blushing.

'Henrietta. To what do I owe the pleasure?' He smiled, in suitably avuncular fashion. 'Do not say you have overspent your pin money on boot laces.'

'Oh no, sir. I do not find myself in reduced circumstances. My allowance is generous, even though silk stockings are a terrible price, and wear to holes faster than one could possibly imagine.'

'Er, well, I am glad to say I do not imagine them at all. So, if it is not a pecuniary paucity, how can I help you?'

'Actually, I came to see the room, and not you.' Henrietta's cheeks reddened fully.

'How lowering. I trust you find it to your taste.' He was still smiling, but a crease of interested enquiry sat between his brows.

'You are roasting me, sir, and that I am sure is not fair. Nieces ought not to be roasted by uncles.'

'I shall remember that in future.' He watched her. 'Why this room?'

'Well, I . . . I am used to being with just Papa, you see, and there is a certain masculinity to libraries and book rooms, less feminine frippery if you will, and I was suddenly missing Papa very much. This seemed a place I might feel closer to him, surrounded by books and leather and no Meissen shepherdesses or embroidered drapery.' As she said it, the excuse became real, and she did indeed feel it brought her closer to 'home'.

'Then please be seated, and enjoy the atmosphere. It is certainly not a chamber frequented by the female members of my family. Do you miss your papa very dreadfully, Henrietta?' Lord Elstead was no longer teasing.

'Not all the time, and sometimes that in itself makes me feel guilty, but yes, very much, and at odd times, just like now, it is quite overpowering.'

'You are close, since there is but the pair of you. That is natural.'

'We do get on very well, very comfortably, and I think that although I miss Mama, both her and her advice, I am privileged to have such a bond with my father.' Henrietta's voice had a slight waver, and she sniffed. To steady herself she brought the reason for her presence to the front of her thoughts. She looked at the picture in the alcove by the fireplace. 'Is that you, sir?'

'Yes, it is, though more "was" than "is". My own

mama thought it a fair likeness, and mothers are very critical of portraits.'

'You were rather dashing,' Henrietta offered hesitantly. He laughed.

'Unlike now. Ah yes, the impetuosity of youth. I was not accounted a bad-looking fellow, I suppose.' He too looked at the painting, and his smile became lopsided as he recalled posing for it, one elbow resting negligently upon a marble pillar, before an imaginary background of general classical style, designed to show that he had benefitted from the Grand Tour.

Henrietta, for her part, was trying to look beyond the old-fashioned clothes and the clubbed hair, and look at him as she looked at Lord Martley or Lord Netheravon or . . . She stopped the list there. He had a good face, strong, but not belligerent, and his figure was trim. There was an appeal, of sorts, she thought, and it was far more likely that he, and not Lord Pirbright, had been the man over whom the two ladies had squabbled.

'You must have had lots of ladies flirting with you over the sticks of their fans, sir.'

'Oh, I am not sure it was lots, but I do not think I was unpopular.' He could not help but preen himself very slightly at the memory.

She wondered if he knew about the reason for the hatred, or whether it was a secret between females. She rather fancied he was in blissful ignorance.

'You are taller than Papa.' Henrietta did not say that she thought the miniature of her sire was the nicer portrait. She sighed. 'I like this room, sir.'

'It is not out of bounds, my dear. Please feel free to come and sit here when you need to escape from the madness of the Season and be quiet and yourself and think of your home.'

'Thank you, I will. Now, I must return to that "madness", for I believe my aunt wishes to take us to see some classical statuary.'

'She does? I confess I had not thought her fascinated by antiquities.'

'Nor I, but I believe it is "a place to be seen", so we shall be seen.' Henrietta rose, made her uncle a polite curtsey and left, hoping to be able to speak privately with Caroline before they went out. It might not advance Lord Martley's cause, but it could not do any harm.

Since most of the younger set were unaware that the Exhibition of Sculpture was 'a place to be seen', they encountered none of the gentlemen they desired to meet, or would have been happy to meet, and in fact after half an hour of rather fruitless promenading, Lady Elstead declared that she had seen more than enough 'arms, legs and urns' for a month. However, since the horses were put to, it gave them the opportunity to stop at Rundell, Bridge and Rundell, where Lady Elstead had sent an emerald earring to be repaired when one of the stones had become loose. Whilst an employee disappeared to see if her ladyship's jewel had already been repaired, Henrietta and Caroline enjoyed themselves surveying the sort of pieces only worn by married ladies, and spending imaginary hundreds of pounds. The assistant returned, apologetic that the earring would not be ready until two days hence, since they had been unaware that her ladyship would be calling for it herself today, but Lady Elstead remained gracious, right up until the moment she left the premises, and stepped in front of Lady Pirbright. If air could freeze from emotion, said Henrietta later, there would have been a frozen wall between them in an instant. Both ladies first tried to pretend that they did not see the other, then feigned delight so badly it would have been laughable, had it not been so important to Caroline.

'Lady Elstead.'

'Lady Pirbright.'

'I trust I find you well, and the young ladies also?' Lady Pirbright stressed the 'young' to emphasise Lady Elstead's age.

'Oh, we are all in good health, I assure you. Of course you and I, Lady Pirbright, are firmly matronly these days.'

'Oh, in years, perhaps, but I have never felt "matronly"; it is such a "round" word.' Lady Pirbright smiled brightly, being so slender.

'Ah yes, you never had much "neck", did you. So "boyishly slim", we always thought.' Lady Elstead made 'we' sound like all the rest of society.

'I am proud to say that my lord can still span his hands about my waist.'

'Indeed, though at times he must wish they were about your throat.'

At this very open insult, delivered with a smile of pure malice, Henrietta and Caroline actually gasped, and Caroline then added a groan. Lady Pirbright matched the smile, and dropped her voice.

'When one is reduced to that level, ma'am, it is an admission of defeat.' She nodded at the girls in a dismissive way, and swept around them to enter the jeweller's.

'Mama,' breathed Caroline, horrified. 'In public too.'

Lady Elstead made a peculiar noise in her throat that was a form of refutation, and said that they were going straight home.

Back in South Audley Street, Caroline went swiftly to her room, and sat upon her bed, her face in her hands. Henrietta followed her.

'Oh, cousin, I cannot imagine a more unfortunate encounter. Such dislike! It dooms us to be forever parted.'

If Henrietta thought this sounded a little melodramatic, she did not say so. 'I was not able to tell you before,

Caroline, but I think I know the cause of the animosity.'

'You do?'

'Yes. We know it goes back to when both made their come-out, and it must have been important. I think they were both hoping to marry the same man, possibly your papa, and certainly not Lord Pirbright.'

'Papa?' Caroline had the natural inability of progeny to imagine their parents as capable of inspiring love or rousing desire.

'Yes, for the portrait in the book room shows him to have been quite personable. What if Lady Pirbright, before she was Lady Pirbright, of course, set her cap at him, but failed, and saw him offer instead for your mama? That would rankle for decades.'

'Would it?' Caroline frowned. 'Really?'

'Well, with some people, perhaps. I mean Lady Pirbright lost, and . . .'

'But Mama ought therefore to feel smug and superior, if anything, but she is just . . . angry.'

'Mm.' Henrietta sucked the end of her finger meditatively. She could not understand that part either, but the rest made such good sense it just had to be true. 'But Caroline, if Lord Martley dares defy his own mama to ask for your hand, would your mama not see that as a victory?'

'I think, Henrietta, she would rather I married a blind beggar off the street.'

* * *

It was a rather sombre pair of young ladies who were to be found at the Sandbachs' rout that evening. Lord Netheravon, who had been watching Miss Gaydon over the last few days and wondering at the change in her, asked her if anything untoward had occurred.

'Not wishing to pry, of course, but you have seemed very thoughtful, but not unhappy, these days past, and tonight you look, well, almost glum, dare I say it.'

'Oh dear. "Glum" is such a glum word too. I will make every effort to be more cheerful, my lord.'

'No, no, dear Miss Gaydon, that was not a command, or even a request, merely an observation. If there is anything I could do to alleviate said glumness I would do so.'

'Alas, I fear it is something beyond your abilities to alleviate, or indeed my own. I think that I must therefore make every attempt to put it out of mind for the evening and sparkle like the diamonds in the bracelet Lady Mary Mortlake is wearing.'

'I confess I have not seen Lady Mary this evening, but I am sure you will "outsparkle" any jewel if you put your mind to it.'

'My lord, you do realise that implies that I shall not do so unless I put my mind to it.'

'Does it? Surely not. Certainly not my intention, Miss Gaydon.' Lord Netheravon shook his head. 'Sometimes a fellow just says the wrong thing.' He put his head on one side. 'I am not sure I ever say quite the right thing with you.'

'Why do you say that, my lord?' Henrietta looked at him squarely.

'Because I think you are an absolutely splendid young lady, but I am not sure I have ever met you.'

'I beg your pardon?'

'I mean You, the real person. You are a delight, witty, charming, but the real Miss Gaydon remains, I think, a mystery to me.' He sounded wistful, and Henrietta felt rather guilty. Was he not correct, for had she not put on the mask of 'witty Miss Gaydon' for the Season?

'My lord, I am not sure what to say, except that I will always be honoured if you will be my friend.'

'Do you know, ma'am, that is a very nice thought.' He bent over her hand. 'Now, since I am at risk of seeming as low-spirited as you admit to being, shall we dance, and be merry?'

'An excellent idea.'

Henrietta offered him her arm and smiled her most charming smile. It was, he thought, such a dashed shame, but friendship was all that lay behind it. He did not, he realised, expect that a woman would adore him, but he did think there ought to be just a little hero-worship, rather than tolerant amusement in her gaze.

The dance set forming contained Miss Yate, and, to Henrietta's discomfiture, Lord Henfield. It was perfectly ridiculous, but she did not enjoy seeing him dancing with other ladies, at least not unmarried ones. Miss Yate was, she thought, less clumsy of late, and rather more cheerful, though having a mama as terrifying as Lady Leyburn was enough to put any girl in a quake. Whilst she attended to Lord Netheravon when the dance brought them together, she also watched Lord Henfield. He really was quite light upon his feet, and he appeared in good humour. They passed each other in the dance, and their eyes met. She felt he must hear the sudden thump of her heart, so loud was it in her own ears.

'Miss Gaydon, good evening.' His words were formal, but his tone familiar.

'Good evening, my lord. Fine playing, is it not?'

'I know not, since what I see subjugates what I hear at this minute.'

Henrietta opened her mouth to speak but the figure of the dance changed, and she was facing another. It had been rather a clever compliment, the sort she might receive from Lord Netheravon, but it was not made lightly, but with an awed sincerity. Could it be that he felt as she did, was confused as she was?

Mr Newbold, observing, even as he spoke with Lady Cowper, came to an accurate conclusion. If he wanted Miss Gaydon for himself, he would have to make an effort, and soon.

Henrietta was still slightly dazed when she left the dance floor. She declined Lord Netheravon's offer to procure her lemonade, but thanked him prettily enough, if automatically. Caroline, who had been dancing with a man who, she whispered, danced like a bear, fanned herself and sighed. She still looked a little pale. Lady Elstead, noting the slight sag to her shoulders, suggested that they need not remain quite so late, if Caroline was wilting.

'Your servant, ladies.' Lord Martley made his bow, and smiled at them. His smile was all for Caroline, and he was instantly concerned at the warning look she had in her eyes. 'A very warm evening, is it not?'

'A very warm evening, my lord,' replied Lady Elstead, without enthusiasm.

'I was wondering, ma'am, if Miss Gaydon, and Miss Felbridge of course, had seen the wild beasts at the Tower during their sojourn in the capital. The Season is quite advanced and it would be a shame to return to the shires without experiencing such exotic creatures that one might only otherwise see in books.'

'I am not sure, my lord, that we are free in the near future.' Her voice now had a chill to it, and he looked confused.

'What if I also made one of the party, ma'am,' offered Lord Henfield, who had approached without them noticing, and smiled at the two girls. 'And if you could also be in attendance rather than maids . . .'

Lady Elstead, seeing the look directed at Caroline, immediately softened.

'Well, in that case, my lord . . . though I have never wished to see wild beasts myself, I suppose they must have an attraction for the young.' She paused for effect. 'We might be able to make time if we put off our visit to the milliner's on Tuesday at eleven.'

Caroline, who knew the visit to the milliner was fictitious, clapped her hands together and thanked both gentlemen very prettily. Henrietta was, unaccountably, less transported by joy.

'Have you an ambition to see a lion, or were you more eager to please my cousin?' she murmured in an undertone, as Lady Elstead received Lord Martley's thanks. Lord Henfield frowned, and cast her a thoughtful look.

'I want you both to experience more of the capital than balls and routs,' he said levelly, and Henrietta was not sure whether or not she believed him. 'I had wondered if you might wish to visit Bullock's Museum, but at the Tower there are the Crown Jewels, which I am sure you will like, and of course the history of the Tower and its inhabitants, though I never thought that history was your favourite subject. Miss Thorney used to praise your understanding of the globes, however, so the regions from whence the wild animals originate will give you a chance to show off your knowledge of geography.' He smiled, remembering.

'I have no wish to show off my knowledge of any subject.' She attempted to look superior, and then gave a very immature grin. 'Though should anyone wish to know where Madras is located, I could show them.'

'Is it a question often asked during morning calls?'

'Alas, not as frequently as I might wish. There are some who might even say I ought to have spent less time with the globes and more with Italian.' She sighed theatrically.

'But you never learned a word of Italian, beyond musical terms.'

'Exactly.'

'Are the wild beasts at the Tower dangerous?' enquired Caroline, to both gentlemen.

'Only if they escape and have not feasted upon English maidens for a month,' responded Lord Martley wickedly. Caroline shuddered.

'Ah yes, they tried them with Portuguese damsels and they were not at all interested,' added Lord Henfield.

'Perhaps they ought to use English tellers of faradiddles,' observed Henrietta dryly.

'Too tough,' said Lord Martley.

'And out of season also,' corroborated Lord Henfield.

'Tuesday, at eleven,' repeated Lady Elstead, not appreciating the funning humour of the gentlemen, which brought both back to formality.

CHAPTER FIFTEEN

MR NEWBOLD, HAVING ONLY MANAGED TO SECURE Miss Gaydon for a country dance, which was not conducive to exchanges of any personal nature, felt that his evening had been rather unsuccessful, but he had ascertained that Henrietta would be at the Sorleys' the following evening, which was a soirée he would usually avoid, since Lady Sorley delighted in showing off the talents of the young ladies making their debut, and it normally bored him. Miss Felbridge was, he learned, due to play a piece upon the harp, but Miss Gaydon happily admitted that she was 'very inferior' upon the piano, did not like to sing alone, and had never set finger to a harp string in her life. He foresaw that this would therefore provide him with the opportunity to amuse her as she expected him to do, and also subtly introduce rather more wooing than he had previously attempted. He doubted that Miss Gaydon had as yet considered him as a suitor, and he acknowledged that Lord Henfield had a head start. On the other hand, all that Henfield had was a habitual relationship which was sliding into something more. He felt that his own abilities and experience would soon put him on a par at least, and from thence he could move to claim the lady's hand. A small voice within wondered whether it was what he really wanted, if he could approach the situation in so cerebral a manner, but he dismissed it.

It was not difficult for him to obtain the required invitation, even at the last minute, since Lady Sorley was to be found in the park, in the comfort of her barouche, every afternoon at the promenading hour if the weather was fair. She took great pleasure in being one whom all ladies with musically adept daughters cultivated, if not showed fawning consideration. It was power, of a sort, and she loved it. To be able to add Mr Newbold's name to those who would attend was an additional feather in her cap.

He therefore found himself enduring an evening of insipid trilling and melodious monotony with a forced look of interest, but in the excellent cause of advancing himself with Miss Gaydon. He was not pleased to see that Lady Vernham was in attendance, with Lord Henfield as escort, nor would he have been delighted to know that only the hope that he might see Miss

Gaydon had persuaded him to accompany her. On the other hand, Martley and Netheravon were not present.

Lady Sorley, wishing to show off Mr Newbold as one would a prize, kept him at her elbow for the first three pieces, but then he was able to escape, and make his way to Lady Elstead and her charges. He bowed with grace.

'I hope we are to hear from you this evening,' he said smoothly, addressing both young ladies, though he knew Miss Gaydon would say no. Henrietta instantly affirmed that she was not so accomplished as to appear before a knowledgeable audience.

'I am down to play, but I am rather nervous, Mr Newbold,' whispered Caroline, clutching her fan rather tightly.

'Without cause, Miss Felbridge, I am sure. You have but to play as if you were alone, and ignore everyone else present.'

'Sound advice, Mr Newbold, but I wonder if you have ever had to put it into practice.' Henrietta looked dubious.

'Of course not, Miss Gaydon, but it remains sound advice.'

'I think my fingers will shake so much I will miss the strings,' bemoaned Caroline. In truth, she enjoyed music in private but hated the idea of performance, and had intentionally omitted telling Lord Martley she would be playing, lest he beg the favour to come and watch. At this minute, however, she felt that his presence would have steadied her nerves.

'Mr Newbold is perfectly right, my dear. Your accomplishment upon the instrument is such that all will be delighted.' Lady Elstead sounded confident but was wondering if Caroline might flounder. Having herself used such consoling phrases as 'really very good, considering' over the failures of others in the past, she was acutely aware that this was 'a test'. She was almost at the point of blaming Caroline for putting her maternal nerves under strain. She was not focused upon Henrietta, and so it was quite easy for Mr Newbold to gently disengage Miss Gaydon from her aunt and remove her just far enough away that their conversation would not be overheard.

'I pity your cousin, Miss Gaydon. I have no doubt she can play, but she is clearly not a natural performer, and all this' – he waved his hand at the assembly – 'is barely better than torture.'

'Then why come and listen, Mr Newbold?'

'Because I knew you would be here.' His answer was swift, and accompanied by a smile that was not merely that of the man making the requisite response. It made Henrietta blush. 'I am sorry, Miss Gaydon. Do you think me over-bold, rather than "Newbold"?'

'I . . .' Henrietta shook her head, unable to form a reply. She liked Mr Newbold, for if he was not as jolly as Lord Martley had been, or Lord Netheravon, then he possessed a certain something, a seriousness beneath his dry wit, that she found interesting. She was not sure that she liked the idea of him playing the lover, however, pleased though Lady Elstead might be.

'Alas, that means you do. I wonder if you realise the very genuine admiration you inspire. I think your natural modesty means that you do not, and thus you construe all compliments as mere funning, or flirtation. The problem is thus that of being believed. I have not, you will have noticed, plied you with such compliments, not because I have not thought them, felt them, but because I did not want you to distance yourself, and treat me as you do Martley or Netheravon' – there was the slightest hesitation – 'or Henfield.'

'And how do I treat them, sir?'

'With charm and wit, and as though it was all a game. You joust with me also, verbally, and it is just as charming, but more honest, I think, and I like the honesty. I have been loth to see you withdraw from that.'

'I am not sure what I can say, Mr Newbold.'

'That you do not object to a slight change in our . . . relationship. I know that is rather a strong word to use, but, forgive me, I think you have begun to treat me as a friend, and that is a relationship of one kind.'

From the other side of the room, Lord Henfield saw the blush, and the confusion, and tensed. His intake of breath made Lady Vernham glance at him, and then follow his gaze.

'Well then, do not stand here and hiss, Henfield. "Engage the enemy" and let her see she has options.'

Having got to know Lord Henfield, Lady Vernham wondered if she was sending him against 'superior forces', but trusted to his uncomplicated decency and lack of artifice. He was so patently genuine, which must stand him in good stead against a man noted for clever words.

'Good evening, Miss Gaydon.' Lord Henfield made his bow. It was not as fluid as Mr Newbold's, but the smile in his eyes was warmer when he lifted his head and looked at Henrietta. 'I hope Newbold here has not been telling you that you ought to be standing up and singing.' His smile lengthened.

'You think my voice so out of tune or thin, my lord?' Henrietta looked warily at him, not knowing what he might reply.

'You sing very nicely, but since I have overheard already that three young ladies are planning to sing "Early One Morning", which I know you to hum as if it were part of you, you would be sadly de trop, and besides, I rather like knowing that I have the advantage over everyone else, because I alone have heard you sing.'

'Every man deserves one advantage, eh, Henfield?' Mr Newbold was not pleased at Henfield's arrival, and there was a hint of challenge in the look he gave him.

'At the very least, Newbold.' The look was returned.

'The trouble with people who have known one from the cradle is that they become positively proprietorial, Miss Gaydon, always wanting one to remain the child of memory. I have an aunt who, even now, persists in the belief that I am an adolescent, presumably to prevent her from feeling old. No doubt Henfield here remembers you singing nursery rhymes.' Mr Newbold's words were light-hearted, but Lord Henfield was under no illusions as to his intent. He glared at him.

'Oh, he must do so, since he even taught me some.' Henrietta, vaguely aware of some undercurrent between the gentlemen, chose to take him literally. 'However, he was very wicked, and taught me the wrong words to "Mistress Mary, Quite Contrary", so that when I sang it, my nurse sent me to bed without any warm milk, and threatened to tell Papa.'

'They were words I had heard, and I believe the version widely known,' declared Lord Henfield, defending himself as best he could.

'That is as may be, but teaching a four-year-old "With silver bells, and cockle shells, Sing cuckolds all in a row" was not appropriate.'

'I had no more idea of what it meant than you did.' He looked a little embarrassed, nonetheless.

'Innocents both, it appears,' drawled Mr Newbold. He was conscious of having been, for a moment, entirely forgotten. 'How charming.' He did not sound very charmed. 'If you are going to indulge in sibling reminiscence, I fear I must withdraw.'

Both Henrietta and Charles Henfield coloured. Henrietta looked at the floor.

'We are not siblings,' averred Lord Henfield, glowering.

'Ah, but as good as, yes?' Mr Newbold saw this had hit home, and not just with Henfield. It cost him a pang of regret that it affected Miss Gaydon, but needs must.

Henrietta told herself that it was foolish to feel upset, but if others thought that she and Charles were as good as brother and sister, did it not strengthen the idea that loving him, in an unbrotherly manner, was wrong? She had come close to realising and accepting the truth, and had been telling herself that her feelings were valid, but this dented her confidence.

'I . . . I think my cousin is about to play,' she murmured, colouring furiously, and looked at neither gentleman.

Charles Henfield was fuming. If Henrietta was not aware of Newbold's intent, he was, and Caroline's taking up the harp and beginning her piece did not help him, since it prevented any further repudiation of the familial connection. Sir John had told him he was a fool to think it, and so had Lady Vernham, and, at long last, he was convinced of it himself, but he worried that Henrietta was holding back for that exact reason. He had been doing so well, and now this. Had not the sound of plucked strings covered the sound, Mr Newbold might have had the satisfaction of hearing Lord Henfield grinding his teeth.

It was agreed by even the most impartial observers that Miss Felbridge possessed a talent with the harp, although one matron, whose daughter had mangled a song in Italian, was heard to say that 'the harp is much overrated for its complexity and leaves the fingers sadly coarsened'. At the conclusion of her piece, and to strong applause, Caroline, almost weak at the knees with relief, returned to her mama. She also found Henrietta in close attendance, accompanied by Mr Newbold and Lord Henfield, who looked preoccupied. Henrietta took her hands, which shook slightly.

'You were superb, Caroline, honestly. I am sure your performance will be the highlight of the evening that everyone will remember.'

'Just for a moment, at the beginning, my mind went entirely blank,' whispered Caroline.

'But you remembered, which is what counts, dear child.' Lady Elstead beamed at her daughter. She could relax, and bask in the reflected glory. She enjoyed basking.

'I hope you were listening very carefully, Mr Newbold. Did I make any mistakes?' asked Caroline diffidently.

'None at all, Miss Felbridge,' announced Mr Newbold decisively, having not listened to a single note, as Henrietta well knew. Having decided that he had put Henfield on edge, but that the man was unlikely to give ground and go away, Mr Newbold played his hand with subtlety, and withdrew, fairly sure that Henfield would manage to make things worse for himself without his assistance. In this he was not totally wrong.

'Thinks himself so dashed clever,' muttered Lord Henfield, watching Mr Newbold as he made another lady laugh.

'Well, he is,' said Henrietta reasonably, also watching the gentleman. That she did so raised Lord Henfield's hackles. She turned to look up at him, her eyes serious, and her look searching. 'Do I treat you as if all this were a game, Charles?'

'Yes,' he answered honestly, and rather heavily. He meant the London Season, but she meant how she treated men as a whole.

'You think I am just a flirt?'

'Of course not, Henry. It is just—'

'I sound like one, act like one?' She was suddenly angry, not at him, but at herself, because Mr Newbold's words had struck deep, and she so wanted to disregard them.

He looked at her, and for a moment his expression was bafflement, because he could not see how she could be at odds with herself, and yet that was how he read her. Then he assumed he had got it all wrong again, and it was he who was the source of her frown and bitter words.

'I do not understand, Henry. Why is everything so very different in London?' It was becoming a familiar cry, but she could not answer him. There was an uncomfortable silence, and then Henrietta turned away to speak with a young lady in a jonquil crêpe gown. Lord Henfield was left feeling at a loss.

Lady Vernham was not much interested in a succession of damsels singing and playing upon the pianoforte or the harp, though she acknowledged that when she brought out her daughter it would be a useful evening. She therefore clapped politely when everyone else did so, and spent her time watching Lord Henfield. She could not quite get rid of the idea that he had become a form of protégé, and she wanted his success. She was not seeing it tonight, and feared that having made several steps forward he had just taken one back. Newbold was not the sort of man to be malicious, but if he had serious intentions about the chit, he would not stand back and invite a rival to take his place. He was experienced in society, and that polish counted, especially when Lord Henfield was not ill at ease, but not in his favoured environment. When he returned to her, Lord Henfield's expression was sober.

'So?' More seemed superfluous.

'So Newbold raised the idea that Henrietta and I are as good as brother and sister.'

'Clever,' acknowledged Lady Vernham.

'I am not very interested in whether or not he is clever, ma'am,' responded Lord Henfield, understandably chagrined.

'No, I can see that perfectly well. What did you do?' Lady Vernham looked searchingly at him.

'Repudiated it, of course, but it made Henrietta look . . . confused, and then angry.'

'Oh, good.'

'What?'

'Try and show a little sense. If she was not inclined to favour you she would not be confused at all. It shows that she is indeed not thinking of you in a fraternal light. You ought to be pleased.'

'Yes, but we were getting on famously only yesterday and now . . .'

'Now she has had to take a breath, and wonder. Let her wonder. Newbold looks as if he wishes to try and fix his interest with her, which may prove a little awkward, for he has considerable address, but if she is so far down the path to regarding you as her heart's choice of partner, then he may well have started too late.'

'But I am not convinced she is "down the path", ma'am.'

'That is because you are in love with the girl. It clouds your judgement, naturally, and you are the sort of man who takes the pessimistic view rather than the over-optimistic in these cases.'

'I think it realistic.'

'Yes, you would.' Lady Vernham laid her hand upon his arm. 'You have to remember that she is but seventeen, eighteen? She is dealing with her first Season, the first time she has been treated as a grown woman by men, and I say that to you, because I doubt you treated her as "a woman", but as "Henrietta", for that is her name, yes? It is sometimes bewildering, like stepping into light from darkness.' She laughed. 'That sounds histrionic, and I never approved of histrionics.'

'I cannot match Newbold.'

'Do not try. He has experience, he has address. Your advantage is that you know the real person.'

'I did know. I am sometimes less sure, and at other times . . .'

'Pah! The chit has not changed her character in two months.'

'A butterfly is nothing like a caterpillar.'

'And she is not an insect. Now, since Newbold has set her to wondering, what are you going to do next?'

'I am due to act as one part of an escort to view the wild beasts at the Tower of London, ma'am.'

'Goodness me. Hardly the ideal location for romance, I would have thought, but there.'

'I did not offer to go for that reason.' Lord Henfield felt chastised without cause.

'No, no, of course you did not, though walking in Kensington Gardens on Saturday afternoon might be a good idea.'

'It would if I could think of anything to say.'

'If you make the offer then you have until Saturday to think of something. That ought to be plenty of time, by my book,' replied her ladyship brightly.

CHAPTER SIXTEEN

I F LADY ELSTEAD VIEWED TUESDAY'S EXCURSION
as some form of trial, the two young ladies foresaw
nothing but pleasure. They were to see one of the most
famous sights of the metropolis, with fierce beasts they
had only ever seen in illustrations, and their escorts
were personable young men. Henrietta, whilst still
having no plan whatsoever formulated to advance Lord
Martley's cause, hoped vaguely that several hours spent
entirely in his company would prove to Lady Elstead
that her antagonism was unfair, and that in fact he
was 'a very good catch', which term made her giggle,
since it made her think of fishing. She was appreciative
of Charles offering his additional escort to make the
outing acceptable, but was not as pleased by the way
in which her aunt greeted it as if divine beneficence.

Caroline was patently smitten with Lord Martley, but if nothing could be done to make that union come to fruition, might she be persuaded by her mama that Charles Henfield was just as good, if not better?

The gentlemen arrived promptly and were both astonished to find that they did not have to wait for the younger ladies, although Lady Elstead was delayed by mislaying her gloves. Once these were found, and her ladyship's barouche brought round from the stables, the party set off, Henrietta armed with the latest edition of Mr Feltham's *The Picture of London*, which, it assured the purchaser, described 'all the curiosities, amusements, exhibitions, public establishments and remarkable objects' to be found in and around the capital.

'I say, Miss Gaydon, you are not expecting us to squire you to every place mentioned in that book, I hope,' complained Lord Martley, with a broad smile. 'I do not think the Season long enough, and if you were out every day seeking them, you would be positively exhausted come the evenings, and unable to dance until the small hours. That would never do.'

'Oh, I assure you that I will be most selective, my lord. However, if you cry craven, I can always ask Lord Henfield to oblige.' She cast a look at Lord Henfield that was full of mischief. It made him think of Henry as she had been, but his smile was wry and Lady Sorley's evening not forgotten.

'You see her intent, Martley? She wants nothing less than us to end up with pistols at dawn over the right to escort her to the dullest locations in London.'

'Any good with a pistol, Henfield?' Lord Martley cocked an eye at him.

'I confess I have experience with a shotgun rather than a duelling pistol.'

'Then I will remember not to choose "shotguns at dawn".'

'Ah, but think of the advantage. We could both delope into the air and bring back some wood pigeon or rabbit for dinner.' Lord Henfield, despite himself, grinned.

'I do not think that very gallant, gentlemen.' Henrietta lifted her chin. 'You would prefer rough shooting to a duel for the honour of my presence?' Her lips twitched.

'One has to be practical, Miss Gaydon,' murmured Lord Henfield.

'And to be honest, I would far rather put lead into something edible than Henfield here.'

'I would prove rather tough, I admit.'

'Eugh, how horrible!' cried Caroline.

'Yes, I rather think he might be,' agreed Henrietta, and giggled.

This morning she was feeling more as she always had with Charles, and it lightened her spirits, as long as she kept from considering Mr Newbold's words.

Lady Elstead, finding it hard to keep up with the levity, announced, in repressive tones, that she did not hold with duelling.

'Quite right, ma'am.' Lord Martley managed to look 'saintly', as Henrietta described it, when she exchanged words with him as he handed her down from the carriage at the Tower.

It was agreed that the barouche should return at two o'clock, which ought to leave plenty of time for viewing the historical, the regal and the animal. Caroline shuddered as they passed into the Tower precincts, with its looming walls.

'Are you chilled, Miss Felbridge?' enquired Lord Martley solicitously. 'We shall be out into the open sunshine in but a few moments.'

'Oh no, it is just, when you think of the poor people who have entered and never left . . . It is most gruesome. One cannot but feel terribly sorry for them.'

'Best not think about that aspect, ma'am. No point in upsetting yourself over people dead for centuries. All very nasty at the time but . . .'

Lord Henfield had accosted a Yeoman Warder, who, recognising quality, not only offered directions to the Jewel House, but now said that he would be only too happy to appraise 'your Honour' of various places of note about the Tower, and some of the historical incidents. Lord Henfield had little doubt that this would be in the expectation of largesse at the conclusion of his tour, but thought it might enliven the proceedings more than Henrietta's guidebook, which had so far furnished them with the length of the ditch about the Tower, being some 3,156 feet, and the calibre of the sixty-one guns they would find facing over the river. Henrietta had read out these facts without huge enthusiasm. The Yeoman Warder, in his archaic garb and with his brightly ribboned hat, was of interest in himself. He advocated visiting about the precincts and then the Jewel House, before returning to see the wild beasts. Since they were housed in proximity to the west entrance, he might lose 'his visitors' if he had to wait for them to finish staring at the animals. Lord Henfield, after a few minutes of the man's story-telling, recognised the fact that it was a well-rehearsed performance. It did, however, enthral the ladies especially, and he obviously delighted in making them shudder and gasp at his revelations of murdered princes, and tragic maidens. At the Tower Green he drew a vivid picture of gruesome beheadings, and Lord Martley, seeing Miss Felbridge's pallor, suggested they move on without delay. The chapel was visited, but the ladies were firm in having no interest in seeing room after room of ancient weaponry, and every desire for viewing the Crown Jewels. At the Jewel House the warder left them, with a crown of his own in his pocket.

After the warm sunshine outside, the Jewel House was dark and cool. The guidebook had already warned them that entry to the 'jewel-office' would cost one shilling per person in a party, but all agreed that seeing the magnificent pieces in close view was worth it. The warder reminded them that there was to be 'no

the cages, recoiled at the 'animal odours'. It had not discouraged a steady trickle of the curious public.

The beasts were contained in small cages, able to lie down or stand, and a rail kept the visitors from trying to touch them.

'You know, they keep the beasts behind bars just as they do the royal regalia,' murmured Caroline.

'I doubt the sceptre would bite you, though, Miss Felbridge,' Lord Martley responded, in high good humour. After all, the day was going remarkably well, and Miss Felbridge had smiled at him on several occasions.

'Where is your parasol, Caroline?' interjected Lady Elstead, holding her handkerchief to her nose, and Caroline felt that it was some form of reproof.

'My parasol! Oh dear,' cried Caroline, in some distress, 'I must have left it in the Jewel House.'

'Never fear, Miss Felbridge,' announced Lord Martley gallantly, 'I will restore it to you within a few minutes. I am sure it will have been handed to the guardian at the door.' He made her a flourishing bow, and almost skipped off to return to the incarcerated regalia. The party remained by the barred cages, Caroline facing away from them and watching Lord Martley as he rushed from the room. She leaned slightly against the rail. What happened next occurred so swiftly that none could have foreseen it. Within the cage was a large monkey. Seeing the spray of bright 'cherries' upon Caroline's hat, it reached through the bars with astonishing alacrity, and took a firm hold of the straw hat's wide brim, tugging it towards its eager mouth as it thrust as much of its head as it could through the bars. Caroline, caught off balance, broke the rail and fell back against the cages, where a monkey in a lower cage grabbed at her skirts, jabbering.

Caroline screamed, and Lady Elstead cried out.

Lord Henfield instinctively moved forward.

'No, no, Charles,' whispered Henrietta firmly, laying her hand upon his arm and holding him back. 'Do nothing.'

'What? Henry, for goodness' sake . . .'

'Lord Martley must "rescue" her, do you not see?' she insisted in an under-voice.

'No, I do not.' He wrenched his arm away. 'Your cousin stands at risk, for those animals would have a nasty bite, and it matters not who keeps her from harm.'

'But it does, it does. Lord Martley will be here in an instant.' Her voice suddenly lost a little of its certainty. 'He must be.'

Lord Henfield ignored her, and, grabbing Henrietta's parasol, charged, in a manner that would have been applauded in an infantryman of the line. He lunged towards the thoroughly frightened beast that was now baring yellow teeth, and still holding the straw rim of Caroline's hat in its grip.

'Untie the ribands, Miss Felbridge,' cried Lord Henfield, jabbing at the lower monkey, and, after a moment of frozen indecision, she did so. Letting go of the parasol with one hand, and keeping his eyes engaged with those of the animal, his lordship held out his hand to Caroline, who grabbed it as though it were a lifeline, and pulled her away quite sharply, the hat remaining in one animal's grasp, and the muslin of her skirt rending to leave a small portion in the hand of the other. He thrust her behind him, in a gesture Henrietta felt was a bit melodramatic, his own form acting as a shield, and began to open the parasol to distract the monkey as he reached to grab the hat. The furore had caused a degree of panic among the other onlookers, and one of the Tower staff came running up the stairs to find a semi-circle of people who were either having hysterics, or watching events as if it were a spectacle laid on for their amusement. Lord Martley, having arrived just too late to perform his act of bravery, was doing the decent thing and trying to calm down Lady Elstead, and begged Henrietta for smelling salts.

'Smelling salts, my lord?' Henrietta had eyes only for Lord Henfield. 'I never carry such things.'

Lord Martley, understandably, felt that in this Miss Gaydon had failed him. He was trying to support a highly agitated lady who was drawing almost as much attention as the incident, and was receiving no assistance whatsoever. He would also far rather be the one protecting Miss Felbridge.

'Stand away, please, nothing to see here,' declared the official, in a nasal tone, which was foolish, since there was plenty to see. 'If you would cease waving the parasol, sir, I will see if we can calm the animals.'

Lord Henfield did as instructed, but kept his hold on the hat. At which point, the monkey glared at him, opened its jaws wide in a gesture that seemed defiance, and then took a bite from the brim of the hat and let it go, so suddenly that his lordship took a step backwards to balance himself. A youth laughed.

'Move on, please, now. The grizzly bear is just three cages along and we have a hyena.' The official made it sound a special treat.

'What's a hyena?' asked a child.

'A beast like a wolf but with raised shoulders and jaws so strong they can crack the leg bone of an ox in one bite.'

At this, Lady Elstead, who had been making fluttering gestures, gave in to her emotions, uttered a high-pitched cry and passed out into Lord Martley's arms. The look he gave Lord Henfield was one of entreaty.

'Give her ladyship some air,' declared Lord Henfield, taking charge of the situation, and going to the prostrate lady's side.

'Let us get out of public view, Martley,' he growled, handing the parasol and ruined hat to Henrietta, and, linking arms with the discomposed gentleman, formed a chair-like support so that they might carry Lady Elstead somewhere less public. 'You,' he addressed the official, 'show us where her ladyship might rest and recover, and have a glass of wine procured for her.'

'Wine?'

'Yes, man, or tea if there is any. I would not trust to the water hereabouts, having seen the state of the moat.'

'Yes, sir, my lord.' The man was out of his depth. If this was a titled lady . . . 'Best take her to Mrs Swifte; she is the jewel keeper's wife, my lord. Follow me.' He edged past them, apologising to the inert Lady Elstead, and led the way from the Lion Tower to the jewel keeper's lodgings in the Martin Tower. Mrs Swifte, summoned by the maid who opened the door, was quite overwhelmed at the quality, and indeed number, of persons introduced to her parlour.

'I would be obliged, ma'am, if you could find some sal volatile, or a vinaigrette,' requested Henrietta. Mrs Swifte went immediately to find her smelling salts, and had recourse to an invigorating inhalation herself before she brought them down to Miss Gaydon.

Lady Elstead had been laid upon a small sofa, and Caroline was kneeling at her side, chafing one of her hands. Whilst not as pale as her mama, she had clearly sustained a shock to the nerves, and Lord Martley was eyeing her in some concern, lest she become ill. Lord Henfield, seeing Henrietta had control over the lady of the house, stood back and observed the tableau. Now that the emergency was over, his annoyance at Henrietta's foolish attitude rose once more. He could not, however, remonstrate with her in front of others.

Lady Elstead, brought back to consciousness by the administration of smelling salts under her nose, was persuaded to take a cup of tea, which she later described as 'a ghastly brown liquid which tasted as if its major components were dust and dried hay, and with as much relation to tea as I have to the Empress of Russia'. Having recovered sufficiently to sit up, and say a few gracious, if entirely mendacious, words to Mrs Swifte, she was relieved to find that Lord Henfield had called two hackneys to convey them back to South Audley Street. The gentlemen did not come into the house, but both announced that they would visit upon the following day to see how the ladies did. Lord Henfield looked as though this would not be merely a social visit, and touched Henrietta's arm as she passed him.

'I wish to speak with you, Henrietta, tomorrow. Understand.' He looked most severe. In truth he was shaken not with the physical events, but with Henrietta behaving in so illogical a fashion. He was annoyed with her, and because he disliked the feeling, it was exacerbated as being entirely her fault.

Henrietta simply nodded, but frowned. Charles never called her Henrietta in private unless he was very displeased with her.

Lord Martley was the earlier visitor next day, and brought flowers for Lady Elstead, which she received graciously, if a little coolly, and he was not granted the sight of Caroline. Lady Elstead, having had it borne upon her how caring his lordship had been of her person, was in the awkward position of having to be grateful to a young man she would have preferred to castigate for the crime of . . . being his mother's son. His tentative questions as to Miss Felbridge's well-being were answered calmly, but it was clear that Lady Elstead had no wish for him to linger.

Lord Henfield was, by contrast, greeted with such a degree of gratitude that he became quite embarrassed.

'I assure you, ma'am, that I did nothing, did not even save Miss Felbridge's hat.'

'But the animals might have caused my poor Caroline untold harm!'

'It is just possible that one might have reached its face far enough to bite her, just.' Privately, Lord Henfield thought the chances about even, hence his actions, but played them down.

'And who is to say such a bite, from wild and ferocious beasts with those awful teeth' – Lady Elstead shuddered – 'would not have festered? No, no, my lord, you are too modest.'

'I think, ma'am, you place too much upon the "might have been". The only casualty was a hat, which can be replaced.' He did not mention the gown as it felt rather more intimate. 'I am glad that both you and Miss Felbridge are recovered from the incident, which must have been a nasty shock to your nerves.'

'Thank you. I shall ring and ask Caroline to come down and thank you herself, of course.'

'No, no' – Lord Henfield raised a hand – 'that will not be at all necessary. I would, however, be grateful of a few minutes with He . . . Miss Gaydon.' He saw her ladyship's expression grow wary. 'You will understand that Sir John and I are in frequent communication, and some messages are best made in person rather than by letter.'

It was a lie, but only the very slightest of changes in his lordship's expression might have revealed it to the observant, and Lady Elstead was not observant.

'Yes, yes. I understand. You stand very much in place of a brother to Henrietta, I know.'

Had Lady Elstead jumped to this conclusion on her own, or had Henry spoken of him in such terms that his 'fraternal' relationship was clear? He wished he might deny it unequivocally.

'I shall leave you and send her here. I hope you will not report that I have been too rash, permitting her to go to see the beasts.' Her smile was false.

* * *

Henrietta stepped into the room to find Charles facing away from her, staring at the clock upon the mantelshelf, his hands locked behind him. Ever since they had parted yesterday, she had been anticipating this interview, the rebuke, and had worked herself up into a temper. She was even aware that it was contrived, and yet felt unable to control it.

'Goodness, Charles, why do I have the sensation I am about to be told off?' She sounded arch, even to her own ears.

'Because you know why I must speak with you.' He turned, his face emotionless. 'Your behaviour yesterday...'

'Was very level-headed.' She sighed. 'I know it is fashionable to be all fluttery and "lost", but really, in such a situation one ought to keep a sense of proportion.' She intentionally misunderstood him. He frowned. It put him off his stride.

'Yes, well, afterwards . . . I admit you were a voice of reason among the ladies present, and that is to be commended, not disparaged, but . . .'

'How generous of you to say so, Charles.' There was an edge to her tone, sarcastic, bitter.

'Do not play games with me, Henrietta. You know full well it is your behaviour when the situation arose that concerns me.'

'I cannot see wh—'

'What were you thinking of? Had I agreed to your lunacy your cousin would have been at risk of being bitten by a wild animal. Why on earth were you so keen to delay, to have Martley show himself the hero? If anything, would it not have encouraged your cousin to think of him in that light?'

'No, since he is already viewed that way.'

'By you?' Charles sounded incredulous.

'Do not be silly, Charles, of course not by me. By Caroline.'

'When he has been doing his level best to win your affections the better part of these last two months?' snorted Charles. 'Hardly credible.'

'Oh dear, Charles, are you so very slow?' she mocked. 'Lord Martley has not fallen in love with me, and I never even gave a thought to it.' That was a lie, but how lowering to admit one had thought it, at least for a while. 'He has been pretending to court me to see as much as he can of Caroline, with whom he is besotted, but his suit would not find favour with my aunt.'

'That is ridiculous. There is nothing said to his detriment, and he is the heir to an earldom.'

'Wherein lies, as they say, the rub.' Henrietta smiled, showing off her superior knowledge.

'Do not tell me Lady Elstead has decided only a marquess or a duke will do for her daughter.'

'No, but I should say any earldom but that of Pirbright.'

'I say again, ridiculous,' grumbled Charles.

'That is as may be, but it is true. I only wish I knew the basis of it, because then we might get around it.'

'We?' Charles looked very suspicious.

'Well, I am obviously trying to help Lord Martley and my cousin,' explained Henrietta reasonably.

'Help them to flout her parents' wishes? Hmm. Do not tell me you are planning some elopement, Henrietta, because I tell you frankly . . .' He was losing his temper, and part of him was wondering why.

'Elopement? I would not dream of such a thing, and take it very hard that you should even imagine it of me.' She pouted. 'No, I am simply trying to help them win Lady Elstead round to the idea of their marriage. I do not, of course, know Lord Martley's financial situation, but I hope that he need not depend upon his parents, since they may choose to cut his allowance.'

'They object also? Good grief, Henrietta, what are you about? These family decisions are not yours to make.'

'Nor ought it to be two silly sets of parents blighting the lives of their children for the sake of some stupid "feud" that dates back over a quarter of a century.'

'They would not.' Charles now looked puzzled as well as angry.

'They have, I tell you. I cannot find out for sure what began it, only that Lady Elstead and Lady Pirbright hold each other in the most violent dislike, and it dates back to when both were single. My thought is that both admired the same gentleman.'

'And you think to play Cupid? Grow up, Henrietta.'

263

'I have grown up, Charles, except you have not noticed, or have tried to pretend I am still a schoolgirl. You stand there, daring, yes, daring to berate me as though you were Papa or my big brother . . .'

'No.' He shouted the word, came swiftly to her, and took her by the elbows.

'Yes, Charles.' She shook him off. 'You have no right, none at all. Ever since you came to London, and why did you come, by the way, you have judged me, judged the people I choose as friends. We were friends, Charles, such good friends as I thought would never be parted.' There were tears in her voice. 'You were witty, and understanding and . . . my best friend. All that seems in a different life, now, and you have behaved as if you had a right to dictate to me. You do not. Leave me alone. I will not obey you, will not listen to you. I am in my aunt's charge, not yours. Let me get on with my own life.' Her voice throbbed, and her cheeks were flushed.

'Very well.' He stared at her, and she thought how suddenly cold he looked. 'You have made yourself very clear, Henrietta, and I . . . Good day to you, Miss Gaydon.' She could not know, must not know, how close he was to taking her in his arms, kissing her, proving how little he thought himself *in loco patris*, and most definitely not fraternal. That would be to betray all they had ever had.

He bowed stiffly, strode past her, flung open the door and passed into the hall, and down the stairs. She heard him ask calmly for his hat and gloves, and the front door close behind him. She stood for a moment, not even able to take a breath, and then she took a great gulp of air, and ran to her room, locking the door behind her. Whereupon she threw herself upon her bed, beating the counterpane with her fists, and weeping her anger, her frustration and her immense sense of loss.

CHAPTER SEVENTEEN

Lord Henfield strode, almost blindly, towards St James's, his mind in turmoil. His first thought was to leave London, which he had never liked particularly, and go home to Shropshire. Doing so would, however, necessitate telling Sir John what an almighty fool he had been, and returning to the world of which she had been such a vital part, and which was now, he felt certain, lost to him. At the same time it would mark him as defeated in her eyes, and he would not have her think him weak. The answer was thus to remain, to brazen it out, pretend he was unconcerned at her childishness. Yes, he told himself, for all that she had vaunted her 'grown-up' status, what he had witnessed was an exhibition that showed the petulance, the frustration, of adolescence. She had become modish in looks, but she was still a green girl, trying to pretend. This reading of the matter eased him a very little, although a part of him doubted its veracity. He told himself that he ought to take the positive from their argument: Martley had not won her heart. Young Felbridge had never counted, for that was the adoration of calf-love, but Martley was not green, was in fact a rather decent fellow, and he had a certain unthreatening charm to him. Perhaps he ought to have offered to assist Henry in her quest to see her cousin betrothed to the man. No, it was none of his, or Henry's, concern.

The removal of Martley from the lists still left Netheravon and Newbold at the head of the 'pack'. Netheravon was, thought Lord Henfield, rather lightweight, and would bore Henry after a few months, and he seemed very social. She claimed she was relishing her Season, but underneath, he saw her as essentially a girl who would be happiest involved in local matters back in the country. All that he had seen of her here had been an elaborate act, a pretence of pleasure. In Shropshire she was natural, at ease, truly happy.

Newbold was the greater worry. He could not accuse him of toying with Henry, because for all the light talk and entertainment he provided, he was not attempting to have her fall in love for sport. Yet even if he were serious, well, he was twice her years, and he was at the other extreme, too knowing, too clever. Henry had novelty value, for she was showing herself to be rather more incisive than most of her peers, which might be mistaken for maturity. Lord Henfield grimaced. Newbold would not have been edified by this morning's display. How would the man react if she behaved like that as his wife?

How had he himself reacted? Was Henry right? Had he presumed? Had he unconsciously, wanting always to protect her, appeared merely as one acting as a damper upon her enjoyment? He could not compete in charm and polish with the other men vying for her affections, so had he turned into an unwanted guard dog? One thing at least was true, and that was they had laughed together more rarely, been close in spirit and able to exchange thoughts by a mere glance less frequently in London. He had feared being so much as he had always been that she would continue to think of him in a fraternal light, but the change was not to lover but guardian. He had done everything wrong, and now there seemed little chance of rectifying the situation.

He stepped into his club and hid himself in a corner in a deep winged chair to brood. It was there that Lord Gorleston found him an hour later, gazing morosely into space, his lips compressed in a hard line.

'I say, you look dashed put out about something, Henfield. Anything I can do, my dear fellow?'

'Turn me into someone else,' replied Lord Henfield miserably.

'Er, bit beyond my powers, but . . .' Lord Gorleston was suddenly struck by a thought. He had seen other men cast down in such a way, and it was always a woman at its source. 'There is only one answer, Henfield, forget about her. Miss Gaydon is a gem, but not the only delightful young woman in London, even if she is in your part of Shropshire. Open your eyes to the others about you and you will soon find another filly that catches your eye.'

'If only it were that simple.' Lord Henfield sighed, and ran a hand through hair that looked as if it had suffered similar mistreatment several times already.

'Well, sitting in gloom will not help you. Come for a toddle about Green Park, and if you feel you can unburden yourself, I am all ears.'

Lord Gorleston, whilst true to his word as a sympathetic listener, was not of any immediate help, although Lord Henfield was of the opinion that his problem was insoluble. The exact nature of the reason for the falling-out was not revealed, since Lord Henfield felt that Martley's situation was a private matter, but he made much of how he had known the depth of his own feelings before Henrietta even left Shropshire.

'Dashed awkward situation, I can see that. Applying for her hand before she even had her Season would have looked mean-spirited, as though you knew she would find someone "better" and dare not let her out of the shire, and was complicated by your having been on such terms with the girl all her life.'

'I cannot compete with the likes of Newbold, or Netheravon,' bemoaned Lord Henfield.

'Er, do you think you ought to try?' enquired his friend.

'I have been doing my b—'

'No, no, my dear fellow. I mean, is trying to be like them the answer at all?'

'I have seen her, the "Town" her, lapping up their flattery.'

'She may have lapped it up, but I have seen no sign that she has developed a tendre for any of her charming admirers.'

'Which is something' – Lord Henfield looked pensive – 'but she now actively dislikes me, I am convinced of it.'

'Not an expert on the ladies, I grant you, but from my little experience of the fair sex, saying what they mean is not their strong point. In fact, they dashed often mean the opposite.' Lord Gorleston pulled a face indicative of perplexity. 'My sisters are a total mystery to me on a permanent basis.'

'But . . . damn it, Gorleston, I cannot win. If I persist and she means it . . .'

'She will throw her fan at you, declare you a beast and burst into tears in public.' Gorleston shook his head at this prospect. 'Puts you in the wrong before the world, and means a rapprochement is highly unlikely.'

'And if I retire from the lists, I will watch her marry a man she will either bore, or will bore her, within a six-month. Your mama says that I must "develop" the art of seduction, which is both alien to me and, well, it sounds indelicate. I mean, this is Henr . . . ietta we are talking about here.'

'Not wishing to be indelicate either, dear chap, but ultimately, are you not wanting to "seduce" her? Not,' he added hastily, 'in the way of making her fall in love with you and then casting her aside, but . . . "to have and to hold" and all that.'

'Of cou—' Henfield stopped, and coloured. Holding Henry, let alone having her, was a lot to think about. 'Yes, I suppose I do, but . . . I have never thought of it that way, in the past.'

'Wherein lies your problem,' sighed his friend. There was a short but heavy silence, then Lord Gorleston brightened. 'Write to her, then.'

'Write?'

'Yes, write a letter, an epistle, a missive, call it what you will. Apologise for your terse behaviour, blame it upon the strength of your feelings, etc.'

'She would tear it up.'

'Ah yes, but at least she would do that in private, which is an advantage.' Lord Gorleston was being pragmatic. 'And you never know, having slept upon it all, she might have second thoughts about sending you off like that.'

'Perhaps. I . . . I am in the deuce of a muddle, Gorleston. I am, have always been, a steady sort of fellow who knew his own mind, saw the path clearly, even if it was going to be steep. It is as though I have no faith in myself any more, no certainties, except the certainty that I love her, and if she marries anyone but me, my life will shrivel to mere existence.'

'Don't like the sound of that, I must say. Is there anything you could do that would win her admiration? Not talking dangerous feat sort of thing, since most of the time females berate one for thoughtlessness if one tries anything daring.'

'There is a . . . situation . . . If it were resolved as she hopes that would please her, but it is not something in which she ought really to involve herself.'

'However true, my dear fellow, it sounds as though she has, so you need to consider which is more important to you: her or "not getting involved". You already know the answer to that.'

'Yes, I do. It is a social problem that I do not even understand, however, let alone know how to solve.'

'Then apply for assistance to someone who may. I say, speak with my mama on it. When it comes to "social" problems a woman with knowledge and experience is probably your best bet.'

'It involves others.'

'Sacrifice niceties. This, Henfield, is a war.' Lord Gorleston was beginning to sound like his mother.

Discussing Martley's aspirations with Lady Vernham was not something Lord Henfield could contemplate without deep reservations. It was not his affair and he did not feel he, Henrietta or anyone else had the right to interfere. It was naïve of Henrietta to think that marriage among the members of the Ton was not as much to do with dynastic relationships as those of the heart, if not more so. He had seen for himself the degree to which Lady Elstead and Lady Pirbright disliked each other, and if that was going to have bearing upon their progeny he could not see how anything could be done. They were hardly likely to become bosom friends upon the suggestion of a girl of eighteen after a quarter century of mutual hatred, and whatever the historical cause of the rift it was going to be embarrassing to both parties. He therefore kept Lord Gorleston's suggestion in reserve, for the time being at least.

He did write a letter, although it was not to Henrietta, but to her father. He then tore it up, and tried again. How could he explain that he was in the right at the same time as being in the wrong in equal measure?

Sir John Gaydon received two letters upon the same day, and they left him out of patience with both parties. He sat with Henrietta's letter upon his lap for some time, for there was much upon which to ponder. He had been distressed that his daughter found the pressure to marry a burden laid upon her, and part of him was delighted that she wanted to return to him at the Season's end, but he understood that it was complicated. To want her at his side was to be selfish, for in the long term Maria Elstead was right: marriage was success, and spinsterhood was failure. He had not been able to address the problem to his own satisfaction in his last letter to his daughter and felt it still weighed heavily.

What he wondered at in this letter, however, was that at no point did it mention Charles Henfield's name, other than to say that he had used a parasol to ward off a monkey from biting her cousin Caroline. This puzzled him and then made him think, not only as to where this monkey had been encountered in London. Henrietta had always been mindful of Charles, even when she railed against him. He featured large in her life, in her thoughts, and it seemed impossible that this should not be so even amidst the bustle of her first Season. Henrietta's letter rambled in a manner most unlike her usual missives and was confused. She was clearly distressed by something, for at times the letter looked very much as if wept over, but she did not say exactly what this might be. There was mention of Mr Newbold and 'unexpected attention', although he was not certain whether this was unwanted or merely a surprise, and disjointed sentences about 'thinking the impossible' and 'I must not let myself be swayed by the practical advantages', followed by 'I have behaved so foolishly as to ruin what chance there was, if it was right to be so', which left her papa completely lost.

Charles Henfield's letter had the advantage of not being smudged by tears and said much that was omitted from his daughter's epistle. Taken on its own, it was a self-castigation blended with an apology and no small degree of desperation, for he had decided to hold nothing back about his failure to his godfather. However, it was lucid, and had a vague chronology. Having opened with the usual wishes for good health, etc., it swiftly got to the meat of the matter.

I regret, most bitterly, that any chance I stood with Henrietta must be at an end. Ever since I arrived in London I have found it exceedingly difficult to judge how to behave with her, for at times she has been as at home, and at others an entirely new and incomprehensible being, who resents me treating her, in her words 'as a child'. I have tried assiduously not to do so, but just when I think we are establishing an understanding, I appear to ruin all. I have accepted my feelings for her, do not question them in the slightest now, and at times hoped, felt, that she in some way reciprocated. However, only two nights past a rival for her hand, Mr Newbold, made a pointed remark about us as 'siblings'. It was clearly intended to create tension between us, and I fear it upset Henrietta considerably. Her manner thereafter was agitated, and we parted somewhat at odds. However, this need not have been an irrevocable division. My impression was that it had upset her equilibrium and that had made her brittle.

Yesterday I accompanied her, with her cousin, aunt and another gentleman, Lord Martley, to see the collection of beasts at the Tower of London.

'Ah,' thought Sir John, 'this at least accounts for the monkey.'

Henrietta seemed in better spirits and was not in any way antagonistic towards me. We viewed the royal jewels before the animals, and it was then that Miss Felbridge was made aware that she had left her parasol in the Jewel House. Lord Martley departed to find it, and at that moment a large monkey grabbed at her hat through the bars and she fell back against the cages. There was some immediate risk that she might be bitten, but even as I went forward to protect her, Henrietta tried to stop me, claiming that we must wait for Lord Martley to 'rescue' her. This was so thoughtless that I was for a moment taken aback before ignoring her plea. I did not make too much of the danger at the time, to prevent Miss Felbridge being rendered insensible as, alas, was Lady Elstead. Henrietta's actions thereafter were those of a woman of good sense, as I would always expect her to be, but I was both perplexed and angered, there is no other word for it, at her initial response.

This morning I went to Lady Elstead, who almost fell upon my neck, which is not something one would wish to happen. I requested an interview with Henrietta, wishing to make clear that her action had been irresponsible, etc. I was a fool. I am sure that Henrietta, after the event, is as aware as I was of the dangers involved and must have chastised herself. However, I took it upon myself to act the tyrant and she jibbed at it, and reacted in a manner you would recognise from years past. She flounced, she berated me as if I had committed the fault, declared it was not my right to tell her off, since I was not her brother, (no doubt thinking upon Newbold's comment) and said she wanted me to leave her alone and go away. She was very angry, and I am not at all sure how to approach her hereafter, since she has expressly told me to keep my distance. My love for her is making it difficult to even think clearly, and I am driven half mad with the fear that she will accept Newbold, who is accepted as 'a catch' by the matchmaking mamas. If he were to offer for Henrietta, I have little doubt that Lady Elstead would advocate the union most strongly. I am not sure of Henrietta's own heart in this. I have seen no sign that she feels any tender emotion towards him, but he knows very well how to make himself agreeable, and if I have bruised her in some way, then she may be responsive to his blandishments.

I had hopes, sir, real hopes, this last week, that Henrietta might have discovered in herself what I discovered some time past, that what we mean to each other is not just the closeness of the past, but a durable, and deep, love. It was too soon to ask, and now I have destroyed what hope there was.

It is all my fault, and you alone may perhaps understand how bitterly I regret what is lost.

'Foolish chit,' said Sir John, out loud, 'and you are little better, my boy. You, of all men, ought to know how Henrietta is when she has done something wrong. I can hardly send to her and order her to fall into your arms.'

He did, however, write to her, gently reminding her that those who loved her best most desired her happiness.

CHAPTER EIGHTEEN

HENRIETTA WAS FINDING IT HARD TO THINK she was loved, just at the present. With her father so far away she felt she had nobody to whom she could turn, since the very person she needed was the one she had cast from her. It would not be fair to say that she was wallowing in her misery, but rather floundering in it, since she had no desire to be so unhappy, or so lost as to what she should do. Explaining to her aunt was impossible to imagine, and even Caroline, bound in her own turmoil, was not one into whose ear Henrietta could pour her woes. The obvious answer, to seek out Charles and apologise, did not occur to her, since she felt she had been so harsh with him that he would reject any contrition. It was thus not surprising that she took what comfort she could, and from Mr Newbold.

It would have been impossible for Henrietta to simply withdraw from society and be miserable in private. She therefore had the exhausting task of appearing her normal carefree self, whilst weighed with troubles. Her more casual swains observed no change, but Lord Martley and Lord Netheravon noticed, as did Mr Newbold. Of the three, only he guessed the cause, although Lord Netheravon did wonder. Out of politeness, however, Lord Netheravon did not probe. Lord Martley was struggling with his own problems rather too much to do more than register that Miss Gaydon was not quite herself, and to regret it.

Lord Henfield's avoidance of Miss Gaydon did not involve him immuring himself within the Vernham residence, since Lady Vernham would not let him linger with what she acerbically described as 'either a bad fit of the sulks, or being a faint-heart'. Thus berated, he did as he was told, and not only appeared in public, but danced with a succession of young ladies with every appearance of pleasure, and found himself gravitating to Miss Yate, who had an air of resigned melancholy which he found suited his own mood. He was unaware that in several quarters this was seen as 'singling her out', and among the mamas, gossip sprang up that Aurelia Leyburn might just get her clumsy daughter off her hands after all. This would have come as both a surprise and shock to both parties.

Dorothea Yate found Lord Henfield consoling. He was happy enough to talk about sensible subjects, and subjects in which she had an interest, such as the plight of rural orphans, and the keeping of bees, and her concern over her younger brother's lack of interest in his studies at Oxford, which, had Lady Leyburn overheard but one word, would have resulted in being lectured on her many failings as a daughter. He treated her as a friend, and Miss Yate, who could not contemplate any but one particular gentleman being more than a friend to her, relaxed, and unfurled.

Henrietta, who could not help watching them together, felt overwhelmingly jealous. It would have been all too easy to act the hurt child and cry out, 'But he is my friend, not yours.'

Mr Newbold watched, and if his heart knew a pang for her pain, it knew stronger beats that told him his chance had come. What he offered was not the adoring lover, but the sympathetic listener, one who could make her feel better about herself, which was the step before feeling more inclined to him. He saw her at a ball three days after the argument, fanning herself, and looking across the room.

'You are not a lady who copes easily in stuffy heat, Miss Gaydon.'

She turned, and for the briefest moment he thought she was too lost in a world of her own to respond.

'I . . . alas, Mr Newbold, you have found me out. I confess to wilting yet again. You must promise not to reveal this weakness. It must be our secret.'

'I think I can be accounted safe with secrets, Miss Gaydon.' His slight smile invited trust, but did not demand it.

Henrietta frowned very slightly. Was he hinting at something more? No, she was being silly.

'It is not, I think, such a secret whose revelation would bring down empires, though, would it, Mr Newbold.' She sighed. '"Young lady is not at her best in hot rooms" is very ordinary.'

'But you, ma'am, are a little out of the ordinary, if I might be so bold. You are not the simpering sort whom one naturally assumes "fades" in heat. You are more confident, brighter . . .' He halted, as her lip trembled. It was a very alluring lip.

'Confident? Bravado, Mr Newbold, would be the word, and it is there merely to conceal the reality.'

'Are you telling me that it is an act?'

'Yes.'

'Well, that is another secret I shall keep, Miss Gaydon. One is bound to wonder why you feel the act is needed?'

'Because . . . I do not really understand all this, sir.' Henrietta indicated the assembly at large.

'That, ma'am, is because you assume there is something deep to understand. It is simply social interaction upon a large scale.'

'Perhaps that scale has overawed me.' She spoke in a softer voice than normal, and he felt she was immensely vulnerable. In response, he was struck by a desire to protect her.

'Ignore the scale, then, and treat it as just so many versions of what we are doing here, exchanging thoughts.' His voice was gentle, and Henrietta knew the urge to unfold her sorrows to him, as he wanted. Yet she held firm.

'But there is more, Mr Newbold, and it is blinkered not to see it. Talking together is not the same as this, for between friends, real friends, one may say anything' – she sounded wistful – 'and here one must be mindful of every word.'

'Miss Gaydon, you need not be "mindful of every word" with me, I promise you.' He paused, and let that sink in. 'I am not considered to be unobservant. These last few days you have not been happy, happy with yourself. With the benefit, alas, of rather more years than you number, might I be permitted to say that being at odds with oneself is a very unprofitable thing. Whatever the cause, turn the page of life, and be once again yourself.' He did not ask why she was unhappy, did not suggest it was an affair of the heart. That would be to press too closely.

'I . . . thank you, Mr Newbold. I take your advice seriously, though I am not yet sure that I can act upon it.'

'"The Slough of Despond" is, I feel, much overrated, as is Milton's poetry, in my personal view, and lingering in it is a waste of life. We cannot turn back the clock and undo what is done, so better to step forward and do new things better.' He pulled a wry face. 'I fear, ma'am, I sound as if I require a pulpit.'

'No, Mr Newbold, what you say is very true, but one needs a certain amount of strength to extract oneself from the "slough", and just at present I do not think I possess enough.'

'Then lean upon my arm, Miss Gaydon, and take strength from me.' His voice dropped a little. 'I offer you whatever support I may humbly provide, in whatever form you require it.' He offered the arm, but it was obvious to Henrietta that he meant more. She laid her hand upon the arm, and looked at him, rather shyly.

'Thank you, Mr Newbold. Thank you, truly.'

It was, he thought, definitely a good start.

The idea of watching a balloon ascension from Hyde Park had rather excited Henrietta, when it had been placed on a list of 'events to attend' as the Season began to take shape. It meant nothing to her now, and it was a listless Miss Gaydon who took her place in Lady Elstead's barouche on Thursday afternoon. To Lady Elstead the actual balloon was nothing, but the situation of the barouche was another matter entirely. Ensuring that it was placed so that she might be able to converse with the most powerful hostesses was paramount, and she dithered over whether to direct her coachman to draw up in the rather narrow space between Lady Sefton and the Duchess of Rutland, and appear to have pushed in, or to settle for the Duchess of Bedford, and a decent gap to Lady Soughton. To Henrietta and Caroline's disappointment, she chose the latter, for Gerald Soughton was sitting with his mother, and from her expression, even she had already tired of his knowledge of aeronautical adventure. She was thus only too delighted to engage in conversation with Lady Elstead, and foist her son, with his inexhaustible flow, upon the young ladies. Caroline exchanged glances with Henrietta. The former was living upon her nerves somewhat, still wondering how her dear Lord Martley was going to win over his parents, and her own, and Henrietta was, despite Mr Newbold's support, as yet not cheerful. Henrietta grimaced, very briefly.

'Of course, the hydrogen gas used to fill the balloon is not without risk, since it is highly flammable. It was the work of Mr Henry Cavendish, whom I had the honour of meeting as a small boy, er, myself being the small boy, of course. The first balloon ascent in this country was by Signor Lunardi a little over thirty years ago, and the following year a small town in Ireland suffered the incineration of a hundred dwellings when a balloon crashed into it and caught fire.'

'Goodness,' cried Caroline, rather alarmed, 'and we are eager to see such a dangerous contraption?'

'You must be, Miss Felbridge, for this is the future!'

'If we survive to see it,' murmured Henrietta.

'Ah, Soughton, should have guessed you would be present. Good afternoon, ladies.' Mr Newbold, who had discovered that Lady Elstead was bringing her charges to the event by the simple expedient of asking her, had spent an increasingly irritating half hour 'sauntering' between the carriages, looking mildly entertained, and really seeking only Miss Gaydon.

Henrietta gave him a look that pleaded, and a pleading look from those eyes would have won more than mere extraction from the loquacity of Mr Soughton.

'Miss Gaydon, would you care to be escorted to the edge of the enclosure before anything of a dangerous nature develops? I believe they are bringing barrels of hydrogen with which to fill the balloon itself and I would rather stand well back from such things.'

'Why, yes, sir. That is very kind, and my cousin also, of course.'

'Of course.' Mr Newbold bowed to Miss Felbridge, and inwardly regretted her presence. 'With Lady Elstead's permission, of course.'

Her ladyship, hearing her name, turned from Lady Soughton, and nodded graciously. After all, the girls acted as chaperonage for each other in so public a spot, and Mr Newbold was a definite feather in Henrietta's cap.

Mr Newbold handed both young ladies down from the barouche, offered an arm to each, and moved away before Mr Soughton had the wits to suggest he accompany them.

'I do hope you will both hang upon my every word about balloons,' purred Mr Newbold, and watched the two young faces dissolve first into disbelief, then amusement as he added, 'They are filled with more hot air, or more accurately, gas, than Mr Gerald Soughton; they go up, and then they come down. There is no more to be said.'

'Sir, you are a terrible tease.' Miss Felbridge shook her head.

'But we owe you a huge debt.' Henrietta was not speaking in jest. 'If Mr Soughton had carried on much longer I would have been wishing for a balloon to float me away.' She shuddered. 'The spectacle is one which I would like to say that I have seen in my life, but to have such a flow of pointless information thrust upon one is beyond all. We are so fortunate that you came upon us.'

'"Fortune" had little to do with it, Miss Gaydon, since I was looking most particularly for . . . Lady Elstead's barouche.' His eyes twinkled for a moment, and Henrietta felt her colour rise. Caroline did not notice, since at this juncture they were hailed by Lord Martley, and she so forgot herself as to wave her little gloved hand in his direction. If Lady Elstead chose not to see that her daughter and the viscount were besotted with each other, Mr Newbold wore no such blinkers, and saw, most reprehensibly, that it could work to his advantage. Without Lord Martley, or the ladies, quite understanding how it happened, the four became two couples, sufficiently apart for private conversation, which was preferable to both gentlemen, and certainly one of the ladies.

'Have you recovered a little yet, Miss Gaydon?' enquired Mr Newbold solicitously.

'That makes me sound as if I have suffered from an indisposition, sir.'

'In a sense you have, but one of spirit, rather than a physical ailment. Miss Gaydon, I have not asked, not intruded, but . . . is this perhaps some "affair of the heart" that has not ended as you hoped? If so, I must tell you that such things give great pain, but nearly all of us suffer at least one in our lives, and thereafter go on to be happy, and indeed to find a better and more suitable partner. I myself suffered one such in my early twenties, and am now heartily glad that the young lady refused me.'

'But you are still single, sir.'

'Ah, very true, but that is from choice. I have become very particular in my tastes, and there have been no ladies who have tempted me to exchange my freedom for the bond of matrimony' – he looked her in the eye – 'until very recently.' The eyes widened. 'Too precipitate? Perhaps. Yet I would have you know, Miss Gaydon, that whoever might have turned from you of late, I am one whose admiration appears to grow, rather than dwindle.'

'I do not know what to say, sir.'

'Then say nothing. I do not press, nor will you find me hammering upon your uncle's door come the morning, but if your heart is bruised, consider, in the near future, whether marriage where there is honest friendship and a very real regard might be a good basis for a contented life.'

Henrietta bit her lip. Had she not just rejected 'honest friendship and a very real regard'?

'I will consider, Mr Newbold. I can say no more.'

'I ask no more. Now, we ought to see this ridiculous bag that will later rise into the air, so that if asked by Mr Soughton, you may describe it in detail.' He reverted to unimpeachable and public topics, but Henrietta was more confused than ever.

Caroline was not confused. She never felt confused when Lord Martley was with her, but she was still worried. He was wonderful, but he had no firm plan that would see them exchanging vows in church, and upon being told of the unpleasantness outside Messrs Rundell and Bridge's premises, he sucked his teeth and shook his head.

'I cannot say but that it does not help us, not one bit. Without being privy to the cause of the rift between them it looks impossible to bring about a reconciliation.'

'My cousin Henrietta is of the opinion that your mama and mine favoured the same gentleman,' offered Caroline tentatively.

'Good Lord! Well, it is hard to imagine but they must both of them have been young and impressionable once. I suppose . . . but for it to fester so? I can think of nothing more likely, but it is da . . . most odd. All I can do is sit down with my man of business and see what I can scrape together, to see if I have enough, even if my father cuts off my allowance.'

'You would risk that for me?' Caroline's eyes filled with tears.

'In an instant, but I would not have you reduced to scrimping and saving, and living in penury. You deserve the best, and only the best.'

'You are the best,' she whispered, and laid her hand briefly upon his arm. He in turn laid his other hand upon hers, and pressed it, just for a moment. She made him feel like a king, except that at present he looked like being a king without a kingdom. He swallowed rather hard.

'Caroline,' he murmured reverently, and her mouth formed a silent 'oh' of pleasure, as if he had kissed her. 'You must have faith, as I have, my dear one, for I cannot believe that we can be kept apart. Something must happen that will enable us to be happy.'

Mr Newbold touched Lord Martley upon the shoulder, and remarked that the barrels were being brought forward.

'You would not wish to risk Miss Felbridge in their vicinity.'

'Indeed not! Let us retire to a safe distance. Er, what distance do you think that would be, Newbold?'

'Safe?' He let his voice drawl. 'I would guess at some fifty yards, but preferable . . . several miles. I declare myself thoroughly bored by balloons.'

'Well, to be honest, they are not very exciting when deflated, and once they are full, do they not float away out of sight? So I will agree with you there.' Lord Martley shook his head. 'Bit like morris dancers. Not that they float away, of course, but . . . I saw some once. Rum set of fellows I thought the lot of them, what with bells and handkerchiefs and hopping about.'

Mr Newbold's lips twitched, and his gaze caught Henrietta's. They shared the moment silently.

When they returned to the carriages, Lady Elstead bore a glazed expression. Mr Soughton was still expounding upon gases and 'rubberising solutions', and she looked thoroughly bored. Lady Soughton's expression was once again of rapt interest, but it might have been that she had learned to cultivate this whenever her son spoke, and did not actually listen to a word. Lord Martley, thinking discretion the better part of valour, slipped away just before the quartet reached the line of equipages, and it was Mr Newbold who handed the ladies tenderly back up into the carriage, and was then invited to take the spare seat, even though it faced the wrong direction, for 'the balloon going off' as Lady Elstead phrased it.

In the end, the ascension was not accompanied by any explosions, nor any sounds beyond the tensing of the ropes before it was let free, or the collective 'ooh' of the crowd as it lifted into the air, at first quite quickly, and then more gently, as the wind took it on a westerly course.

'How do they know where they will end up?' enquired Henrietta softly, lest Mr Soughton overhear and give a long answer.

'I think they work upon the direction of the wind at the time, and simply continue until there is insufficiency of gas within the fabric to keep them at a decent height. Then they let out the gas in a measured way, and hope to land in open country.'

'But "open country" could mean "miles from anywhere", sir.'

'Then they will have to walk to the nearest village where they can arrange for transport for themselves and the balloon. I find it all rather ridiculous, really.'

'Absolutely,' agreed Lady Elstead, whose attempt to engage Her Grace the Duchess of Bedford in conversation in her carriage on the other side had been doomed from the moment Lady Jersey's carriage had drawn up beyond it, and 'Silence' had let her tongue run on more than Mr Soughton, though more interestingly to the duchess. Had it not been for the fact that Mr Newbold was now clearly making a push to engage Henrietta's affections, Lady Elstead would have declared the whole afternoon a waste of time.

CHAPTER NINETEEN

THERE FOLLOWED A WEEK BOTH HENRIETTA and Caroline preferred to forget. Henrietta was watching, as covertly as she might, Charles Henfield bringing Miss Yate out of her shell, and Henrietta was now jealous enough to wish that young lady were a crustacean that could be boiled. In addition, Mr Newbold was being 'attentive', and Henrietta was divided once more. It was a delicious feeling to have a man courting one, with envious eyes looking on, and it made one feel very pampered, but . . . Deep down there was that 'but'. She tried telling herself that she was being missish, and what more could she want? That, of course, was fatal, because she knew just what the 'more' was, and the 'more' was invited to a very select dinner at Lady Leyburn's house, select because her ladyship possessed few close friends, and was already giving out hints that her 'dear Dorothea' might well be about to contract a very good alliance. So, if Charles was lost to her, through her own stupid fault, it would be foolish in the extreme to not take advantage of what was, in the eyes of the world, a brilliant match, would it not? Yet she dreaded at every meeting that Mr Newbold would announce he wished to have a private interview with her uncle. She knew that Lady Elstead would say, with reason, that Mr Newbold was not only an eminently suitable husband but that he fulfilled the requirements for compatibility. Henrietta could not say that she disliked him in any way; in fact, she rather liked him. It was just that he was not Charles, the Charles she loved but had thrust from her. She ought to be clapped up in Bedlam.

Caroline was simply a nervous wreck, fearing that her mama would meet Lady Pirbright every time they as much as left the house, seeing the laying of a plot when Mama suggested that 'Lord Staines has very nice manners', and resorting to her smelling salts when it was suggested that if the Season was taking such a toll upon her, perhaps they ought to retire into Buckinghamshire for a week for her to rest.

Lord Martley, seeing his love's increasing pallor, began to feel pressured, and was also aware of the advancing of the Season towards its conclusion. However, at the end of the week, he received news which seemed to indicate that Providence was on their side. He sought out Henrietta at a rout at Lady Lavington's, before he spoke with Caroline. He approached her far more circumspectly than normal; one might almost say that he sidled. He was obviously having difficulty in schooling his features into impassivity, and then gave up completely and beamed at her.

'My great-uncle has died.'

'My condolences.' Henrietta made the obvious response, though in the face of his expression that sounded out of place.

'Well, I cannot claim to be badly cut up about it, Miss Gaydon, because I did not know him very well. The thing is, he has left me his estate in Sussex, and a very tidy sum in funds. Even if my parents decide to cut me off without a penny for marrying against their express wish, I can afford to offer for Miss Felbridge in the knowledge that I can support her as she deserves. I am going to present myself in South Audley Street tomorrow. Could you tell me what time would Lord Elstead be most likely at home and breakfasted?'

'He is not a man who lingers in his bed. I believe him to be generally up and dealing with his correspondence before eleven has struck.'

'Thank you. I . . . shall be informing Miss Felbridge, of course, but it occurred to me that she might be in some trepidation as to the outcome. Do you think you could try to be with her, as support?'

'Of course, my lord, and one would have to say that there is no cogent reason why Lord Elstead should refuse you permission to pay your addresses to Caroline, when you have the means to give her all that a lady could desire . . .' Henrietta suddenly blushed, and added in a rush, 'in terms of home and comforts.'

'Just what I was thinking myself, Miss Gaydon. I have every reason to think that you will be wishing us happy by noon.'

Caroline, when he imparted this news to her shortly afterwards, was not so sanguine. Her hand flew to her cheek, and she paled even further.

'Oh dear!'

'But surely this is what we have hoped for?' Lord Martley was understandably rather taken aback at his beloved's less than ecstatic response.

'Yes, but I am still very afraid that my mama will be set against our marriage.'

'But it is Lord Elstead's decision.'

'And he will heed Mama. Imagine if it were the other way about, my lord.'

He did, and knew the truth.

'But there is nothing, nothing I tell you, that renders me ineligible for your dear hand. Whatever antipathy exists between our mamas can only be between them, and will not cloud good sense. I have no wish to boast, but I am of good character, have excellent prospects and, in the final analysis, you will equal Lady Elstead in rank from the moment my ring is upon your finger, and in the fullness of time will be a countess. She cannot sniff at that.'

'I agree, in theory, but, oh, I am so afraid that we will be parted, forever.' She wrung her hands together, and looked so frightened that Lord Martley had to control the urge to take those hands in a very firm hold. He urged her to be positive, but this was to no avail, and she even urged him to leave her, lest her mama should see them together.

'But, my dear Miss Felbridge, we have been "seen together" at functions these three months past, and all you have to do is appear as though I were but another gentleman soliciting you for a dance.'

'I cannot dance. My knees are knocking.'

Lord Martley strove very hard to dismiss the thought of Miss Felbridge's knees, knocking or otherwise, from his mind, and was not totally successful. He was actually relieved when Lord Chilwell joined the conversation, and he could withdraw with what he hoped was the appearance of a man who had merely engaged in a few minutes' casual conversation with a young lady.

Thus it was that Caroline loitered upon the first-floor landing as eleven o'clock approached next morning, gazing frequently over the banister rail and alternating between telling Henrietta something unnamed but awful would prevent Lord Martley arriving, and dreading the sight of his elegant form entering the vestibule. The most unfortunate consequence of this was that Lady Elstead, emerging from the small parlour, found niece and daughter almost hanging over the aforementioned rail, and demanded to know what on earth they were doing. Henrietta, as she told Caroline afterwards, would have lied. Caroline could not lie to her parent, and therefore revealed that they were in expectation of Lord Martley arriving to request an interview with 'Papa'. Lady Elstead went white, and her eyes nearly started from their sockets. She almost ran down the stairs, and the girls heard the book room door shut with such vehemence that it might have been termed a slam.

'We are lost,' cried Caroline, gripping her cousin's hand. 'My life is ruined.' She burst into tears, and Henrietta led her gently to her room, which they entered just as Lord Martley handed his hat and gloves to Barlow, and sent his card, with his compliments, to Lord Elstead.

When he was admitted to the book room, he found Lord Elstead a very sombre man. His lordship had been exposed to his wife at her most emotional, which was not a pleasant thing, and he was aware that he was about to crush a decent young man's hopes based solely upon hysteria. He offered Lord Martley a seat, which the nervous viscount rejected.

'I, er, well, I would hope that you have some idea why I have asked to see you, my lord.' Lord Martley wondered why he had tied his own neckcloth so damned tight it was strangling him.

'Yes, I think I do.' Lord Elstead did not sound delighted, in fact rather more as though he had just been informed of a death in the family.

'Good. I mean, excellent, sir. Whilst the reason for my interview is known, I hope that the news I bring will surprise you in the best of ways. I am come into an inheritance, a very tidy inheritance, though I say it myself, from a great-uncle who lives, lived, in Sussex. He has left me his estate, which has a fine little house of eight bedrooms, and three acres of pleasure grounds, four farms with tenants sitting, totalling six hundred acres in the vicinity of Storrington, and a home farm. There is some ten thousand pounds in funds, and an income from the property of three thousand pounds per annum. I will, of course, inherit Hazelton House, and the lands and title upon the demise of my father, though I am delighted to say he is currently in good health. In short, sir, I can offer your daughter, for whom I entertain the most tender emotion, every comfort upon a modest scale as a newly married lady, and the position of chatelaine of Hazelton and Countess of Pirbright in the future. I am not in debt, other than what I owe my tailor for this quarter's purchases, and I feel confident that nobody could say anything against my character. I therefore formally request permission to pay my addresses to your daughter, Miss Felbridge, and hope that the announcement of our bet—' Lord Martley stopped. Lord Elstead had raised a hand.

'I realise that this must appear most contrary to you, Martley, but despite all those very reasonable reasons why your suit should be accepted, I have, with great reluctance, to deny you what you seek.'

'My lord? I know Lady Elstead and my mama are on poor terms, sir, but Miss Felbridge and I are deeply attached, at least deeply without obviously having overstepped the mark when permission had not yet been granted but . . . Forgive me, my lord, but it feels unfair, damned unfair.'

'I am sorry. I feel for you, for you both. However, it would appear there are insurmountable obstacles that prevent me from . . .'

'What are they, my lord?'

'I am not at liberty to reveal them to you, Martley. Look, do not make this more difficult than it is, my boy.'

'I do not think it could be more difficult, sir,' Lord Martley managed, a little hoarsely. 'I love your daughter, and she has indicated that the feeling is reciprocated. I . . . we . . . are left without hope.' He took a deep breath. 'I thank you for at least being honest with me, my lord, and not inventing some blemish just to fit your exc . . . reason. I will, with your permission, wish you good day.' He swallowed hard, made Lord Elstead a stiff bow, and left.

A minute later Lady Elstead re-entered the room.

'Well, did you tell him?'

'I told him, madam, but it is not well, not well at all. I hope that your "overwhelming reason" is true, Maria, because if it is not, you have made two decent young people very, very unhappy, and in all possible respects that I could see, Martley would be an excellent match for Caroline. This has been your work, your decision. You tell her.' He looked grim, and walked out. Lady Elstead gripped the back of a chair and closed her eyes.

Caroline was sitting upon her bed, with Henrietta beside her, and with a cousinly arm about her waist. They both looked to the door as it opened. Lady Elstead was not smiling, and Caroline's heart sank.

'Mama?' Her voice was already tear-laden.

Lady Elstead looked acutely embarrassed, and also distressed.

'I am sorry, Caroline, deeply, deeply sorry, but we simply cannot permit you to marry Martley.'

'Is there anything in his character, Mama, that makes your decision just? Has there been a breath of scandal to his name? Is he some secret gamester?' Caroline cried, in anguish. 'Tell me if he has deceived me in any way.'

'My dear child, I . . .' Lady Elstead reached out a hand to her daughter, who shrank away. 'You are young, so young. You cannot know everything.'

'And if he was so "bad", why have you encouraged Henrietta to look favourably upon him?'

'I . . . we . . . He is a personable and decent young man. I can quite see why you would find him attractive, my dear. It is not your fault for developing a . . . tendre for him.'

'I love him, Mama.'

'You think you do, now, but . . . I am very, very sorry, Caroline, but you simply cannot, must not, will not, marry Martley. It is unthinkable.' Lady Elstead pressed her handkerchief to her lips. She looked quite ill.

'Just because you and Lady Pirbright were at odds when you were my age?' Caroline's cheeks flew spots of high colour, and she no longer attempted to sound reasonable, or calm. 'How fair is that, Mama? You would blight my life out of an old spite?'

'There are reasons . . . things you cannot know, Caroline. If it could be otherwise, I promise you . . . We will not discuss this further . . . I cannot . . .' With which Lady Elstead stepped back, opened the door and rushed from the room with a rustling of skirts and a sob in her throat, and Caroline sank slowly to the floor, and sat, utterly broken, rocking to and fro.

Henrietta, wondering if there was anything she could have done to prevent this calamity, was yet taken aback to see her aunt so evidently unhappy at prohibiting the match. If she had done so for the reason Henrietta had surmised, she ought more likely to have been defiant. She frowned, and went to put her arms about her cousin Caroline weeping upon the floor.

'Dearest cousin, oh dear!'

'It is . . . too cruel . . .' sobbed Caroline. Henrietta had no response, for she agreed with her, totally. She hugged her cousin tightly, murmuring soothing words she knew must do nothing to assist. She was herself made miserable by the thought that her cousin, to whom she had become deeply attached, and Lord Martley, of whom she was fond, were both cast into such depths of distress. There seemed nothing that she could do.

Caroline was distraught. She made it clear that she did not want to go out, could not face company, but Lady Elstead insisted.

'You cannot hide yourself away, and give cause for gossip.' She did not add that seclusion would also not provide her with alternative suitors.

It was therefore a very pale and serious Miss Felbridge who accompanied her mama and cousin to the opera, which, ironically, suited Caroline's mood, since it seemed full of doom-laden love. At the interval Mr Newbold came to their box and it did not take a gentleman of his perspicacity to tell that something was severely amiss. The atmosphere was so heavy with grief that he was confused. If there had been a death within the family the last place the ladies would be was the opera house. Henrietta's responses were mechanical, and at times she was not attending him. This made matters difficult, since he was keen to ascertain something very important. He had come to a decision, after much soul-searching, and he wanted to make his intentions known to Henrietta before visiting Lord Elstead.

It had been, he acknowledged, a very odd Season, and that was entirely down to Miss Henrietta Gaydon. He rather enjoyed his freedom, his bachelor existence, and had not previously considered giving it up since the failed romance of his youth. Now he had considered it, considered it very seriously. He was an analytical sort of man and had therefore attempted to analyse why he found Miss Gaydon so attractive. She was undoubtedly beautiful, but then he had seen many beauties without ever considering marriage. She was unusual. She was quite bright, though of course not highly educated. She did not look at him with blank incomprehension when he made dry witticisms, unlike the majority of young women. He had sat down and imagined actually living with her in his house, seeing her upon a daily basis, and found the thought appealing. That the physical aspect of having such a wife would be appealing he took as read, and set to one side. Thus, in a way, he had fallen in love with Miss Gaydon in a cerebral and clinical manner, and had come to the decision that he would make her an offer having weighed upon the scales both advantages and disadvantages.

He had let her know that he was serious, this last week, and she must be aware that an offer for her hand was imminent, but he had just one small doubt about whether such an offer would be accepted, and he would not ask where he might meet rejection. He had no doubt whatsoever that Lord Elstead, prompted by his wife, would welcome his request, which ought to be the same as Miss Gaydon accepting him, but she was not the sort of girl whom he considered totally malleable, and that was one of her attractions. When he had first shown interest in her she had been as divorced from deep emotion as he was himself, but of late she had seemed as though she was not impervious to him, for her eyes brightened when he approached, and she seemed pleased to see him.

'Miss Gaydon,' he whispered, 'I am inopportune. I have something I wish to ask you, but this is, I can see, not the time, and almost certainly not the ideal place, but . . . Are you attending to me, Miss Gaydon?'

'Mr Newbold? Oh, I am so very sorry. What must you think of me?' He did not answer that. 'It is just that my cousin has had some . . . distressing news today, and . . . I share her sorrow.'

'I am sorry, ma'am. I take it this is not some family bereavement, however.'

'No, no, and yet, in some ways much worse.'

He looked suitably astounded. 'Worse?'

'Well, worse than the death of some relative one barely knows, and may never have seen, yet for whom one has to wear black gloves or abstain from dancing.'

'Ah, yes, I do see what you mean, now.' He paused. 'I shall not enquire further, for it would be unfair, and you would not wish to spread a private sorrow, but I believe I may not be totally unaware of a potential cause, and if that be so, Miss Felbridge has my sympathies. It makes it an even less propitious time for me to . . . so we will attempt, Miss Gaydon, to pretend that the only sorrow before us tonight is the tragedy played out for us upon the stage. Do you like this opera?'

Henrietta, who had been holding her breath in anticipation of an aspiration she dreaded, let out a sigh.

'I do, and the story of Orpheus and Eurydice is one with which I am familiar, so it is easy to follow.'

'I think, Miss Gaydon, that you ought to be prepared, for in this version of the story, the tragic is replaced by Love, and, although your cousin may not be in the mood for it, Love triumphs.'

'Oh, well, I am glad I am warned, Mr Newbold, for I shall feel almost cheated if I do not leave the theatre with a damp handkerchief.'

She sounded so genuinely aggrieved that he laughed, and received a reproachful look from Miss Felbridge. He would bide his time with Miss Gaydon, and await another day. He asked Lady Elstead if they would be attending the opening of the Waterloo Bridge three days hence, and received, as he had hoped, not only an affirmative, but an invitation to accompany them. Lady Elstead was not going to let Mr Newbold slip through her matchmaking fingers if she could possibly help it. He feigned surprised delight, and arranged to join them in South Audley Street at one o'clock for a light luncheon before setting out.

Charles Henfield was not absorbed in Miss Yate, and for his part, he regarded Robert Newbold's swift assumption of 'suitor in chief' with a jealousy which actually matched that of Henrietta. The man, unscrupulous swine, had seen that Henrietta was unhappy, and had used that as a means to worm himself into her affections. Having correctly recognised that unhappiness, it would have been a logical step for Charles to assume that she regretted her dismissal of his own person, which in turn indicated that her feelings for him were strong. He instead told himself that she was unhappy because she regretted that Martley had not been able to make his 'rescue', appear as a hero to Lady Elstead as well as Miss Felbridge, and be welcomed into the Elstead fold.

Had he told all this to Lady Vernham, she would have probably assaulted him with her reticule for being a prize idiot, but he had not told her. Instead he watched, and grew ever more miserable. The day after

Mr Newbold's unsuccessful approach at the opera, Lord Henfield almost literally bumped into Henrietta in Piccadilly, outside Hatchard's bookshop. She was accompanied by a maid, but not by her cousin, which was unusual. Henrietta had been walking, eyes lowered, and he had been walking without thinking where he was going. He came up short with a garbled apology, and only then did it sink in that it was Henrietta. There were shadows under her eyes, and her expression was one of desolation.

'Miss Gaydon, Henry . . . I . . .' He stared at her.

Henrietta's heart gave such a lurch she felt that she would collapse at his feet. 'My lord.'

'Something has overset you. Tell me, is there any way . . .'

'It is too late, too late for everything,' she murmured, and her eyes swam. 'My poor cousin's heart is broken, for Lord Martley's offer has been refused.' She took a deep breath. 'No doubt you will say that the decision was fair, but . . .'

'I have never suggested that.'

'It was not fair. Lord Martley now even has the means to support Caroline even if his parents object but my aunt . . . You would not help.' It was a cry from the heart, without thought, for there was no realistic way in which Charles Henfield's support could have affected the outcome, but suddenly she felt that if he had been in agreement with her it would have made a difference in some unspecified way. 'So you see, we end up married as we are told.' It was an accusation that blamed him, and he was without an answer. 'My poor, sweet cousin!' She gulped, and sniffed.

'Henry . . .' His hand went out to her, and she was filled with a desire to throw herself into his arms and weep upon his chest, but this was Piccadilly, and she could not.

'Who would be a woman,' she breathed, and moved to step past him. 'Good day to you, my lord.'

He could not prevent her, could not take her by the arm and force her to walk with him. He raised his hat, made the polite response and strode on, filled with self-loathing. He went not to his club, but back to the Vernham residence, where he met Lady Vernham in the hall, pulling on her gloves. She halted, and began to remove them.

'Barlow, tell Caxton I will not require the carriage after all. And bring coffee to the Green Sitting Room.'

'Yes, my lady.'

'Lord Henfield, a moment of your time.' It was a command. He did not want to talk, but he felt incapable of refusing her, in her own house.

'Of course, Lady Vernham.' He handed his hat and gloves to a footman, and followed her up the stairs. He was left waiting but a couple of minutes before her ladyship, divested of her spencer and hat, entered the room.

'The time has come, Henfield, when you either have to do something, or leave London, and by doing something I do not mean making an even bigger mess of your existence by offering for Miss Yate. She is a decent enough young woman, but there is bad blood in the Leyburns, through her mother. I have heard her brother seems determined to ruin himself and the family name in short order, and I would be most distressed if Gorleston looked in her direction.'

'I have no intention of offering for Miss Yate,' declared Lord Henfield, surprised.

'Well, I wonder if she is thinking the same or not. Lady Leyburn is certainly living in hope.'

'Then she is doomed to disappointment, ma'am,' he replied acerbically.

'That is something, I suppose. Now, what final catastrophe has driven you to look as if you would like to shoot something, possibly yourself?'

'I . . . I bumped into Henrietta, Miss Gaydon, in Piccadilly. She is . . . she looks heart-broken.'

Lady Vernham said nothing as to why she was not surprised by this statement. 'Really?'

'Yes. You see, when we . . . when we fell out, it was because she had done something, something thoughtless, trying to advance the cause of Lord Martley with her cousin.'

'Well, any but a fool could have told you they were smelling of April and May for weeks.'

'Yes, but it seems that there is some very deep dislike that exists between Lady Elstead and Lady Pirbright.'

'I know of it.'

'Well, from what I gathered, even though Martley was able to offer Miss Felbridge every comfort, even without his parents' approval, Lord Elstead turned him down, at Lady Elstead's insistence.'

'Foolish woman.'

'This has made Miss Felbridge deeply unhappy, and thus also Henrietta, who is most attached to her cousin. Never having had a sister, I think she has taken her to heart as she would a sibling. If you had seen her face this morning . . . And she threw at me that I was in some ways culpable, because I had not agreed to help machinations to bring the marriage about. In fact, I had told her she should not dabble. Even so, there was nothing I could have done, was there?'

'No.' Lady Vernham was not quite listening to him. 'Nothing you could have done, Henfield, except, perhaps, tell me.'

'Tell you, ma'am?'

'Yes, for you see I know exactly why Maria Elstead and Augusta Pirbright hate the very sight of each other. I am also perhaps the only person who may be able to resolve not the animosity, for that is in their bones by now, but the bar to Martley making the Elstead girl a very good husband.'

'You are?'

'Yes, and what is more, if that particular mess is sorted out, your Henrietta' – she raised a hand before he could interject – 'I say again, your Henrietta will be made happy, and happier still when you reveal that it was you who set the resolution in motion.'

'But I had no idea . . .'

'That, sir, is immaterial. Now, go away and do not shoot anything. I have to prepare for a morning call upon Maria Elstead this afternoon. I am going to enjoy myself, very much.' Lady Vernham smiled at him, in a way that made him feel, just for a fraction of a second, sorry for Lady Elstead.

CHAPTER TWENTY

A T TWO MINUTES TO THREE, LADY VERNHAM stood in the vestibule of the Elstead house in South Audley Street, having sent up her card. Barlow returned with the information that the ladies were receiving visitors. Her ladyship removed her gloves, and handed her parasol to a footman, who was hovering in anticipation.

'If you will be so good as to follow me, my lady.' The butler led the way up to the morning room, where Lady Elstead, accompanied by Caroline, and a hastily summoned Henrietta, were sitting in attitudes of studied nonchalance as though in mid conversation. Lady Vernham did not so much as bat an eye at the presence of the two girls, both of whom were pallid, and for perhaps ten minutes made general 'morning call' small talk. Then, much to Lady Elstead's amazement, she looked straight at her hostess, whom she thought looked strained, and suggested that the young ladies had better things to do than listen to matriarchal gossip. It was clearly a hint that they ought to withdraw. Lady Elstead, sightly flustered, concocted some excuse which, had it not been but a form of words to all present, would have sounded foolish. Henrietta and Caroline made their curtsies and withdrew, puzzled.

The door closed behind them, and the two older women stared at each other.

'You know, you have no reason to prevent your girl from marrying Martley.' Lady Vernham did not believe in circumlocution.

Lady Elstead blinked, and her mouth opened slightly, then shut again. She tried to marshal her thoughts.

'There are reasons, reasons which must remain private—' she began, but was interrupted.

'You are a fool, Maria.' Lady Vernham shook her head, and Lady Elstead stiffened. 'You were a beautiful fool, I grant you, even prettier than that nice chit of yours, but a fool. Augusta Paulton was a fool too, of course, but only about men, and learning her lesson has left her very bitter.'

'I do not wish to discuss this.'

'No, I am sure that you do not. Nor do I, actually, but since it is influencing another generation, I shall do so.'

'It is none of your business.'

'True, but when have things being "our business" stopped us?' Lady Vernham raised a well-shaped eyebrow. 'You think Martley is Elstead's by-blow, do you not?'

'How dare you . . .' Lady Elstead blushed to the roots of her hair.

'I asked a simple question. Your face answers me. You are wrong.'

'You cannot have any . . .'

'Idea? Oh, you see, I have more than an idea. Do you think that nobody watched you and Augusta fight for the man? It was not edifying, but it was certainly entertaining, and you won, more by default, but you won.'

'I refuse to listen to this.' Lady Elstead stood, wavered, and sat down again.

'No, it is just that you prefer not to do so. You need to know, Maria, that you have built a past based upon rumour and guesses, and it is erroneous. You may even have been torturing yourself through over a quarter century of marriage, since I doubt you ever voiced your "belief" to Elstead, poor man, for him to deny. What happened at Ranelagh Gardens that night, and you know which night, was not as you have assumed.'

'She would have done anything to entrap him,' hissed Lady Elstead, remembering.

'That I do not deny. The fact is, however, that she did not do anything, or rather not the "something" you have always thought. She had an assignation with Elstead, except Elstead never knew of it. She committed the folly of telling her sister how she was going to meet Elstead and persuade him to run away with her, and Sophia was ever a tale-teller. She told "Papa", who had the note intercepted, and it was her brother whom she encountered in that secluded bower. I doubt it was a very pleasant interview, but then Vere Paulton was not a nice man at the best of times. From what happened thereafter it is safe to assume that he informed her that she would not be marrying Elstead, who was not the family's choice, but the heir to her papa's friend Pirbright.'

'She would not have agreed.'

'I doubt very much she had a say in the matter. She was what, sixteen? Seventeen at the most.'

'But I saw her, saw her with her hair dishevelled and down her back, and her brother dragging her away so roughly that she stumbled and he pulled her along the ground.'

'As I said, Vere was not a nice man, not at all. He probably enjoyed every minute. He was also, like his little sister Sophia, not one to keep a secret. A couple of bottles of claret and . . . I am not proud that my brother accounted himself his friend, but he did. When the rumour started about her first child, and I always wonder if it was you yourself who started it, my brother Ludovic let slip that it was all a hum.'

'But Martley, as he is now, was early.'

'He came promptly, I grant you.'

'He came early. They had scarce been married eight months, and by licence not banns, remember, within a week of Ranelagh.'

'Banns? How rustic! I can barely name a handful of our peers who were married by banns. I am sure you were not.'

'But I did not need to rush.'

'Nor did she. Sweet heavens, Maria, look at young Martley. Can you see anything of Elstead in him?'

'No, but nor can I see anything of Pirbright.'

'That is because he looks like Augusta in colouring, and you do not want to see Pirbright in him. Besides, Pirbright is a very ordinary-looking man with no features that are memorable. The only person who really ever believed the rumour of illegitimacy was you, and I am certain that Augusta knows it was you who tried to circulate the idea. No wonder she hates you.'

'I saw the way she used to look at Elstead, when we were younger.'

'If you were married to Pirbright, would not you look longingly at the man you did not get? Pirbright is decent, dull and depressingly "nothing". Augusta Pirbright is a bitter woman, and it has told upon her looks. She is married to a man she despises, loathed her brother, and her sister, and disliked her parents. She also appears to have no interest in her progeny. There is no affection in her life or in her, and it has dried her up like a stick.'

At this, Lady Elstead appeared much cheered. 'That is true.'

'Gloating does not look well, Maria.' Lady Vernham's lip curled. 'Young Martley is a surprise, because he is neither dull like his sire, nor twisted like his dam. I can only assume he has had little to do with either of them over the years. His lineage is good, he is of average intelligence, and above average sweetness, and he is besotted with your Caroline.'

'She could do much better.'

'She could do much worse. Who is on that list you must have, tucked away? Siddington? Evercreech? Not Kidlington, I hope.' Lady Vernham snorted. 'You married for love, Maria, yet you would deny that chance to your daughter?'

'No, but I . . . the Pirbrights would not countenance the match.'

'Augusta would not, but even if Martley is tied to their purse strings, and I hear he is not, he is not going to find his father disinherits him, whatever Augusta may threaten. She can hardly tell Pirbright that her objection is that you have been hinting for two decades that Martley is not his son.' Lady Vernham watched all this sink in. Lady Elstead's face was easy to read. 'Yes, I thought you would reach that conclusion eventually.

You are right, giving your blessing may scotch an old rumour only you recall, but it will also thoroughly upset Augusta Pirbright.'

'She would hate it.'

'Yes, she would, and she would probably make Pirbright's life a misery for a month until it was shown that it achieved nothing. I suggest you make it known to Martley that if he wishes to renew his suit, he would receive a more favourable answer. The boy must be head over heels if he swallows that, after being sent away, tail between legs, but he might do so.'

'What do I tell my lord?'

'Oh, for goodness' sake, Maria, I will not give you the lie. That is for you to concoct, and as a married woman you must have had plenty of practice. We are always giving our husbands versions of truth to cover rash purchases, thoughtless words and "headaches".'

'Yes, I will think of something. But how do I get word to Martley? I cannot face walking up to him and . . . I could not.'

'No, perhaps you could not, but suffice to say, I can arrange that, through a third party. Leave it to me, but speak with Elstead, and make it today. Your daughter looks fit to go into a decline, and why make her suffer more.' Lady Vernham rose. 'There, I have said all that must be said. I will leave you to your thoughts, and hopefully these will be wiser than all those years ago.'

She left, leaving Lady Elstead much agitated, her hands clasped together as if she were about to wring them.

'Remind me, Henfield, not to play some form of benign godmother to all and sundry in the future. It is positively tiring.' Since Lady Vernham did not look the least tired, and in fact rather pleased with herself, Lord Henfield did not answer. Her ladyship fanned herself, since the afternoon was still very warm. 'You do not ask what I have achieved.'

'No, ma'am, but it is bound to be . . . impressive.' He gave a lopsided smile. He had not dared to emerge from misery, and even her demeanour could not rally him completely.

'Well, I cannot say it is guaranteed to bring about a miracle between you and Miss Gaydon, but it has every chance, and it will certainly make two blameless souls happy. I have "persuaded" Lady Elstead to withdraw her objections to Martley marrying her girl Caroline. Whether he renews his offer is up to him but . . .'

'How on earth did you do that, ma'am?'

'I am not prepared to say, since much of it is water long under the bridge, so to speak, but it is now up to you to find Martley, before the fool throws himself off some other bridge, and tell him that if he is prepared to brave his mama, then Miss Felbridge is his for the asking.'

'I shall certainly do so, but—'

'No questions. You make all well between Martley and the girl, and her cousin will thank you for it, more I cannot say.'

'But I do not want her to favour me out of gratitude.'

'Better that than not favour you at all, my boy. Get into her good books, and all may yet come about.'

'If she does not already have an understanding with Newbold,' sighed Lord Henfield gloomily.

'Well, there is no announcement as yet, and, if you were to ask me, nor will there be if you act like a sensible man. She is throwing herself at Newbold, politely of course, but wants you to be jealous.'

'Then she has succeeded.' He still looked glum.

'So do something about it, Henfield.'

'What do you suggest, ma'am, kidnap her?'

'Of course not, but just occasionally it does a young woman good to know that she fires a man.' Lord Henfield blushed. 'The only passion you have shown before her is anger. If she wants you to be jealous it is because she wants you to react. Well then, react. Tell her what it means to you, seeing her with Newbold. Declare yourself. If she repulses you, then you have not lost more, since you have nothing left to lose. She may as likely throw her arms about your neck in a reprehensible manner, and weep upon your chest in joy.'

'Do you think that, really?' He dared not hope.

'I think it a fair chance. I have daughters, Henfield, and though it may appear impossible, I too was young once.' She smiled wryly.

Charles Henfield stepped forward, grabbed her hand and kissed it. Her smile twisted the more.

'Off with you, and find Martley.'

'Yes, ma'am.' He nearly ran from the room.

'Why is it,' Lady Vernham addressed a particularly smug-looking, bewigged figurine supporting a tall candle sconce, 'that everyone but me is sadly lacking in an ability to actually do something?'

The china figurine simply continued to look smug.

Lord Henfield strode down St James's with a very slightly absent look upon his face, since imagining 'reacting' with Henrietta made his throat tighten. He realised that just by allowing the thought, admitting it was what he wanted, accepting it, and hoping it was secretly what she wanted too, liberated him. He had held back, fought his instincts, but now he as good as shouted them in the street. He did not want Henry in another man's arms, he wanted her in his, wanted her full stop. It put 'fight' back into him where only despair had lain supine. He would encourage Martley, and when Henry found out he had been instrumental, well, helped, in achieving her cousin's happiness, she would forgive him enough to speak with him, somewhere privately, and then he would lay his heart before her, tell her the truth of his feelings, and . . . It was possible she might be shocked, slap his face for his temerity, but if Lady Vernham was right . . .

A swift glance about the clubrooms showed no sign of his quarry, and the waiters with whom he spoke said that they had not seen Lord Martley for several days. Perhaps the man was in his rooms, moping. Charles Henfield had some sympathy for moping. He ascertained his direction, and headed for Half Moon Street, hoping that he was not going to spend the rest of the day on a wild goose chase, or even worse, that Martley had made a bolt for the country. It was with huge relief that he heard the doorkeeper say that he was sure his lordship was at home, and would take him up to his chambers.

Lord Martley was not looking well. Consuming the amount of claret he had the previous evening, not that he could recall much after the third bottle, would do that to a man. He was dressed, in that he had a silk dressing gown about his person, but he looked rather sickly, and had not shaved. His valet was clearly a worried man, for his lordship was not one to imbibe more than might make a fellow merry and affectionate, and perhaps break into ditties, and he always shaved upon rising.

'Martley,' declared Lord Henfield briskly, thus making the viscount cringe and hold his head, 'you have to sober up.'

'I do? What the deuce for? M'life's blighted, that's what it is.'

'No, it is not. Listen.' Lord Henfield, seeing the degree of alcohol-induced fogginess that clung to Lord Martley, sent the valet for a pot of coffee. 'Martley, all is not lost.'

'It is, I tell you, all lost.'

'No. You must go back to Lord Elstead and repeat your desire to pay Miss Felbridge your addresses. He will agree.'

'He said no, but yesterday.'

'And now he will say yes, my dear fellow. You love Miss Felbridge. She is worth the embarrassment of making your case once more.'

He now had Lord Martley's undivided, if confused, attention.

'But nothing has changed.'

'Yes it has. Lady Elstead has been persuaded to rescind her prohibition on your betrothal to her daughter.'

'How?'

'That I am not at liberty to say.' Lord Henfield thought that sounded a little pretentious, but it implied his own influence had been used, and that would filter back to Henry. 'Just you make yourself presentable, and get yourself to South Audley Street. The longer you delay, the more Miss Felbridge will be lost in despair, and you do not want that.'

'No, by Jove, I do not.' Lord Martley sat up straight, winced and groaned. 'Might take an hour, getting presentable. Head not good, in fact nothing very good.'

'Well, you will feel a lot better when Miss Felbridge says "yes" and' – Lord Henfield remembered Lady Vernham's words – 'throws her arms about your neck in a reprehensible manner and weeps upon your chest.'

This appeared to do Lord Martley as much good as at least one pot of coffee.

'I will,' declared the viscount, perking up. 'Not sure how I can ever thank you, Henfield.'

'No need. Make Miss Felbridge happy, and that makes Miss Gaydon happy, which is all I want to do in life.'

'Ah, thought as much. You know, she has not looked so "Miss Gaydon" since the Tower. I take it there was some misunderstanding.'

'"Almighty row" is what you mean. Since when she has been showing Newbold every encouragement.'

'I would not read too much into that, my dear old fellow. I would have said her heart was not in it, if you get my drift.'

'I sincerely hope so. Anyway, the first thing is to sort out your problem, and then we shall see about mine.'

'Yes, yes it is. I must shave, dress . . .'

'And I will leave you, since you do not need directions to South Audley Street, nor moral support. Good luck.' Lord Henfield extended his hand, and Lord

Martley shook it firmly. The two men then parted, one to his ablutions and the other to Green Park, where he felt he might stroll and think, imagining how he might engineer a meeting with Henrietta, and what he would say. He was so lost in his reverie that it was only upon being hailed a second time by a female voice that he turned.

Miss Yate, followed by a worried-looking maid, was hurrying towards him.

'Lord Henfield! Oh, my lord, you are just the person . . . The only person . . . What else can I do?' Her disjointed words were followed by a caught breath and sobs, and she wrung her hands.

He raised his hat, rather automatically. He was not familiar with young women who wrung their hands, and spoke in half sentences when worried. Henry was more inclined to frown and keep silent, which always made ascertaining the cause of her perturbation more difficult.

'Miss Yate, what is the matter?'

'My brother,' she cried, and covered her face with her hands. Aware of their very public situation, Lord Henfield looked at the maid, took Miss Yate's arm, and guided her to a seat set back from one of the pathways.

'Calm yourself, ma'am, and tell me what has occurred.'

'I will try, sir.' Miss Yate gripped her hands together, and took deep breaths. At last she spoke, and this time her voice was low, and steady. 'My brother, Leyburn, is in his second year at Oxford. He . . . he has taken every opportunity to "raise a rumpus", being beyond Mama's control, and has behaved very foolishly. He has, in a desire to reject all that she commands, taken to gambling and, I fear, low female company. I heard from him this morning in a missive that fills me with fear. He has been rusticated for the rest of the term for some prank which overstepped the mark, but he has been trying to remain in Oxford so that Mama does not find out.' She bit her lip, and then continued. 'It appears he has exhausted his funds, which ought to have been more than adequate, and has been living in a very insalubrious part of the city and has caught a fever. His note was in a very scrawling hand, and I fear he is exceedingly unwell. He asked me for money but if he is so ill . . . I must go to him.'

'Then ought you not to tell Lady Leyburn, regardless of his wishes?'

'I thought of doing so, but if I do and she . . . I do not want my brother to feel he cannot trust me, my lord, for if he will not attend to Mama, he may yet attend to me. I want to go to him, but I have neither the money to hand to do more than travel by the mail coach, and am most reluctant to travel on my own, or with just my maid. I wondered . . .' She looked at him in mute appeal. 'You are the only friend, male friend, I believe I possess in London, my lord.'

Lord Henfield rubbed his chin. He could not, in honour, let this young woman down, and he was conscious of having shown her a degree of friendship over the last few weeks in the same manner as he hoped Henry had Mr Newbold, to fan a flame of jealousy. He was not proud of that. However, haring off to Oxford with only her maid as chaperone did not sound the action of the wise.

'You think the situation that desperate, ma'am?'

'I do.'

'And what do you intend when you reach Oxford? To nurse him? Bringing him back to London would defeat your object, since Lady Leyburn would know all upon arrival.'

'But I might persuade Jasper to return of his own accord, when improved, and I have a pearl ring that I could sell in the meant—'

'That would be unnecessary, Miss Yate.' Lord Henfield was silent for a minute. 'It is too late today to make the journey and arrive at an hour that would not be inappropriate. If we were to set off tomorrow morning, at eight of the clock, with a post-chaise and four, we could be returned that same evening, and if your brother is very ill, it would be best to deliver him to the infirmary in the first instance, so that he might better travel when a little recovered.' Lord Henfield was already worrying over the thought that if the boy was at death's door, he might have a hysterical sister with whom to deal, and a potentially rather compromising situation, which had clearly not occurred to Miss Yate.

'Yes, I can leave the house then, for Mama never rises before nine. Thank you, my lord, thank you. I . . . I shall endeavour to reimburse you, somehow.'

'That is unimportant, ma'am. Just write down your direction and I will be there at eight tomorrow morning.'

She took a small pencil from her reticule, and wrote her address on the back of one of his visiting cards. Then with a watery smile, she left him.

She might have been less confident had she seen his frown.

Lord Martley was not used to being quite so hungover, but on the other hand, he had a very, very good reason to be stone-cold sober, and looking refreshed in short order. His valet found himself instructed to lay out raiment, concoct a guaranteed 'pick-me-up' and bring his lordship's razors, almost in one breath. The viscount gave vent to one final, and very heartfelt, groan, and then set about turning himself back into 'Viscount Martley, suitable husband for a well-brought-up young lady'. It was, in the circumstances, a remarkable transformation, and if his lordship still felt that his stomach would prefer not to encounter food in the near future, this did not mean that he looked anything less than dapper when he made his way to South

Audley Street, under an hour and a half after Lord Henfield's departure. He only hoped that Lord Elstead was at home, and was not gone up early to dress for dinner.

It was only as he knocked at the door that Lord Martley became aware of the awkwardness of his situation. He could scarcely tell Lord Elstead that he had been informed that renewing his suit would meet with better success, and facing the butler, who was bound to know what had happened, since butlers knew everything that happened in a house, made him blush and hesitate. The door was opened by a footman, who bowed him within, and there was Barlow, his face a mask to all expression.

'Er . . . I wonder if Lord Elstead is at home.'

'I shall enquire, my lord. Do step this way.'

Barlow, of course, did know everything. The art of being a butler was to know all and say nothing. 'Omniscience and reticence' had been the watchwords of the butler who had trained him, and Barlow held fast to those precepts. Whilst he would have denied, even under torture, knowing that a 'highly unusual situation' had developed, he was aware that Lord Martley's return to the house, barely more than forty-eight hours after leaving it in stunned dejection, would be greeted with pleasure, relief or ecstasy, according to the personage. He therefore showed the gentleman into the book room for a second time, and bade him wait, with just a hint of fatherly beneficence. He withdrew with all the studied calm of his profession, but when he informed Lord Elstead of his visitor, it set in motion much dashing to and fro upstairs. His lordship, who had thankfully not begun to dress for dinner, but was paring his nails in quiet contemplation, said that he would come down 'in a moment', and requested that Barlow inform her ladyship of their visitor.

Lady Elstead did not greet the news with the calm of her spouse. She had been reclining upon a day bed in her chamber with a most outlandish and melodramatic tale keeping her just on the wakeful side of dozing. Upon hearing that Lord Martley was below, she let out a most unrefined squeak, and sat up so fast she felt quite dizzy.

'Miss Caroline, Barlow. Has Miss Caroline risen from her bed?' Lady Elstead had recommended that her daughter try and recoup the lost hours that she spent in tearful wakefulness during the hours of darkness.

'I could not say, my lady.'

'Then send Hayes to her and have her dress immediately.'

'Yes, my lady.'

'And send . . . no, I will tidy myself. After all, it is not how I look that . . . Thank you, Barlow.'

'My lady.' Barlow withdrew, and, being a God-fearing soul, thanked Providence for making all turn out for the best.

* * *

Neither gentleman in the book room knew quite how to begin. Lord Martley could not say, 'I am back, and hear you have reconsidered', and Lord Elstead could not say, 'You were unsuitable yesterday, but now I am only too happy to let you marry my daughter'. There was an awkward silence.

'I . . . If you, sir . . .'

'Yes, I understand. Only too pleased . . .' Lord Elstead coughed, and extended his hand. 'I only want my daughter's happiness.'

'Of course, sir, as do I.'

It was not a loquacious exchange. Lord Elstead poured his future son-in-law a stiff brandy, which Lord Martley, acutely aware of an empty stomach, sipped very gingerly. Lady Elstead did not quite erupt into the room, but her feigned surprise and 'Oh, my lord, I did not know you had company' were so false as to make both gentlemen blink. She then, at the announcement, burst into tears and clasped Lord Martley by the hand so strongly that he feared the next move would be that she would clasp him to her bosom instead.

'I will send our beloved Caroline to the morning room. Do you join her as soon as . . . Such wonderful news.' For a woman who had been, apparently, only prepared to see Lord Martley marry her daughter over her own lifeless body, this was a remarkable change. She whisked away, leaving her husband and Lord Martley looking confused.

'Women,' declared Lord Elstead.

'Indeed,' agreed Lord Martley.

Caroline sat very still, on the edge of her bed. Henrietta held her hand, and chafed it occasionally.

'It is not a dream, cousin?'

'No, Caroline, it is not.'

'I am so happy, so very, very happy.' In proof of which, Caroline burst into tears. At least they were tears of joy, thought Henrietta, holding her. What had stunned Henrietta even more than the volte face by Lady Elstead was the information that 'kind Lord Henfield' had been instrumental in the change of heart. How, and indeed what, he could have done she had no idea, but Lord Martley had said, very clearly, that it had been Lord Henfield who had come to him and urged him to make haste and make representations to Lord Elstead, in the knowledge that he would meet with the answer he so fervently desired.

Henrietta then asked herself 'why'. Why would Charles untangle the knot that kept her cousin from happiness? The only answer that presented itself was that he had been moved by her own distress in Piccadilly and knew of, or had discovered, some incredible way to make the impossible possible. He had thus done this thing for her, even after she had treated him so cruelly. Could he still have a fondness for her? Or was it the last offering before he offered for the hand of Miss Yate? Henrietta simply did not know, and her tears joined those of her cousin, but from a different cause.

CHAPTER TWENTY-ONE

LORD HENFIELD ORDERED THE POST-CHAISE FOR a quarter to the hour next morning, which made Lady Vernham's butler blink, and his lordship's valet speechless, and was a few yards along the street from Lady Leyburn's hiring just before eight o'clock. He did not expect Miss Yate to be on time, and was quite surprised when two female figures, one with a basket, emerged from the house and hurried towards him. Three in the post-chaise was not ideal, and the basket was large. He could foresee it being a major encumbrance, and covering not just the knees of the maid. He bowed to Miss Yate, and handed her into the vehicle, then assisted the maid, who was struggling with the basket. Finally, he climbed up and requested the postillions to set them off.

'Might I enquire as to the contents of the basket, Miss Yate?'

'I sent Matty to buy such things as my brother might find useful. There is calf's-foot jelly, some potted meat, a bottle of tonic, some goose grease in case his chest is bad, and also a pair of clean sheets.'

She sounded as though this list was worthy of praise, so he made appropriate noises. Privately, he was convinced that what he was doing was madness, and might prove a very difficult situation when they reached Oxford. This was strengthened when he asked if her brother had given his address. Miss Yate dragged a note from her reticule and gave a lane he did not recall, but then said 'St Ebbe's'. He groaned. The parish might be not that far from Christ Church, but the other side of that road was an area of squalid tenements running down to the gaol and ancient castle. It was not an area suitable for genteel young ladies. In his time at the university, only a few years past, it had been an area of strumpets and low drinking dens, and he dreaded what they might find.

They made good time, and pulled up at The Angel, on The High, a little after one o'clock. Miss Yate was all for rushing to her brother's side, but Lord Henfield was firm that she must take sustenance first, after a long journey. His legs were cramped, and he had spent five hours in close proximity to a large basket, a maid of 'homely' proportions and a young woman who had alternated worried silences with fear-filled imaginings of her brother's condition and what her mama would do if she found out about both his situation and her 'rescue mission'. At the same time, Lord Henfield admired the fact that Miss Yate, the downtrodden and browbeaten Miss Yate, had taken positive action, and against what she knew her mama would want.

'I assure you, my lord, I could not eat another morsel.' Miss Yate shook her head. 'How can I eat when Jasper . . . ?'

'Very well, ma'am, we will go and find him.' Lord Henfield paused. 'I take you with some reluctance, and would rather go alone, for it is unlikely that . . .'

'You think he may have already expired?' Miss Yate went white.

'No, but the area in which he resides is not . . . is not suitable for you to see.'

'But I am his sister, my lord, and it is my duty and desire, however unsuitable. I shall . . . be resolute.'

It had been worth the attempt, thought his lordship, calling for the bill.

Miss Yate, walking upon his lordship's arm, and with the basket-laden maid behind them, thought that Lord Henfield had been over-sensitive as they made their way towards Carfax, and then turned left. The impressive grandeur of Christ Church looked more than respectable. However, once they crossed the road and headed south and westward she began to cling more tightly. The streets were narrow, and filthy. Barefoot children scampered like rats, a man sat upon a house step, hunched, and with a large bottle of spiritous liquor at his side, slatternly women with grimed hems and greasy necklines watched them with hard and calculating eyes. Matty the maid gripped the basket in fear of it being snatched from her. A man in clerical garb, but fading from black to a greenish hue, was coming towards them. He looked tired. Lord Henfield, much relieved that here was someone who might give them honest directions rather than send them into a blind alley to be robbed, showed him the scribbled address.

'Ah.' The priest looked at Miss Yate. 'Are you sure?'

'It is the address where my brother lies ill, sir,' said Miss Yate softly.

'Ill? I see. I think it perhaps best that I lead you to it. My presence may . . .' He looked at Lord Henfield, who nodded understanding. The odd quartet threaded their way via a narrow alley to a house with a door that had a man standing before it in the manner of a guard. The priest, who had named himself as the Reverend Octavius Preston, spoke to the man, who touched his forelock with a grudging respect, but remained impassive, and denied the presence of any 'sick coves' within. Upon further pressing, he agreed to speak with his employer, and opened the door just enough to slide within.

'You know who lives here, Mr Preston?'

'Yes, my lord, and he is not one who is known for his . . . charity. In short, he owns both properties and, in effect, those within them, in this parish. He is not an honest man.'

Lord Henfield's worst fears seemed likely to be real. The large door guard returned, and with a few whispered words and a jerk of the head, indicated that they might enter. Within the house a narrow passage led back to where a flight of bare wooden stairs rose to the next floor, and it was up these that they were directed, and thence the second door to the right. Lord Henfield led the way, with the priest to the rear, and opened the door into a chamber that was clean, if simply furnished. Sitting upon a hard chair before a table by the window was a young man, coatless, his brow furrowed, and his cheeks thin. He did not, however, look at death's door.

'Jasper!' cried Miss Yate, and rushed forward to clasp her brother to her bosom. For his part he looked both shocked and horrified.

'Good God, Dorothea, you cannot be here!'

'But you are ill?' His sister seemed only now to realise that the brother before her was not as he had claimed. 'Are you so soon recovered? I came as soon as I could, for your case sounded desperate.'

'But I asked but for money,' bemoaned the youthful Lord Leyburn.

'And money is what 'e needs, see, not cold compresses, nor a sister's 'and.' A man with thinning hair had entered behind them, and leaned back against the wall, arms folded. He looked at the clergyman. 'Not parish business, Reverend, so best you leave.'

Mr Preston stood firm.

'I do not understand,' said Miss Yate, still looking at her brother. She put out a hand to touch his brow, but he scowled and brushed it away.

'Why could you not just do as you were asked and send money,' he grumbled.

'Because you are a fool, Leyburn.' Lord Henfield spoke, and his firm tone made the 'householder' narrow his eyes. 'You wanted money, presumably to furnish debt, so applied to your sister, who is unlikely to have any large sum, upon the pretext of illness. What loving sister would not come, post haste? The truth now, before I lose all patience, and remove your sister from this hole.'

Lord Leyburn looked at Lord Henfield. 'Who are you?'

'Henfield. Friend to your sister.'

'Oh, like that, is it?' The youth looked at his sister.

'No, it is not "like that", you insolent cub. What has brought you to this and in what state do you stand?'

Before Leyburn could answer, the man by the door spoke up.

'I'll tell you, guv'nor, the state 'e stands in. 'E can leave 'ere as soon as 'e pays 'is dues, for board an' lodgin', the money 'e borrowed, and "services rendered".' The last was accompanied by a lewd wink.

'How much?'

'All in all, a ton would see 'im clear.'

'That is very expensive "food and lodging" for a place of these "amenities".' Lord Henfield had a pretty good idea what was coming.

'Well, see, most of it is debt, since 'e 'as borrowed a pony off me and not paid the interest all this last quarter.'

'Leyburn, how long have you been here?' Lord Henfield turned back to the young man.

'A fortnight. If Crimble will not let me out of the house, how can I pay him?'

'You ain't got the readies anyway, boy,' sneered Mr Crimble.

'So, you have lent money at an extortionate rate to a youth under age, which cannot legally be reclaimed, and you have kept him here against his will, which is kidnapping,' remarked Lord Henfield almost conversationally. 'I feel your claim for a hundred pounds looks . . . ambitious.'

'Think what you like, guv'nor, but possession is nine tenths of the law, so they says, and I 'ave possession of 'is lordship 'ere, and you.'

'Ah, but that, Crimble, is purely temporary. I will grant that the chamber is tidy, and he does not look starved. I will give you the sum of ten pounds, to cover the bed, board and "other services", and we will leave.'

'Oh ho, you will?'

'Yes. Leyburn, if you still possess a coat, please put it on. We, all of us, are leaving.' Lord Henfield reached within his coat and extracted a note with his left hand, and placed it upon the bed. His other hand slid into a pocket upon the other side and emerged with a small but very serviceable pistol.

'No violence, my lord,' pleaded the clergyman.

'No violence indeed, Mr Preston. All Crimble here has to do is take his money and walk just ahead of me all the way back to Christ Church, where he will shake me by the hand and wish us a safe journey back to London.'

'Will I . . .' the man began to expostulate.

'Ladies present, Crimble. Look at it as a form of education, for which Oxford is rightly proud. The lesson you have learned is that even foolish greenhorns have relations, relations who are not fools, and even if those relations are female, there are likely to be gentlemen connected to the family who are not easily blackmailed, or in any other way threatened.'

'You can't do this.'

'I am doing it. Mr Preston, if you will be so good as to escort the ladies, with Leyburn in front of you.' Lord Henfield kept his eyes firmly on Crimble. Crimble was used to violence, at least dishing it out, and saw before him a man who was calm, and perfectly certain of his actions. Crimble evaluated the risks, unfolded his arms and shrugged.

'You can't trust Quality,' he bemoaned, as he walked down the stairs, and shook his head as he passed the doorman.

They made their way back towards what Miss Yate could only term 'civilisation'. When they emerged once more onto Fish Street, Lord Henfield extended his hand to Crimble.

'We will not meet again, Crimble, nor will Lord Leyburn meet with you or yours. Thank you for your "assistance" today.'

Crimble looked at the hand, and then, to everyone's surprise, laughed, and gripped it.

'Done over I've been, good an' proper. As long as you keeps away from me, I'll be 'appy, guv'nor.' With which, he turned back into his own world.

Lord Henfield looked at the priest, and then at the large basket. He was already wondering how to get four persons into the post-chaise.

'Mr Preston, this basket, which contains nutritional items and some bed linen, is our donation to the poor of your parish, with Miss Yate's thanks.' He nodded at Matty, who in turn looked at her mistress. Miss Yate smiled and nodded.

'Thank you, my lord. You were not really going to use that pistol, were you?' The gentle clergyman sighed with relief.

'I did not want to do so, but if our lives had been threatened, I would have had no compunction, I am afraid.'

'Then Providence has looked upon us all, including Crimble.'

'It has.' Lord Henfield held out his hand, with genuine thanks, and shook Mr Preston's. He then offered his arm to Miss Yate, smiled encouragingly at her, since she looked rather overwhelmed by events, and set off back to The Angel, where he bespoke a parlour, ordered tea for the ladies, and took Leyburn to one side. Lord Leyburn did not look as grateful as he ought, in the circumstances.

'And just what am I to tell my mama when I stand before her? She will flay me,' he complained.

'Be a man, Leyburn, not a snivelling schoolboy. Tell her the truth, tell her you have behaved like an idiot, and that it has taught you a lesson, because, by God, if it has not you are heading for a short and unpleasant life and will be the ruination of your family.'

'Have you met my mother?'

'Of course I have. She is, to put no fine a point on it, a bully. Well, playing games like this, kicking over the traces, just makes her feel the stronger, proves she is right in treating you as if in short coats. You have stepped upon the Road to Ruin, seen, if you had the courage to keep your eyes open, where it leads, and yet have come back. Use the lesson, as Crimble has learned his lesson.'

'Look, Henfield, if you think all this is going to make me stand up for you with Mama . . .'

'Stand up for me? Oh, you still think that, do you? Well, I tell you yet again, you are wrong. Not every man does things only when he sees they play to his advantage.'

'But you came all this way? Why?'

'Because your sister requested my aid. That is enough. Now, I am going to have the horses put to, so go and tell her that we need to be ready to depart in five minutes.'

Lord Leyburn, whilst not happy at being ordered what to do, raised no demur.

If the outward journey had been cramped, the return one was decidedly uncomfortable, and Lord Henfield, his shoulder pressed into the frame of the side window, and with Leyburn, whose clothes smelled rather stale, rammed up against him on his other side, resigned himself to hours of discomfort. Added to this was his embarrassment when Miss Yate, now recovered sufficiently to go over in her mind what had taken place, began asking questions which illustrated her innocence, but which could not be answered because of that same innocence. That they were directed at her brother as much as himself did not make them any easier. Leyburn, anticipating the dreaded meeting with his mama, was in a sullen mood, and snapped at his sister, who looked hurt. Lord Henfield felt rather sorry for her. She had put herself into a position where her mama would be highly unpleasant when she found out about her actions, done so out of sisterly affection, and was being berated for stupidity and 'lacking any feeling'. Eventually Lord Henfield could listen to no more.

'Either speak to your sister with gratitude, be quiet, or walk back to London. I see no reason why you should sit there, blaming everyone else but yourself for your predicament, and upsetting your sister, in a vehicle which I have hired. Behave or walk.'

Miss Yate, very conscious of just how much his lordship had done for her and her graceless brother, began to apologise profusely, which was not what Lord Henfield had intended at all. Lord Leyburn sat in sulking silence for the next four changes of horses. At the final change, at Barnet, he complained of cramp in his feet, and demanded to be set down while the horses were changed, so Lord Henfield descended, to let him out. Miss Yate asked for the hour, and Lord Henfield consulted his pocket watch.

'It is a little after six, ma'am. We ought to have you at your door within the hour, or just over.' It suddenly occurred to him that Miss Yate had deserted the house ten hours previously, and even so uncaring a mother as Lady Leyburn must have been worried if her whereabouts were unknown. 'Miss Yate, did you leave word for Lady Leyburn, saying what you were doing?'

'No, my lord. I could not reveal the truth and did not know what to say.'

'So all that she knows is that you left the house this morning, with your maid. Miss Yate, you do realise she may well think you have run away, or, dare I say it, eloped.'

'With my maid in attendance?'

'She may ignore that aspect if she is overcome by the idea that you are alone and friendless. She may even have contacted the Bow Street Runners to try and find you, though your departure would not be a crime.'

'Sadly, my lord, my mama might be in a frightful fluster, but only at my disobedience, and the fact that I have acted without referral to her and her wishes.' Miss Yate gave a lopsided smile. 'You think me lily-livered, and it is true, but I am not blind. If there were any way out for me, and please, do not raise the option of matrimony again, I would take it. There is none.'

'She may ring a peal over you, but you are not a child, forgive me, to be sent to bed without supper.'

'No, and going without supper would be easy.' She sighed. 'You see, it becomes habitual, and just one's life, always being wrong, always being told that whatever one does is not up to standard. Perhaps one begins to believe it is true, I do not know. It is a constant drip that wears one away as water does upon a stone. I cannot "run away" because I possess nothing, excepting three hundred pounds my grandfather left me, and that would not last for very many years. I am not well educated enough to be a governess, and, well, I had considered going to Bath under a new name and trying to get employment as a companion to an old lady, but would that not be much the same as the situation I find myself in now?' She sounded tired, and defeated. 'I do not relish walking into the house any more than Jasper does, but I see no point in complaint.' She rubbed a gloved finger at her temple.

'You must be very wearied, Miss Yate.'

'No more than you, my lord, and before Jasper returns, I want to say that I am grateful, eternally so, for though we did not find him in extremis, we found him in, I believe, a dangerous and unpleasant situation from which your own forethought and courage has rescued us all. Thank you, from the bottom of my heart.'

Lord Henfield brushed away the thanks, and Lord Leyburn, now complaining that he could not see why they might not remain at the posting inn to dine, resumed his seat. Lord Henfield said nothing, and shut his eyes, pretending to fall asleep.

CHAPTER TWENTY-TWO

WHEN THE POSTILLIONS BROUGHT THE HORSES to a standstill before Lady Leyburn's house, Lord Henfield opened his eyes, having achieved a half-doze where he had lost track of time, and descended from the chaise a little stiffly, turning to offer his hand to Miss Yate. He therefore did not see the gentleman who was at that moment leaving the house. The gentleman, thunderous of face, came down the shallow steps in two bounds, and as Lord Henfield turned at the sound, planted the unsuspecting viscount a facer.

Lord Henfield fell heavily upon the pavement, momentarily stunned, as Miss Yate cried out. He got up shakily, rubbing his chin, and stared into the face of a man in regimentals who looked very much as though repeating the blow was the least of his intentions.

'No, no, Clement, you misunderstand.' Miss Yate stepped forward, and pressed her hands to the broad chest of the irate officer.

'I do, do I?' He did not sound at all convinced. 'I come to London to seek you out, Dorothea, and find you have . . . absconded with a man, this man.' He began to set Miss Yate aside.

'How could you think that I would . . . Oh, Clement!' Miss Yate dissolved into tears, which left 'Clement' caught between the natural inclination to clasp her to his manly bosom, and the equally natural desire to blacken Lord Henfield's eye, or, more probably, break his neck. Taking advantage of the momentary hesitation, Lord Henfield raised a placating hand, and managed to speak.

'I do not know what faradiddle you have been told, sir, but I assure you that I accompanied Miss Yate not on any clandestine escapade, but upon an errand of urgency and mercy. We went to Oxford, where her brother was assumed to be very ill.'

'And yet his mama has not gone to his side? I find that hard to believe.' The officer still looked bellicose.

'Well, it turns out that he was not ill, but that is beside the point.'

'Beside the point? I do not see . . .'

'It is true, Clement. Jasper has got himself into debt and was rusticated and did not dare tell Mama, and then he wrote to me saying that he had caught a fever and needed money . . .'

'That brother of yours ought to have been taken in hand, Dorothea. Loose fish, that is what he will become if he does not mend.'

'I resent that, Hathersage.' The youthful Lord Leyburn climbed down from the post-chaise, and scowled at the officer.

Lord Henfield, having now gathered his wits to such extent that he recalled the 'suitor from Norfolk', lowered his hand from his aching jaw, and extended it.

'My name is Henfield, and all I can assume is that you are long acquainted with Miss Yate.'

'Clement Hathersage, captain, Second Dragoons.' The hand was taken in a strong, if not vice-like, grip, and shaken with more vehemence than enthusiasm. 'I . . . we . . . not that Lady Leyburn has changed her mind . . . but . . .'

Miss Yate clasped Captain Hathersage's free hand, and drew it to her wet cheek. Lord Henfield made a decision.

'I would prefer not to discuss matters in the street, Hathersage, but needs must. Forgive me for asking you, Miss Yate, but how old are you?'

'Two and twenty, my lord.'

'Thank heavens for that. It makes things simpler.' He looked past her to Captain Hathersage. 'I take it that you and Miss Yate have an understanding of some duration, thus far unpalatable to Lady Leyburn?'

'Yes. I came today with some news. I have inherited a small property in Cambridgeshire, not huge, but . . . Lady Leyburn scoffed at it and said that I was too late anyway, since Dorothea was about to marry you.'

'Well, I think I can safely say neither of us have the inclination, nor is there any need, since we can be vouched for by Leyburn here that we went to his aid. If you can afford to keep Miss Yate in a sufficient degree of comfort, and I take it that is what you came to tell Lady Leyburn, and Miss Yate is not a minor, why not obtain a special licence from Doctors' Commons, and marry her anyway. It will be legal, and if Lady Leyburn, forgive me, Miss Yate, never speaks to you again, I can see that as an advantage.'

Captain Hathersage blinked, then looked down at Miss Yate.

'It answers, indeed it does. I had not got further than imagining being accepted when I presented my new circumstances and . . . I cannot offer you luxury, Dorothea, but I can offer you comfort. You may choose to "follow the drum", and we have not just my pay but income from the estate rents and the house rented out, or I will buy myself out and we will live in Cambridgeshire, as you wish. Would you accept that?'

'I would have accepted without your recent good fortune, Clement, you know that.'

'Then the only problem remaining is that obtaining the special licence must wait until tomorrow, and if Miss Yate returns to Lady Leyburn there will be the deuce of a lot of unpleasantness this evening.' Lord Henfield was thinking ahead.

'Yes, and mostly directed at me,' declared Lord Leyburn pettishly, but he then brightened. 'However, if I tell her of Dorothea's p—' He stopped, as Lord Henfield and Captain Hathersage glared at him in such a way that he felt extremely intimidated.

'I do not care.' Miss Yate lifted her chin, and gripped Captain Hathersage's hand tightly. 'I have never stood up to my mama, ever, and I have paid heavily for it. Now, I shall be brave. What can she do to me, when tomorrow I can leave her?'

'She could lock you in your room?' Captain Hathersage suggested.

'Oh.'

'However, if you do not make our rendezvous tomorrow morning, I shall hold Leyburn personally responsible, and' – Captain Hathersage looked at the young man – 'brother or not, I will make him wish he was indeed lying sick of a fever in Oxford.'

'I never said—'

'Be quiet, puppy,' interjected Lord Henfield, aware that the five of them on the pavement might yet attract attention from within the house. 'Miss Yate, if you are going to explain your absence, and indeed, your absence with me, do you require my presence, at least to ensure your brother gives his tale honestly?' Lord Henfield was pragmatic.

There was a silence. Both gentlemen looked at Dorothea Yate, whose brows knit together.

'I do not think so, my lord, although I am grateful for your offer.'

'Then we need to plan tomorrow. If you would care for me to accompany you to Doctors' Commons for the special licence, Hathersage, and also find a church, I am happy to oblige.'

'Thank you, Henfield. I, er, am sorry about knocking you down. No great harm done, I hope?' Captain Hathersage looked a little shame-faced.

'No loose teeth, and I am sure a cold compress will leave my jaw without visible signs of bruising.' He sounded very serious, but his face, admittedly aching, broke into a smile. 'Now, let us decide when and where we are to meet.'

There was some short discussion, after which Lord Henfield directed the postillions to take himself and Captain Hathersage to his club, where they might dine, and finalise arrangements.

Miss Yate ushered her brother, already complaining, to the front door of the house.

* * *

It had been agreed that Miss Yate would meet with her intended and Lord Henfield at nine in the morning, in Hanover Square. At such an hour it was almost deserted, which made her feel safe, but also conspicuous. Her maid, Matty, who had proved her loyalty with the journey to Oxford, carried a band box, and a valise, containing those few things Miss Yate felt she could least do without, which ranged from a nightgown to her late grandmother's pearls. Although the day looked set to be warm, she had a cloak over her pelisse, as the best means of carrying it, and she presented an unusual figure, making circuits of the square. She was most relieved when Lord Henfield stepped from a hackney, and bowed to her.

'Good morning, Miss Yate. I see you have managed your "escape", presumably without resort to a drainpipe.'

'Indeed, my lord. Our exit, whilst attended by nervousness upon my part, was remarkably easy. I had my maid place the valise and my cloak outside, by the tradesman's entrance, with a scullery maid paid a shilling to guard it, and once we had left upon the grounds of an urgent repair to a hat, she went down the steps and collected those incriminating items.'

Lord Henfield did not like to say that going out to have a hat repaired before nine in the morning looked suspicious in the extreme, and so commended Miss Yate upon her forethought.

'I am here as yet without Captain Hathersage, whom I left awaiting the opening of Doctors' Commons, ma'am, and very much upon the fret. If they do not open upon time, I think it quite likely that he will simply break down the door. He suggests that we await him here, or rather within St George's church, where I may speak with a clergyman and explain the situation.'

'That sounds very sensible, my lord, but I was wondering, if I leave the valise and band box, and my cloak, if I might take my maid and make some necessary purchases in Bond Street – things that I neglected to bring with me, or rather ignored for the sake of items of sentimental importance. It is so close by. If I am to be estranged from my mama, I would not be without such mementoes as I treasure, even though it means I am lacking in other items.' She omitted to say that she had just enough money on her person to buy a hat that her mother had declared 'far too embellished for one with such a plain face'. She was not the most beautiful young woman, but this had been but the harshness of a woman who did not want to spend money upon her daughter when there were things she desired for herself. Well, the final act of defiance would be that hat, but Dorothea Yate decided, wisely, that gentlemen would not see buying a hat as important. 'I shall not be long.'

This, of course, was incorrect, because the milliner did not open her doors to her aristocratic clients until half past ten, since none would be likely to be abroad before that hour. Dorothea bit her lip, caught between the desire to commit this symbolic act of rebellion, and also to delight her Clement with the sight of herself in the nicest hat she had ever seen, and the fear that he would think she had met with an accident or, worse, felt unable to go through with the ceremony. She became quite agitated, wringing her gloved hands, and muttering 'Should I?', which the maid correctly interpreted as not requiring an answer from herself.

When a junior assistant unbolted the door at half past the hour, Miss Yate almost burst into the premises. Never had the assistant, or indeed Mme Perigord, the proprietress, ever been faced with a client who breathlessly demanded a hat from the window display, placed it upon her head, took one look in the mirror and immediately drew forth the required sum from her reticule. When the young lady departed, Mme Perigord shook her head, and remarked that, whilst it was always good to know one's creations were wanted, what had just passed was closer to being held up by a highwayman than selling a hat. By this time Miss Yate, new hat upon her head, was all but running back to St George's, and with a breathless Matty struggling to keep up.

This unforeseen delay meant that Captain Hathersage arrived with the special licence a quarter hour after ten o'clock to find that Lord Henfield had successfully assuaged any ecclesiastical qualms and was himself already waiting at the door of the church with this good news, and the less good news that the bride had disappeared on a 'minor shopping excursion'. Captain Hathersage did not take this news well, initially blaming Lord Henfield for not escorting his intended, but then accepting that his lordship could not do that and simultaneously negotiate for the wedding to take place at exceedingly short notice.

'Er, one thing, Hathersage. Do you possess a ring?'

'A ring?' Hathersage looked blankly at him.

'Yes, a ring for the "with this ring I thee wed" part. Generally considered a required item at a wedding.'

'Good Lord! I completely forgot about a ring.'

'Well, may I suggest a "minor excursion" of your own into Bond Street where there are several jewellers'.'

'But what about the size of her finger?'

'Guess. It can always be altered a little, but err on larger rather than smaller, since a fight to get it on her finger would not be . . . conducive to a pleasant ceremony.'

Lord Henfield was then left to pace up and down beneath the colonnade at the front of the church.

Captain Hathersage was blessedly swift, but this meant Lord Henfield dealing with a worried groom. At ten to eleven he sent the poor man inside to sit in a pew, and pray that his love would arrive shortly. The captain was obviously a righteous man, for just before the clock struck the hour, Miss Yate, with her maid trailing in her wake, hurried up to the church, quite breathless, and pink of cheek.

'I am so terribly sorry, my lord. The shop was not yet open and . . .'

He held out his hand and took one of hers.

'Compose yourself, Miss Yate. Captain Hathersage has not yet become so desperate as to throw hymnals about the aisles. Take a deep breath and . . .'

'Do you like it?'

'I beg your pardon?'

'The hat. My mama said it would be wasted upon me but . . .'

'It is a . . . divine-looking hat, Miss Yate. Shows off your face charmingly. Now, if you will be so good as to take my arm, I shall escort you into the church and give you away to a gentleman who will cherish you as no other.'

'Oh, my lord.'

It was at this moment, as Miss Yate smiled tremulously up at Lord Henfield, and laid her hand upon his arm as instructed, that Mr Newbold, passing along Maddox Street, happened to look down St

George's Street, and saw them. For a moment he did not recognise Miss Yate, Miss Yate in a very elegant hat, and looking inexpressibly happy, but then she half-tripped going up the steps, and he knew it was her. He frowned, for it made no sense, but it might also be very useful to know. He did not stop, but continued on his way.

It was not, of course, a grand wedding. The bride, beautiful hat notwithstanding, wore a serviceable pelisse and the hem of her gown was a little dusty. The groom had the advantage of regimentals, and Lord Henfield was reminded of a pair of pheasant, where the cock bird had all the show, and the hen retained practical drabness. The maid sniffed rather a lot, but did provide the second witness without them having recourse to asking someone off the street, and Lord Henfield was relieved to find that, however laboriously, she could write her own name. Captain Hathersage had decided that the best course was to leave the capital and make for Cambridgeshire at the earliest opportunity, since the road to Cambridge possessed some good inns, and they could halt upon their journey and arrive at their new home next day. However, his new wife had not been able to break her fast before leaving her home, and partaking of an early luncheon would prevent her fainting from hunger somewhere before Bishop's Stortford. Lord

Henfield decided it was better not to ask if the captain had thought to warn the staff that he and his new wife were about to descend upon them, rightly assuming that holland covers and drawn blinds would not be in the thoughts of either party. He would happily have left them to eat à deux, but they were both insistent that he join them in their celebratory repast.

It was as he watched them, eyes only for each other, and attempting not to touch hands as if held by magnetic attraction, that he realised he had spent the better part of two days sorting out the love lives of others, and had paid no attention to his own. He wanted to see Henry, wanted to see the look on her face, knowing he had helped her cousin, just because the girl was her cousin, and she cared for her. Then an awful thought struck him. What if she had not yet heard, what if Newbold had sought the interview with Lord Elstead already? His blood ran cold. It lacked but a quarter hour to one o'clock. He could not just turn up as they were about to sit down to a luncheon. He would have to bide his time until three. No, he would call early, at two o'clock, hoping that was after any meal and lie, if he had to, to see Henry alone.

Mr Newbold thought that Henrietta looked charming in a gown he could not recall seeing before. It was a new promenade dress, and since they did not want to arrive for the bridge-opening ceremony so late that the carriages could get no closer than Charing Cross, Lady Elstead had decided that they should be dressed ready to depart as soon as they had eaten. She also selected Henrietta's new dress. Mr Newbold had become so particular in his attentions that a declaration must surely be imminent, and nothing would spur him on better than Henrietta looking her best in a new gown. Lady Elstead was so sure that she had crossed all the other names off Henrietta's list of suitors.

It was a slightly odd luncheon 'party', since he was the only person not part of the family, and its significance was not lost upon him. Lady Elstead's 'hint' irked him. Lord Martley was present, and combined the look of a man in a blissful dream with the insecurity of one whose suit had first been rejected.

Of course, Lady Elstead just had to tell Mr Newbold how 'absolutely thrilled' everyone in the family was that Lord Martley had offered for 'our dearest Caroline', which made Lord Martley squirm. Mr Newbold gave no sign that he had every reason to think this had not been the case a few days past, though what might have changed he knew not. It made Henrietta the happier, so he was quite genuine in wishing the young couple well.

The truth was that Henrietta was happier, and yet also a worried young woman. Charles still felt something for her, she was sure of it, and in her view he had achieved, by whatever means, nothing short of a miracle. She had expected yesterday that he would seek her out, and he had not been at the party she had attended, although she had seen Lady Vernham, who had commented favourably upon her dancing. Yet surely, she reasoned, he must want to see her delight, receive her thanks? Where was Charles?

The opening of the Waterloo Bridge, on this, the second anniversary of the Great Victory, was going to be a grand spectacle. The bridge itself had been built for some time, and had been renamed, having initially been designated the Strand Bridge, but today was the grand, official opening. His Royal Highness the Prince Regent, who revelled in the reflected glory and loved the uniforms, was going to perform the opening ceremony. There would be enormous crowds, and of all sorts of persons. Fortunately, Lord Elstead had a cousin who held a senior civil position within the Navy Board, and had secured an offer to view the event from the security of Somerset House, which was very conveniently situated at the north bank end of the bridge. The Elstead party set off in two carriages at half past one, but found the thoroughfares already congested, and Lady Elstead, who viewed large gatherings of the populace as intimations of revolution, looked quite agitated, gripping her reticule tightly, and staring straight ahead of her. Every time the carriage was forced to halt, she shut her eyes. By the time they reached Somerset House, at a snail's pace, it was a quarter past two, and when her ladyship alighted, her knees almost gave way beneath her.

'Thank goodness,' she declared, as they passed through the Strand entrance and into the open space of the courtyard beyond. 'There are just too many people in London.' She sounded vaguely affronted that anyone other than the Ton, and those whose services they required, should inhabit the capital.

CHAPTER TWENTY-THREE

Lord Henfield strode purposefully through Berkeley Square. It was impossible to dawdle, and if he was early, well, he could wait. As he entered South Audley Street he consulted his pocket watch, which told him that it was only five and twenty minutes before two. He stared at the face, willing it to be wrong, but then shook his head and continued. Miss Yate, quiet, downtrodden Miss Yate, had been bold and seen her hopes fulfilled. He would also be bold.

He rapped assertively at the door, only to be informed that Lord and Lady Elstead, and party, had departed but a few minutes beforehand, bound for Somerset House. This was a blow, but Lord Henfield was not to be put off. He made his best pace to Piccadilly, where he could be sure of finding a hackney, and hailed one as it turned onto the thoroughfare. When given the direction, the jarvey sucked his teeth.

'Can't trust to get you there soon, guv'nor, there bein' so many folk goin' to see 'is 'ighness open that there bridge. Best I can suggest is to take you along Long Acre and down as far as I can on Drury Lane.'

'Then do so, as swiftly as you may.'

By heading north before going further east, there were no delays until the vehicle reached Drury Lane, where its pace was reduced to a walk. Two thirds of the way down, Lord Henfield tapped on the roof and said that he would walk the rest. He paid the jarvey, with thanks, and made his way through the flow of humanity heading towards the river. He arrived, feeling fortunate to still have his watch and purse about him, to be greeted with the news that the man at the Strand entrance of Somerset House had seen various vehicles arrive, and would have to consult his list. This he did with painstaking slowness, before confirming that Lord Elstead's party had arrived. There then followed a short altercation, since the man was reluctant to allow Lord Henfield access to the building on a day when a view of the proceedings was worth its weight in gold. This 'hint', and the proffering of a sovereign, facilitated Lord Henfield's admission.

He had no idea where to find Henrietta, except that logic told him it would be in the block facing onto the river, and which housed the Navy Board. He entered the building, and, looking right, saw a small group of people being ushered along the passageway. He could not identify the ladies, but Lord Martley's voice reached him, and he made an educated guess that he would be with his intended. He all but ran along the passage, and called Lord Elstead's name as the party reached a magnificent stairway spiralling upwards.

'Lord Elstead.'

Lord Elstead, who was already on the fourth stair, turned. 'Henfield.'

'I am sorry, my lord, but I need to speak with Miss Gaydon, privately.'

'Papa!' cried Henrietta, hearing the urgency in Charles' voice.

'Not bad news, I assure you, Henrietta.'

'How unusual,' drawled Mr Newbold. 'I have never before heard of a man who abandons his bride to tell another lady of his nuptials.'

'What do you mean, Mr Newbold?' breathed Henrietta, her eyes on Charles.

'Why, only that I saw Henfield with Miss Yate, on the steps of St George's Hanover Square, at eleven this morning, and she did look, Henfield, quite radiant, for Miss Yate.' He was looking very directly at Lord Henfield.

'Oh Charles, how could you,' whispered Henrietta, leaning against a wall for support. She was very pale.

'I did not, have not . . .'

Mr Newbold raised an eyebrow. 'I was not mistaken in what I saw, Henfield.'

'My lord, may I speak with Henrietta, please?' entreated Lord Henfield rather desperately.

Lord Elstead, who disliked the idea of some emotional outburst on a grand staircase that ascended many floors and would make everything available to any who might care to listen, looked at his lady, whose lips were compressed, but made up his own mind.

'Yes, of course.' He looked at the gentleman who was conveying them to the chamber where they might view the spectacle. 'Is there anywhere . . . ?'

'There is a small room, if you would care to follow me upstairs, my lord.'

Lord Henfield joined the rear of the party as far as the second floor, where the gentleman bowed and indicated a short corridor, off which he opened a door into a small and currently unoccupied office.

'This room is at your disposal, sir,' he said mildly. 'The rest of Lord Elstead's party will be upon the fourth floor, second chamber to your left, overlooking the river.'

'Thank you.'

The man bowed himself out. Henrietta had said nothing, but her eyes accused. She did not think, could not think. That it would be ridiculous to imagine a man getting married, as Mr Newbold had suggested, and then rushing to inform another woman of the event, did not penetrate her shock.

'Henry . . .' Charles stepped towards her, but she backed away.

'It is Miss Gaydon, remember, my lord.' She flew two spots of high colour on her white cheeks, and her eyes sparkled, with anger and unshed tears. Her voice throbbed. 'So have you sent the announcement to the *Gazette*?'

'Don't be silly, Henry.'

'Do not tell me she had a change of heart at the altar.'

'Of course not. What I mean is . . . Henry, this is not like you,' he floundered.

'Then what am I like?' Henrietta threw at him.

'Normally? Everything a man could want.' There, it was out, in the open.

'Except to you.' Her bosom rose and fell swiftly in her agitation. She hurt, hurt so much that only her anger kept her from sinking to the floor.

'Well, I am sure the polite world will agree with Lady Elstead that Newbold is the better match,' Lord Henfield riposted bitterly.

'What?' Her eyes widened, and then, quite suddenly, she laughed. It was not a happy laugh, but jangling, and near hysterical. Her hands shook, and she seemed to shrink before his eyes, the angry young socialite melting into the girl he had laughed with, chastised, applauded, grown to love. She said nothing, but shook her head, and the tears blinked from her lashes began to run down her cheeks.

'Henry?' he whispered. A seed of doubt was watered by those tears, and sprouted.

'I . . . You have made me so miserable,' she sobbed.

'But I saw you, throwing yourself at Newbold.'

'I did not know what else to do.' Her voice wavered, and she trembled. 'I thought I would be very grown-up, and I could make you jealous, but she . . . How could you marry her, Charles?'

'There is no "her", Henry, and I am not married. There never was a "she", only a "you",' he said simply, taking hold of her arms, and gripping her tightly. 'I escorted Miss Yate to the altar, it is true, but to give her to the man who loves her, and to whom she gave her heart long ago.'

'Not married?' Henrietta sounded dazed.

'No. How could I marry another woman, when I love you, Henry?'

'You can't.'

'Is that I cannot marry another, or love you, Henry, because the first is correct and the second oh so very wrong.' His voice shook a little.

'But we . . . people think . . .'

'I love you, Henry. When you were a child I loved you as a brother loves a little sister, yes, but you are not a child, have not been this year or more past, and I do not love you as a brother, but as a woman. There is no bar, my darling girl, except that which we have placed in our own heads, though not our hearts, I hope. I did not fully recognise it until you left, and came to London, and at first it felt . . . wrong. But it is not wrong, Henry. The

371

feelings I have for you, the grown-up you . . .' She was staring at him, her cheeks still wet, her lips slightly parted. 'Just occasionally it does a young woman good to know that she fires a man', those had been Lady Vernham's words, and Lady Vernham had been remarkably astute. Well, Henry most certainly fired him.

He bent his head, negotiating the awkward angle of avoiding the brim of her bonnet, and kissed her, far from fraternally. He had wanted to kiss her for so long, and the frustration and yearning blended with the desire. When he pulled back to draw breath, Henrietta made a small squeaky noise, and freed her arms, but only to throw them about his neck. He correctly interpreted this as an invitation to kiss her again.

She was trembling, overwhelmed both by the physicality and the knowledge that he loved her, loved her after all, and her knees gave way. He felt her weight, and, laughing, scooped her up and sat her upon the edge of a desk. He looked down at her face.

'You are shaken. It shakes me too, Henry, how close I have been to losing you, how much I want you. It was your papa who told me I was a fool, sitting at home, pining. He saw what we did not, or thought we could not. They say love is blind, Henry, and I pretended I was blind.'

'As did I,' she whispered. 'I have had fun in London, but oh, how I have dreaded where this is all meant to lead. At first I thought it was just that I wanted to go back to Papa, to the world in which I feel comfortable, and then I realised it was not just that, but that I could not imagine another man in my life, except you, Charles. I have been such a fool, and when I . . . I was angry with myself, Charles, but took it out on you and pushed you away. Forgive me, forgive me.' Her hand went to his cheek and touched it. He pressed a kiss to the palm.

'Nothing to forgive, my love. If you were a fool, then that makes a pair of us. I was so jealous of the London beaux, felt so inadequate, I got it all wrong, trying to make it right. The more I tried, the more I made a complete mess of things. I was trying to be what I am not, because you seemed different.'

'And I am "just your Henry".'

'Not "just", but "uniquely, gloriously, my Henry".'

She laughed, and was suddenly shy. 'We ought not . . . They will wonder.'

'If they have not guessed then they are bigger fools than we have been, my darling.'

'Charles.'

'Yes?'

'I was dreading Mr Newbold asking for my hand. I did not know how I would be able to refuse, when it seemed . . . And I think he does like me.'

'If he is disappointed, I think he will get over it, you know, and that is what I could not do. It is why I have almost run after you this afternoon, fearing I was too late.'

'You made it possible for Caroline to marry where her heart lies. You did that for me, yes?'

'I . . . was involved. You may even say I set it in motion, but the credit lies elsewhere. One day, I will give you the full tale.'

'One day?'

'When we are married.'

'Married.' Henrietta sighed. 'Will you write to Papa?'

'I shall do better. I shall take you home to him for his blessing, and then . . . soon, Henry.'

She blushed.

'The bridge may be open by now,' she murmured, as he kissed beneath her ear.

'Mm.'

'And we will have missed the excitement.'

'This is far more exciting.' He stood her on her feet once more. 'Henry, there will be days when you flounce at me, when I play the dread husband and tell you off, when I make mistakes, and when you castigate me for being "a typical man", but I will always love you, with all that I am.'

'That is both realistic, and very sweet.'

'Sweet?' He laughed, and took her hand. 'Let us go and reveal our news, which is news to none, before I say anything too "sweet". "Sweet Lord Henfield" sounds all wrong.'

They entered a large room, where several parties were gathered at the windows, the sashes raised, and were peering at the granite arches. Only Mr Newbold turned around. Seeing them together, he knew his cause was lost, and if his smile was twisted and his tone a little bitter, then at least his words showed a good grace. It might smart for a day or so, being 'beaten', but it would be ungallant to appear petty.

'The happy couple, I take it? Yes, of course you are.' He paused, and gave a smooth lie. 'I think, Miss Gaydon, that you and I both have narrowly escaped a . . . mistake. I was going to offer for you, you know, and if we were unfortunate, you would have accepted.' He held out his hand to Lord Henfield. 'I will not go so far as to say she picked the better man, Henfield, for my ego simply could not stand it, truly it would not, but I think she has made the right choice, for her.'

The hand was grasped, shaken. Mr Newbold took Henrietta's hand and kissed it.

'I . . . am sorry, Mr Newbold.'

'No, no, do not be sorry. You have given me the most entertaining Season in years, Miss Gaydon, and I thank you for it.' He managed to sound just sufficiently detached. 'I think you have reminded me that bachelorhood need not be the only way of going on, and, you never know, I might find your equal, next year, or in the year after that.'

'I hope not, sir. I would rather you find my better.'

'Charmingly said, and with the beauty of being honestly said also. You will need your wits about you, Henfield, married to this young lady.'

'They will be kept exercised.' He grinned at Henrietta.

Lady Elstead turned at that moment, and saw the way they looked at each other.

'Oh dear,' she said, 'what a pity.'

'Aunt!'

'Well, my dear, it will be said that I had nothing whatsoever to do with the match, and it will do my standing no good at all among the matrons. There may even be a suggestion that the match was decided before you ever came to London, which is most lowering.'

'But you have Caroline's success, ma'am.' Henrietta ignored that the betrothal had been more in spite of her than because of her.

'That is true, and Martley is heir to an earldom.' Lady Elstead found this consoling.

'Which puts me in my place,' murmured Mr Newbold to Lord Henfield.

'I heard that, Mr Newbold. Rank is not everything, not always. You have excellent breeding, and you are very rich.' Lady Elstead smiled graciously upon him.

'Such solace as that is, ma'am.' Mr Newbold bowed to her. She did not even notice the irony.

Caroline, hearing Lord Martley's name mentioned, stepped back from the window. Henrietta smiled at her, and she recognised it as the same smile she had seen in her own mirror over the last day and a half.

'Oh, cousin! How wonderful!' She came forward, hands outstretched, but Henrietta went further, and hugged her.

'We are both so lucky,' she whispered in Caroline's ear.

What followed was a more general exchange of congratulations within the party, which only ceased when the other people in the room began clapping.

'It is open,' declared a young man.

'The opening of the bridge may be more important to London, and be remarked in the histories,' said Lord Elstead calmly, 'but I think the opening of new chapters in young lives is far more important overall.'

Despite Lord Henfield's desire to take Henrietta back to Shropshire as soon as possible, Lady Elstead was determined to throw a betrothal party for both Caroline and Henrietta before they left, with the logical excuse that Sir John had already given his implicit blessing by sending Lord Henfield to London in the first place. The notice was sent to the *Gazette*, but Charles himself wrote to his godfather so that he should receive the good news at a more personal level than reading it in the newspaper. As she feared, there were some ladies who whispered behind their hands how Maria Elstead had aimed 'at the moon', pretending her niece could catch Mr Newbold, but most congratulations were genuine, for Henrietta was accepted as a very nice girl, and her marrying a gentleman who did not generally grace the London Season was not seen as her lessening the chances of her peers. She could have done better, but Henfield was a decent enough man, and of course, if it had been in the offing long before the Season began . . .

The only problem with the party lay in the invitations. Lady Elstead sat with her quill poised above paper for a very long time before she could bear to inscribe one to the Right Honourable Earl and Countess of Pirbright, but thought that at least they would find themselves 'otherwise engaged'. However, to everyone's surprise, possibly even Lady Pirbright's, they did come. The earl, to whom the reason for the estrangement between the ladies could never be revealed, dug in his dull and normally submissive heels, and declared the girl was a good match for their only son, and he would not have tongues wagging that suggested otherwise. Lady Pirbright might look as if she were sucking lemons and treading barefoot upon glass, but come she did, and was invited by Lady Elstead to stand beside her at the top of the stairs. Only in her own head did she admit that she would like to have pushed her down them.

Lady Vernham was, as far as Lord Henfield was concerned, as important a guest as the Pirbrights, although he told her that privately.

'Without you, ma'am, none of this would have been possible.'

'It does make it sound a feat of prestidigitation, Henfield, but I thank you for the sentiment. For my part I only hope that when Gorleston seeks to tie the knot, he does so with less soul-searching and wearing of hair shirts. In fact, it might be preferable if I only hear about it all when the decision is made. This Season has made me see that he is not so dim-witted as I had been led to believe in his early youth, and I actually trust him to go about the business like a young man of sense.' This, from Lady Vernham, was praise indeed.

Mr Newbold was sent an invitation, but sent a handwritten note excusing himself upon being previously promised to a friend for racing at Newmarket.

It was thus nearly a fortnight later that Charles escorted 'his Henry' back to the Marches, and when he handed her down outside her father's door she was wearied but blissfully happy. Sir John came out into the early evening sunlight, with a pointer pup dancing at his heels. He shook Charles' hand enthusiastically, and clasped his daughter to his bosom, as the pup barked and bounced about them.

'Thank goodness you are back, Henrietta.'

'Papa?'

'When you have washed, and eaten, you must start immediately.'

'Start? What?'

'Why, a new pair of slippers, my dear. There is not a soft item of footwear left in the house.' He smiled at her, and then laughed.

SOPHIA HOLLOWAY describes herself as a 'wordsmith' who is only really happy when writing. She read Modern History at Oxford, and also writes the Bradecote and Catchpoll medieval mysteries as Sarah Hawkswood.

@RegencySophia

sophiaholloway.co.uk

ALSO BY SOPHIA HOLLOWAY

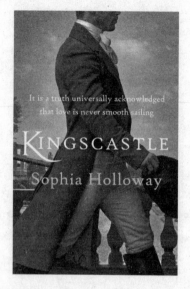

Captain William Hawksmoor of the Royal Navy never expected to inherit Kingscastle, his family's estate, and finds himself all at sea when he does so. Especially when he learns that he must marry within a year or be forever dealing with trustees.

As the new Marquis of Athelney, the captain takes command of Kingscastle and discovers much to be done to set it in order. He must also contend with his aunt, Lady Willoughby Hawksmoor, who is determined that her daughter will be his wife. When she discovers he is far more interested in Eleanor Burgess, her underpaid and much put-upon companion, Lady Willoughby shows she will stop at nothing to keep them apart.

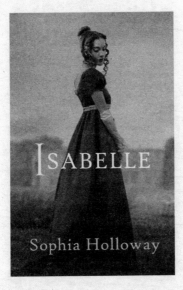

ISABELLE

Sophia Holloway

Isabelle Wareham has not seen much of the world, caring for her beloved widowed father. At his death, she finds she is no longer her own mistress but under the guardianship of her unscrupulous brother-in-law, Lord Dunsfold, who sees her as a way to improve his own fortunes.

The outlook looks bleak until events throw Isabelle and the impoverished Earl of Idsworth together. However, Dunsfold is determined to force her into a more lucrative match and Isabelle will need to rise above her circumstances to reach her chance of happiness.